Let Her Eat Cake . . .

"It is you," I said to Chantilly when I pulled up next to the open door of the van. Even with her face turned the other way, I'd recognize Chantilly's long brown curls anywhere. "Honey, you shouldn't be here. It's not good for you."

Chantilly swiveled round in the driver's seat. White icing and cake crumbs smeared her lips and a glob of raspberry filling dripped down her chin. A pink buttercream rose stuck to the front of her brown uniform blouse. "Dear God in heaven! You went and ate the wedding cake!"

"One slice," she mumbled around a mouthful. "Who's going to miss one little old slice? The freaking thing is five tiers high. It took three Cakery Bakery employees and that owner, Delta Longford herself, to lug it in. They even made GracieAnn Harlow stand on a ladder to get the bride and groom thing on top."

Chantilly held up a chunk of mangled pastry. "This here should be *my* wedding cake, except for the pink roses. This should be *my* wedding day, my wedding colors of creamy peach and blue morning rain. Simon is *my* man. We were engaged! How could he go and do this to me?" Chantilly wailed, a tear sliding down her cheek and cutting a path across a white icing smear. "Waynetta is a man-stealing little witch."

Berkley Prime Crime titles by Duffy Brown

ICED CHIFFON

KILLER IN CRINOLINES

Killer in Crinolines

DUFFY BROWN

BERKLEY PRIME CRIME. NEW YORK

THE BERKLEY PUBLISHING GROUP
Published by the Penguin Group
Penguin Group (USA) Inc.
375 Hudson Street, New York, New York 10014, USA

USA | Canada | UK | Ireland | Australia | New Zealand | India | South Africa | China

Penguin Books Ltd., Registered Offices: 80 Strand, London WC2R 0RL, England
For more information about the Penguin Group, visit penguin.com.

KILLER IN CRINOLINES

A Berkley Prime Crime Book / published by arrangement with the author

Berkley Prime Crime Books are published by The Berkley Publishing Group.
BERKLEY® PRIME CRIME and the PRIME CRIME logo are trademarks of
Penguin Group (USA) Inc.

For information, address: The Berkley Publishing Group,
a division of Penguin Group (USA) Inc.,
375 Hudson Street, New York, New York 10014.

ISBN: 978-0-425-25215-4

PUBLISHING HISTORY
Berkley Prime Crime mass-market edition / May 2013

PRINTED IN THE UNITED STATES OF AMERICA

10 9 8 7 6 5 4 3 2 1

Cover illustration by Julia Green.
Cover design by Diane Kolsky.
Interior text design by Kristin del Rosario.

~Acknowledgments~

For Ray and Carolyn Castelluccio, best brother and sister-in-law ever. Thanks for your support and terrific Christmas parties.

Thanks to Marie Lynott for the hours of Zumba/belly dancing classes. They sure came in handy with this book.

Thanks to my Street Team for your encouragement and hours of hard work. You guys are wonderful.

To Ann Kruetzkamp, who thinks every book should be dedicated to her.

Chapter One

MAGNOLIA Plantation wasn't really a Southern plantation, the guests milling about the wide verandas and lush green lawn weren't really extras from *Gone with the Wind*, and that wasn't Scarlett descending the curved staircase but my auntie KiKi in a green flouncy dress with enough crinolines to cover all of Savannah.

"Honey, what are you doing here?" KiKi said to me when she got to the bottom. "I don't recall seeing Reagan Summerside on the wedding guest list, and you're wearing a regular old skirt and toting your yellow pocketbook instead of a nice parasol. Are those new black flip-flops?"

Auntie KiKi was my one and only auntie. She lived next door to me in a perfectly restored Victorian that had been in the Vanderpool family since Sherman saw fit to park his unwelcome Northern behind in Savannah. "How do you go to the bathroom in that thing?" I asked, eyeing her hugeness.

Auntie KiKi cut her brown eyes side to side at the others in full Southern regalia, chatting politely, trying not to look as if the beads of sweat dotting their upper lips and foreheads bothered them one bit. "I'm not even thinking about such a possibility and neither is any other woman here." KiKi fluffed her voluminous skirts. "Why on earth couldn't Waynetta have a normal August wedding? I do believe it's ninety-two in the shade, and the AC in this place isn't keeping up for diddly."

"When you're the only child of Reese Waverly, horse owner, ranch owner, fat-portfolio owner, you get whatever you set your mind to, including someone else's beau," I whispered the last part with a good deal of upset in my voice since the particular someone who had her beau stolen happened to be my friend.

"Waynetta had it in her mind to get married," KiKi whispered back. "Simon Ambrose had it in his mind to get his name on a Waverly bank account. Marriage seemed the fastest way to accomplish both. One of these days Chantilly will appreciate that she's better off without that no-good, middle-Georgia, low-rent Simon hanging around." KiKi parked her dress over an AC duct to catch a breeze.

KiKi added, "And we're all just hoping Chantilly does her realizing right quick and gets back to being our efficient UPS delivery girl. Last week she was in such a state over this here wedding that she delivered the new girdle I ordered from the JCPenney catalog to Dinky Landers' house. Dinky thought her husband went and got it for her since she's been putting on a few pounds of late. Nearly caused a divorce right there on the spot." KiKi flourished her fan to get some air circulating as Doreen-the-wedding-planner hurried up to us.

Doreen-the-wedding-planner went to school with Auntie KiKi back in the days of Rubik's Cubes and Pac-Man. Now Doreen-the-wedding-planner organized all notable weddings in the area to the point where no one ever referred to her as simply Doreen. She was calm, cool, and efficient, pulling off the most difficult ceremonies without a hitch or even breaking a sweat. Today her hair stuck out in tufts of gray, her petticoat hung a full inch below her blue dress, her nails were chewed to the quick, and she snagged a peach martini right off a passing waiter's tray.

"Have you seen Simon?" Doreen chugged the martini, her left eye twitching.

I unraveled a strip of black material from my purse. "Here's the bow tie you asked me to bring right over for him." That trip had translated into a forty-dollar cab ride from my consignment shop in town. My present financial status left me carless, pretty much furniture-less, and was the reason I wound up in the consignment shop business in the first place. "How in the world could the groom go and lose his bow tie?"

Doreen slurped the peach slice from the martini and lowered her voice. "Honey child, how could I lose the groom?" She swiped her hand across her mouth and burped. "I've had bridesmaids go missing, mothers-in-law, ring bearers, even a reverend and justice of the peace a time or two, but never the groom . . . until now." She held the glass up to the balcony overhead. "Simon's room's up there, last one on the end. Take the back stairs not cluttered with big dresses and Colonel Sanders look-alikes. Can you see if by some heavenly miracle Mr. Blue-eyes-with-goatee has managed to return himself to where he belongs? He needs to propel himself outside for pictures; the photographer's having palpitations. You'd think Simon would be there front and center. I declare, that man's so full of himself he wouldn't go to a funeral unless he could be the corpse."

KiKi rolled her eyes at me and gave Doreen a reassuring pat while prying the empty glass from her finger before she hurried off. Auntie KiKi said to me, "I best go find Putter. He camouflaged that golf club of his as a fancy walking cane, but he's not fooling anyone. I bet that man's chipping pinecones out of the flower beds right this very minute. I'll keep an eye out for Simon and send him your way."

The entire population of Savannah called my uncle Putter because he carried one everywhere . . . restaurants, church, rounds at the hospital. Auntie KiKi maintained it was in case a golf ball dropped to Earth and he had to sink a birdie to save the planet. Thirty years ago KiKi married the perfect Southern gentleman and first-class doctor. Seven years ago I'd married the perfect Southern philanderer and real-estate bum. Then I was twenty-five, stupid, and thought love conquered all. Now I was thirty-two, divorced, living in a partially restored Victorian house with my consignment shop on the first floor and knew beyond a shadow of a doubt that overdue bills conquered all.

I hitched Old Yeller, my beloved yellow Target-special pleather purse, onto my shoulder and cut though the crowd munching cucumber sandwiches and inhaling remarkable amounts of alcohol. I took the back stairway and glanced out the clerestory window to a manicured lawn. A muscled guy sporting a ponytail and clad in a bad-fitting suit sprinted across. Bouncer? My guess was he'd been brought in to keep wedding crashers away and that probably included a brown van with gold lettering parked back in the bushes and out of his view.

Sweet mother in heaven! No, it couldn't be . . . could it? UPS? Chantilly? Here? Now! Maybe it was some other UPS driver who used to be engaged to the groom in her UPS truck and visiting Magnolia Plantation to deliver wedding gifts?

I trotted back down the stairs and ducked out a rear entrance, then hustled across the grass. A weeping willow did a fair job of hiding the truck, but big and brown with gold lettering was downright conspicuous surrounded by rose gardens, white columns, and horse-drawn carriages.

"It is you," I said to Chantilly when I ran up next to the open door of the van. Even with her face turned the other way I'd recognize Chantilly's long brown curls anywhere. I'd been restoring my house for five years now, and

Chantilly had delivered everything to me from offset hinges to an antique brass coatrack I scored on eBay. Usually Chantilly had all those curls stuffed under her brown uniform ball cap. "Honey, you shouldn't be here. It's not good for you."

Chantilly swiveled round in the driver's seat. White icing and cake crumbs smeared her lips and a glob of raspberry filling dripped down her chin. A pink buttercream rose stuck to the front of her brown uniform blouse. "Dear God in heaven! You went and ate the wedding cake!"

"One slice," she mumbled around a mouthful. "Who's going to miss one little old slice? The freaking thing is five tiers high. It took three Cakery Bakery employees and the owner, Delta Longford herself, to lug it in. They even made GracieAnn Harlow stand on a ladder to get the bride and groom thing on top."

Chantilly held up a chunk of mangled pastry. "This here should be *my* wedding cake, except for the pink roses. This should be *my* wedding day, my wedding colors of creamy peach and blue morning rain. Simon is *my* man. We were engaged! How could he go and do this to me!" Chantilly wailed, a tear sliding down her cheek and cutting a path across a white icing smear. "Waynetta is a man-stealing little witch."

I climbed up into the van and hunted a tissue from my purse. I wiped Chantilly's eyes. "You're making yourself miserable. You need to go on home."

She gave me a watery look. "What are you doing here?"

Uh-oh. I couldn't tell Chantilly I was dropping off Simon's bow tie. That would mark me as an accomplice and make Chantilly more upset and maybe bring on another cake attack. "Auntie KiKi," I blurted. Now I needed to come up with something about KiKi. I silently promised God at that moment that I'd help with the St. John's thrift sale at the end of the month if he'd tell me what to say. I was so bad at lying I required divine intervention to pull it off. It occurred to me that was like asking the FBI to help in pulling off a bank robbery.

"KiKi needed her headache medicine and called me," I said. "It's hot inside, people are melting. Everyone's having a painfully horrible time. Downright pitiful. Worst wedding ever. The only reason people came is that no one wants to cross Reese Waverly. The man carries too much weight in this town."

Chantilly brightened a bit. "Really?"

I made an *X* over my heart. "Now promise me you'll get out of here? If you don't deliver the rest of your packages, you'll lose your job. Look at it this way: Waynetta's a spoiled brat and Simon's a donkey's butt. The brat and the butt deserve each other." I squeezed her hand. "You can do better."

She took another lick of icing off her thumb. "This cake is drop-dead delicious and that's just what Simon deserves, the dead part, not the delicious part. Truth be told, Waynetta deserves dead even more." Another tear escaped, and I held her hand tighter.

"Hollis divorced me for a twenty-four-year-old cupcake,"

I reminded. "I understand the *who deserves to die more* dilemma better than most." I gave Chantilly a sympathetic wink and hurried off. Wedding music drifted across the faux plantation, which had opened last year for the sole purpose of hosting gatherings in need of Southern hype, notably Southern brides with more money than sense. Ribbons and roses decorating the gazebo and rows of white chairs caught a much-welcome summer breeze. Guests began to take their seats, set far apart to accommodate hoop skirts, petticoats, parasols, and canes.

Once inside I made a mad dash for the steps. I should have found Simon ten minutes ago. Doreen-the-wedding-planner was probably having a stroke by now, and Waynetta must be in full-blown hissy-fit mode. Everyone in town had witnessed Waynetta in this particular state at one time or another and it wasn't pretty, though it did keep the gossips clucking for weeks on end.

When I got to the second floor, KiKi was leaning over the railing, studying the guests below as they made their way outside. "Have you seen Waynetta?" she asked me.

"Jiminy Christmas! Now the bride's missing?"

"For Doreen's sake let's just go with no one can find Waynetta at this particular moment in time. One of the bridesmaids seems to have misplaced her dress and the photographer has threatened to leave the premises."

"Chantilly's here. UPS truck parked out back."

KiKi's jaw dropped a full inch and she stared at me bug-eyed. "Heavenly days. Doreen-the-wedding-planner has already fainted twice, and Waynetta's daddy is having chest pains. Putter's with Reese now. This wedding cost the man a blooming fortune and I'm not all that sure he's thrilled about the marriage to begin with."

It was always nice to have a cardiologist on the guest list. I said to KiKi, "Simon's a loan officer at the bank. You'd think Reese Waverly would welcome someone in the financial field with open arms. You help Doreen find Waynetta and I'll get Simon into a bow tie if I have to strangle the man to do it." The strangle part had definite appeal. KiKi hoofed it down the hall as fast as billowing yards of taffeta, lace, and chiffon would allow. I knocked on Simon's door. "It's Reagan Summerside."

"Well, have you found him?" Vidallia Ambrose hissed, pulling my purse strap and hauling me inside the room. Vidallia was Simon's petite mamma and socialite wannabe. "Where is that blessed bow tie? You should have had it here a half hour ago"

"Do you know where Simon is?"

"Do you believe that Chantilly person dared show her face around here? I saw her truck out the window. I called the Savannah police myself. Can't leave it up to the locals to take care of something so important. What if she causes another dreadful scene like she did at the engagement party? It'll ruin the wedding."

From what I heard, that particular scene involved being naked and on a horse, but Chantilly was a friend so I ignored the details.

"I do declare," Vidallia went on, adjusting her hat, which was nearly as big as her matching dress. She looked like a piñata. "Why can't that truck-driving trollop understand Simon is marrying someone with more class in her little finger than Chantilly has in her whole body." Vidallia went dreamy-eyed for a second. "This wedding will be in all the society pages. *I'll* be in the society pages. The photographer promised to make me look divine."

Vidallia shooed me toward the door like a pesky fly off an apple cobbler. "Now get a move on and find Simon. Tell him he best behave himself and not mess up this here wedding or he'll have to answer to me. He didn't meet Waynetta just by chance, you know. Sometimes cupid needs a good shove, and I did a pretty fine job of it if I do say so myself."

I stepped into the hall and the door slammed closed behind me. Mamma matchmaker, or was troublemaker closer to the truth? But where was Simon? Where was Waynetta? Not that I cared so much for their sakes as Doreen's. I'd been in six weddings over the years and Doreen-the-wedding-planner and I had bonded, proven by the fact that she sent a lot of customers to my consignment shop for wedding attire.

My guess was that Simon and Waynetta had made their way to the van. Both thrived on drama and the ex at the wedding screamed drama. I headed for the back steps, the slapping of my flip-flops echoing in the now-empty hallway. Everyone was seated outside, wanting nothing more than to get back to air-conditioning and chilled champagne quickly as possible. I turned for the atrium in time to hear Delta from Cakery Bakery arguing with Tipper, her ex, over the color of the buttercream roses and collided head-on with a waitress coming out of the dining room.

"Have you seen the bride or the groom?" I asked breathless, my hundred and twenty-three pounds and Old Yeller taking the worst of the impact. Okay, a hundred and twenty-eight pounds, but I swear I'm on a diet and just thinking ahead.

The waitress's side ponytail drooped down around her ears and she leaned against one of the fake marble columns, her blue eyes with even bluer eye shadow not focusing. "What am I ever going to do?" She slid to the marble floor, her black-and-white uniform inching up to her thighs.

I hunkered down next to . . . Suellen, or so her badge said. "Hey, are you all right?"

Suellen shook her head, blonde hair pulling free. She sobbed. "How could this happen?"

"We just ran into each other, is all, honey. Take a few deep breaths." I rummaged around in Old Yeller and came up with a half roll of Life Savers and peeled off a red one. "Here, eat this. Sugar cures all. Are you okay?"

"This is terrible, just terrible." Suellen slurped the candy and pointed a shaky finger to the double doors leading to the dining room. A chill replaced the August heat cooking me to near done.

I stood and entered the dining room, quiet and still, dust motes floating in the setting sun. Round tables were decked out in peach-tone linens with white flower arrangements of roses and forget-me-nots. Candlelight danced about the room and Doreen-the-wedding-planner lay crumbled in a heap on the floor.

"Oh dear Lord!" I starting for Doreen but then stopped in my tracks because Simon was there, too. He was face-down in the five-tiered wedding cake with a silver cake knife sticking out of his back.

Chapter Two

THE dining room door opened behind me, letting in the first strands of Pachelbel, the music of brides everywhere, and Auntie KiKi.

"Reagan, thank heavens I found you," KiKi huffed, her dress swishing softly across the ivory carpet as she came my way. "I still can't find Simon or Waynetta anywhere and what in the world are you and Doreen-the-wedding-planner doing down there on the floor like that and—Jesus, Mary, and Joseph! Lord have mercy and saints preserve us!"

I figured the last part enlisting the powers above meant Auntie KiKi had found Simon after all. I helped Doreen to a sitting position and the three of us stared, saying nothing till KiKi whispered, "That looks like a mighty fine cake."

"Raspberry filling and buttercream icing to die for."

KiKi gave me the *You didn't really just say that* look and I made the sign of the cross for disrespecting the dead. KiKi and I hoisted Doreen onto a chair. She wobbled a bit, then plopped her elbow in the middle of a white china plate right there on the table and rested her forehead against her palm in how-could-this-happen-to-me expression.

"I take it you called the police?" KiKi said to me, her voice sounding weak, sirens approaching.

"I ran into a waitress out in the hall. She must have seen Simon and made the call."

"There wasn't anyone out there when I came in, Reagan. I wonder who—"

Before KiKi could finish her sentence, Detective Aldeen Ross and two uniformed officers barged through the double dining room doors as if they owned the place. Detective Ross looked from me and Auntie KiKi to Simon. Frown lines wrinkled her forehead, her brown eyes beady, her gaze fixed on me and KiKi. "You two again. Why am I not surprised?"

It was a flat-out statement, not even a polite Southern question asking how we were holding up or wasn't this a mighty hot day to be dead. Detective Ross and KiKi and I had history and it wasn't a great one. Ross happened to be the detective when KiKi and I stumbled on another dead body four months ago. It suddenly occurred to me that KiKi and I were developing very bad dead people karma.

"I didn't do it, I swear!" KiKi blurted, raising her hands in the air, the stress of murder and Detective Ross getting the better of her.

"I never said you did," Ross groused.

"How'd you all get out here from town so fast?" I wondered aloud.

"Got a call there was a UPS truck stashed in the bushes. Everyone knows Mr. Waverly's daughter's getting married here today and the man's always been right supportive of the SPD, donating to the widows and orphans fund and all. We came out to take a look. Thought I'd see to things myself but I never expected this." Her eyes narrowed inquisition style. "Why aren't you dressed like the others around here?"

"Making an emergency delivery." I pulled out the bowtie from Old Yeller and eyed the corpse. "Seems he lost his."

Ross used to be as wide as she was high and always dressed in navy polyester that undoubtedly stood up well under the occupational hazards of blood, guts, and gore. The navy poly part still held, but she was now packing a good thirty pounds less pudge, her skirt held together with safety-pins to take up the slack. I started to say how great she looked but proper etiquette toward a woman with a gun strapped to her hip was a complete mystery.

Ross slid a chair out next to Doreen. KiKi—now the same shade as the carpet—wilted into it, her green skirts billowing around her. Ross handed KiKi and Doreen bottles of water from her brown shoulder bag, which rivaled mine in size. Aldeen Ross had the dead-person routine down pat.

"You best tell everyone outside there's not going to be a wedding today," Ross said to the two policemen standing beside her. I recognized one as Officer Dumont, who had happened upon me when I swiped a military memorial wreath from Colonial Park Cemetery. Normally I would never do such a terrible thing as that's how people wind up in hell. I was truly in a desperate way.

Ross added, "Make sure no one leaves the grounds."

The other officer, who I didn't know, stroked his chin. "I do believe a seafood delivery truck just headed down the drive."

"Well, go fetch him or at least find out who it is." Ross turned to me and exhaled an audible sigh. "And what are you doing here?"

"I was looking for the bride and groom."

"The quartet is playing Pachelbel, the ceremony's ready to start, and you couldn't even find the bride?"

"Or groom. It's been that kind of wedding," Doreen-the-wedding-planner said, massaging her temples, her eyes crossed. "I heard noise and came in to see if it was Simon or Waynetta. I saw Simon in the cake and that's all I remember till Reagan showed up beside me. This will kill my business." She rolled her eyes at the *kill* reference, then buried her head in her hands. "You wouldn't happen to have a peach martini in that bag of yours instead of water? I could do with a peach martini right now." Doreen's head jerked up as if spring-mounted and she looked Ross in the eyes. "Peach."

"Lady, I don't have a martini or any other alcohol in my purse. Do you have any ideas how many calories are in a martini? One hundred ninety if you only have one olive." Ross yanked out a baggie of carrot sticks from her handbag and dropped it on the table. "Deal."

Doreen-the-wedding-planner pointed to the rear emergency exit door across the room. "When I came in, someone in a peach dress, a bridesmaid dress I do believe now that I think about the color, went hurrying out right through there. One of the bridesmaids said her dress went missing and that must have been it. I spied Simon surrounded by cake and icing and fainted dead away and—"

"Where is he!" Waynetta burst into the room, the train of her silk-and-pearl wedding gown draped over her skinny arm. Word had it she lost twenty pounds for the wedding and, only being a size 2 to begin with, that made for one boney-looking bride. She stopped, peered at Simon, threw down her bouquet, then kicked it across the room, flowers and trailing ribbons landing smack on top of Simon.

"That man has gone and ruined everything!" Waynetta screeched. "You can never trust men to do what they're supposed to do. It's always about what they want. What about me?" She poked herself in the chest and I caught a glimpse of her diamond the size of a duck egg.

"This is my day. I made all the plans. I did all the work. I chose everything just the way I wanted it with no help from Simon. All he had to do was show up and he couldn't even do that right! Just look at him, he's a mess!"

"The flowers are a nice touch."

Waynetta gave me a hateful look, then turned to Doreen slumped in the chair with KiKi splashing water on her face while I fanned her with a napkin. Waynetta said, "Tell the kitchen staff to serve dinner outside. See what they have for a suitable dessert, cake is out of the question. Tell those Cakery Bakery people their services are no longer needed.

The roses were more pink than peach anyway and I have no intention of paying for such an atrocity. Can't anyone do anything right around here?"

Waynetta tipped her chin and straightened her spine, her dress nearly sliding right off. She hitched up the front. "I certainly hope no one expects me to return the wedding presents. They're mine, all mine. Lord knows I deserve them after all this commotion."

Waynetta swirled around on her little heel, snagged a carrot stick, and left in a cloud of white, her dress not all the way buttoned up the back. Didn't bridesmaids check such things? Aldeen, who had undoubtedly come across almost every scenario in her detective life of murder and mayhem, looked perplexed. I suspected it took a lot to perplex Aldeen Ross. "Piss and vinegar," she said. "Never seen anything quite like that before. One for the books."

For sure Waynetta Waverly was the most self-absorbed person in Savannah, but this reaction bubbled right over the top even for her. Not a hint of a whimper or a tear of love lost anywhere unless you counted the possibility of her returning presents.

KiKi took my napkin and patted Doreen's face dry. "Don't you worry about a thing, sugar. You just rest for a spell. I'll see what the kitchen can do about dinner. That might calm folks if they're going to be here for a spell." She turned to me. "You get Doreen upstairs. She needs to get herself into bed and settle her nerves."

Auntie KiKi stood, steadied, then wobbled. Giving up on proper Southern decorum, she kicked her green shoes under the table, then shuffled off in bare feet to the kitchen.

I hooked my shoulder under Doreen's arm and helped her up. Aldeen made her way to the cake, plucked off the bouquet, and took a closer look at Simon. She made a call on her cell phone, saying something about needing a meat wagon. I guessed that was cop-speak for *coroner* but I'd had enough death for one day and didn't ask.

When Doreen and I reached the top of the stairs one of the bridesmaids came out of her room dressed in denim shorts and a halter top and looking as if she'd been caught in a windstorm. "Do you mind if Doreen here uses your room to lie down for a bit."

"Lie down!" the bridesmaid wailed and ran her hand through her hair, making it stick out even more. "Doreen-the-wedding-planner can't do that. She needs to . . . plan. She needs to find my dress. It's gone, I tell you, gone! Look at me. There won't be enough bridesmaids. The wedding will be ruined. Waynetta will hate me." Terror lit her eyes and she growled, "Lord have mercy, do you know what happens when Waynetta Waverly hates you? Your life in Savannah is ruined, that's what. You're blackballed from dances, ostracized at church, ignored at dinners, snubbed everywhere."

Doreen pushed open the door to the room and flopped back on the bedspread spread-eagle, staring at the ceiling. "The wedding's off," she said in a flat voice. "I suppose you could say the groom got creamed. I should have been a librarian like Mamma wanted." Doreen closed her eyes, draped a black bow tie across her forehead in defeat, and was instantly asleep.

"I don't get it. What in the world is going on?" the bridesmaid asked me.

I studied the bow tie draped across Doreen, knew I had the replacement for it in my purse, and wondered the same thing. What *was* going on? "Simon sort of . . . died."

"Dead? Simon? Oh my God! How could this happen to me?" The perky little bridesmaid's scream could have stripped wallpaper, and she ran down the steps and out the back door. Doreen-the-wedding-planner didn't even flinch.

I closed the door to the room and went looking for KiKi to see if she needed help with the dinner plans. The UPS truck still sat in the weeping willow tree, but now a swarm of big dresses of every color and their escorts headed right for it. Considering the heat of the day, these folks were truly on a mission of some significance.

Oh, Lordy! Chantilly? Did the crowd think she did in Simon and they were all upset about it? The man was far more liked than I expected. Personally I thought he was a traitorous, money-grubbing slug of a human being. I ran down the steps to find Aldeen Ross standing in the hall, writing in her spiral book. I grabbed the book away. "I think there's going to be a lynching."

She snatched back the book, a scowl on her face. "Keep that up and you'll be volunteering for the event."

More out of curiosity than concern, Ross followed me across the lawn to the brown truck surrounded by Southern belles and gentlemen in cream-toned suits complete with tails, top hats in hand. Chantilly was nowhere in sight, but Elsie Abbott had wedged her lavender fluffiness into the van opening and was reading off a UPS package in a commanding schoolteacher voice.

Elsie and her sister, AnnieFritz, were retired teachers

and lived on the other side of me in a small Greek Revival left to them by their cousin Willie. Three years ago Cousin Willie dropped dead over at the Pirate House restaurant after too much fried chicken and gravy and not enough green veggies and whole grains.

"Putter Vanderpool?" Elsie Abbott called out from the truck. Uncle Putter's hand shot up and a long, narrow package of golf-club proportion got passed on back to him.

"Uh, do you have any idea what's going on here?" Ross asked, an exasperated edge in her voice as I'd clearly wasted her valuable time.

"It's not a lynching."

"Least not yet." She glared my way as AnnieFritz called out GracieAnn Harlow's name.

"You see," I tried to explain. "Chantilly Parker is our beloved UPS delivery gal and has been under some stress of late and not getting the packages to their rightful destination. Being neighborly and sympathizing with the situation, everyone just takes it upon themselves to exchange parcels. My guess is now that most are here in one place they're claiming what rightfully belongs to them." *Like killing two birds with one stone,* I thought, but Detective Ross didn't seem in the mood for morbid levity so I kept my mouth shut.

"Why is this Chantilly person here on a Saturday in her truck? What's this all about?" Ross asked.

"Simon and Chantilly were once . . ." Uh-oh, this was another time to keep my mouth shut. Chantilly had motive enough for polishing off Simon twice over, not that Ross needed to know that. "Friends," I added quickly. "Chantilly and Simon were dear friends. She was probably out making deliveries and must have wanted to wish him well. I was concerned people might be upset over the package situation of late and things would get out of hand so I came to get you."

Ross gave me an *I'm not buying that piece of garbage* look as Chantilly came around the side of the plantation house, crying for all she was worth. "Someone killed Simon." She pulled up beside me. "I had to use the little girl's room and when I came out I heard the terrible news." Chantilly hiccupped and rubbed her eyes. "He had it coming, that's for sure, the no-good rotten bastard. He deserves to have his entrails eaten by hyenas and to be dead and buried in a shallow grave, but he should have been *my* no-good rotten bastard."

"You might want to rethink that," I said to Chantilly as Ross swiped a dribble of icing from Chantilly's brown uniform and Elsie Abbott held up a peach dress from the van. "Well, looky what we have here. I do believe there's a little hanky-panky going on over at UPS. Someone's done left their dress behind in this truck, crinolines and all. My oh my, what is this world coming to."

The crowd laughed. Ross didn't crack a smile. "That's your truck? Your dress? Your deliveries?" she asked Chantilly, cop face firmly in place. "You need to come downtown to the station with me for a chat."

"Detective Ross," Officer Dumont huffed as he hustled toward us from the house. He held a brown cap. "We found this under the cake table."

"Why, that there's mine," Chantilly said, all little Miss

Clueless. She made a grab at the hat with gold UPS stitched on the front. "I must have dropped it. You see, I was sort of in a state when I cut a piece the wedding cake that should have been *my* wedding cake, being as that Simon Ambrose and I were once engaged, and then he went and fell for Waynetta because she has money and . . ."

Chantilly gazed at me, her eyes widening at the realization of what she was saying. She cut her eyes to Ross. "You think I, little ol' me, killed Simon?"

"Chantilly Parker," Ross declared as if she were Saint Peter making a declaration from the Pearly Gates. "You are under arrest for the murder of Simon Ambrose."

"What! You can't be arresting me." Chantilly shook her head, curls flying out into the breeze. "I loved Simon even if he did do me wrong, screw me over, kick me to the curb. Lord knows Simon was an ignoramus, but I'd never kill him, especially in a crinoline of all things. They're itchy; Mamma made me wear one every Sunday to church. I'd choose a waiter uniform or musician outfit, even one of the cook's aprons but never a stupid old crinoline."

"SOME PEOPLE NEVER KNOW WHEN TO JUST KEEP their mouths shut, and I think after today Chantilly is at the top of that particular list," KiKi said to me. She finished off the last of her two-olive martini as we sat on the front steps of Cherry House. Savannah humidity had finally dipped below 90 percent and a crescent moon hung over the cherry tree in the front yard that gave my house its name. "Heard tell Chantilly went and got her cousin Percy Damon for a lawyer," KiKi went on. "I suppose that's all she can afford."

"Percy? He's what, twenty-three? Been out of law school six months? Chantilly made good money at UPS; you'd think she'd have saved for a rainy day."

"And this here is an out-and-out monsoon." KiKi bit a skewered olive, and Bruce Willis performed his nightly ritual of sniffing, leg lifting, and scratching. This Bruce Willis was not the manly man of *Die Hard* and *The Sixth Sense* fame but a rough-around-the-edges dog of indiscriminate parentage. Four months ago he had taken up residence under my porch, then maneuvered his way into my house.

"Heard tell Doreen-the-wedding-planner is giving up the-wedding-planner part of her name," KiKi added. "She's fixing to write a book on the ten virtues of elopement."

"I bet Percy's never even been in a courtroom," I said, the idea of Chantilly's innocence resting in his inexperienced hands a little unnerving.

"Did you hear that Lila Lamont's husband caught her doing the deed with one of the waiters at the wedding? Right there in the boxwoods of all places. Lord only knows how she managed such a thing in a hoopskirt. She said it was the stress of the day that brought on her fornicating behavior. Personally I think what brought it on was tall, dark, handsome with a big do-da."

"Why in the world did Chantilly come to the wedding in the first place?"

"I'm redoing the parlor in teal and cream. What do you think?"

I swirled my olive around in my glass. "Chantilly's got

to be innocent; no guilty person with two ounces of sense in their head would spill their guts to Ross the way she did. How's Percy going to prove it?"

"Putter just told me he wants to book us passage on the next space shuttle to Mars and we're going to live there for a year."

"Do you think Percy can get Chantilly out on bail? It's one of those things covered in Lawyer 101, don't you think? Bet he can't do it till Monday and poor Chantilly will have to spend all tomorrow in jail. How could this happen?"

KiKi snapped my untouched martini right out of my hand and took a long drink. "Reagan, honey, I know where this is headed, and it's not a good place to be going. You're working yourself up to getting involved with finding who did in Simon and not listening to one blessed word I say. You haven't touched your martini, meaning you're thinking and fretting, and that's going to lead straight to trouble."

I took back my martini and ate the olive. "Chantilly helped me get the Prissy Fox up and running," I said around a mouthful. "She sent out tweets to her friends to get them to shop here and bring in clothes to consign. She gave me ideas on how to do the bookkeeping system to keep consigners straight and track sales. Maybe we can help her out. What's the harm in a little assistance when needed; that's what we do here in Savannah, right?"

"We?" KiKi choked. "How did this suddenly become a *we* situation?"

I wagged my empty toothpick. "Nothing's going on in Savannah in August, it's too blessed hot to even move around here. We all sit on our porches and overdose on sweet tea and alcohol depending on the time of day and who's looking. You don't have dance lessons scheduled 'cause there's not a cotillion or social gala till late September. What are you going to do with yourself all month, tell me that?"

KiKi grabbed back the martini. "Hibernating inside my fridge with a gallon of Leopold's Old Black Magic ice cream has definite appeal. Think about the last time we went hunting for the bad guys." She held up her fingers and counted off. "There were abductions in dark alleys, guns, break-ins, hunting through smelly shoe closets, late-night rendezvous, and hunky Italian gardeners. I have to confess I didn't mind the hunky-gardener part so much. And then there's your mamma. If she finds out you're sleuthing again, she'll have a conniption."

Mamma had been a single parent since I was two and Daddy went boar hunting with some good-old-boys from the Oglethorpe Club and a bottle of Johnnie Walker Red and never lived to tell the tale. Over the years Mamma escalated from conservative lawyer who named her one and only child Reagan, to Judge "Guillotine" Gloria, feared by lawyers and criminals alike. Mamma did things by *the* book. When sleuthing, my book read more like *Crooks, Criminals, and Catastrophes.* When not sleuthing my book kept the catastrophe part.

"Mamma's knee-deep in election mode with running for city council," I told KiKi. "We shouldn't bother her with such things as—"

"Murder?" KiKi gulped the rest of my martini and stood. She kissed me on the forehead like she had when I told her I was marrying Hollis Beaumont the Third and she knew I was an idiot for doing such an asinine thing but there was no stopping me.

"I'm going to bed," she said. "Spare key for the Beemer is under the floor mat if you're in need of a car. Don't ding anything or Putter will skin us both and bury our poor lifeless bodies in the sand trap on the fourteenth green over there at Sweet Marsh Country Club since he spends so much time in that particular location. And for heaven's sake, stay away from Aldeen Ross. She might be skinnier these days, but she sure is crankier. The girl's in need of some serious cheesecake therapy, if you ask me."

Chapter Three

I PICKED up a Conquistador sandwich at Zunzi's, then drove down Presidents Street, which was still hopping with locals and even some tourists on a Saturday night. Why anyone visited Savannah in August on purpose was a complete mystery to me. April, now that month belonged to Savannah.

I took Route 80 out of town, heading for Whitemarsh Island. The closer I got to the ocean, the worse the humidity; my two-toned head of half-blonde and half intending-to-be-blonde hair curled into corkscrews around my head. I could turn on the AC but I liked being part of the smells, the sounds, and surrounded by water even if I did have sweat dripping down my back. A night heron cut across the moon, a sea breeze ruffled the oats. I passed the sign proclaiming the next stretch of road a turtle crossing and watched the lights of the city fade away in the rearview mirror as I drove off into the pitch black where sky met ocean.

The red neon announcing Uncle Bubba's Oyster House, which had little to do with Uncle Bubba and everything to do with Paula Deen expanding her food domain, glared from the side of the road. I took a hard right onto Bryan Woods Road and slowed. The tide was in, marshland close by, and the need to stay vigilant particularly important with alligators ready for a midnight snack. The white plantation house loomed in the distance, and even without a murder happening on the premises the place would have a guard or two prowling the grounds. I parked the Beemer behind bottlebrush bushes, their blooms this time of year long and red. I took the car keys, my sandwich, and a flashlight from Old Yeller, which held enough stuff to sustain life for a week. I quietly closed the car door.

Keeping to the shadows, I hid in the weeping willow where Chantilly had parked her UPS van that afternoon. I wondered what happened to it. Did the police take it as evidence? The locals drive it off, holding it hostage till a more reliable driver took over? I wanted to look around, see if the killer left something behind. I had no idea what and went with the idea that I'd know it if I saw it. Yellow crime-scene tape drooped across the front pillars, with a few lights on inside the plantation house for security reasons. A whip-poor-will called into the darkness, no doubt looking for a little night action.

"Checking the place out for your next wedding?" a deep voice breathed behind me, a hand sliding across my mouth.

A scream lodged in my throat, every hair on my body standing straight up. I spun around and faced Walker Boone, who was not the late-night stalker I feared but the ornery whoreson cretin lawyer who took me to the cleaners in my divorce from Hollis. That I'd signed a prenup might have had something to do with the *cleaners* part.

Boone operated on the right side of the law most of the time, but back in his pubescent years he ran with the Seventeenth Street gang. He was a head taller than me with perpetual scruff, buzz-length back hair, black eyes, a hard, lean body honed in a youth of gang days dodging bullets, knives, and baseball bats, and no doubt kept up by daily gym visits, and had the capacity to make grown women whimper by doing nothing more than walking down Bull Street. "What are you doing here?" I whispered.

"Heard there was a wedding."

"You're seven hours and one dead groom late; go away."

"What brings you out to this neck of the woods at this hour?"

From past encounters, I knew there was no getting rid of Boone unless I answered him. I also knew he was here for a reason. "Chantilly Parker seems to be suspect number one in killing Simon Ambrose, and Chantilly and I are friends. It looks like she might have stabbed the groom out of jealousy and maybe a bit of revenge." I gave that some thought. "There could have been some rightful indignation and blatant anger involved and passion—yeah, lots of passion—but she didn't do it. Heaven only knows why, but she loved the conniving piece of crud."

"Word has it logic and Chantilly parted company a few

months back. Something about being naked on a horse and swearing she'd see Simon dead and in the grave before she let him marry someone else."

"I didn't know about the dead-and-in-the-grave part."

"What you don't know fills volumes, Blondie." Boone tucked his finger under my chin and my gaze met his unwavering stare that never gave anything away. "Go home," he said. "Feed our dog."

Boone had once paid a hefty vet bill and now maintained that he owned BW's tail and a leg. "What are you doing out here in the middle of the night?"

"An associate has the same notion as you do about Chantilly not killing Simon. I got black-eyed pea sandwiches from Matthews and the security guard and I exchanged pleasantries. He also happens to be a gravedigger out there at Bonaventure Cemetery. His life is about as exciting as yours."

"My life is plenty exciting."

Boone tapped my Zunzi's bag. "Conquistador with special sauce?"

Good eats and drink will loosen any tongue in Savannah, and I wasn't the only one who knew such things. "Since you beat me in food bribes," I said. "The least you can do is tell what you found out from the guard."

I took out the Conquistador sandwich and held up half. Nothing like fresh-out-of-the-oven French bread, grilled chicken with tomato and lettuce all smothered in special sauce dripping down my hand to tempt a man. Boone hesitated a second, his eyes on the prize, drool forming at the corner of his mouth. He snatched the sandwich and bit into his half, doing a feeding-time-at-the-zoo routine as I did the same.

He leaned contentedly against the trunk of an oak and licked sauce from his thumb. "The way I see it, Chantilly had motive. The peach dress that the killer wore was found in her UPS van, her hat was under the cake table, there was icing on her face and her fingerprints on the cake knife, making this case a slam dunk for the local authorities."

I licked a dribble of sauce off my own thumb and had a come-to-Jesus moment. "Chantilly cut into the wedding cake because she thought it should be *her* wedding cake and that's why her fingerprints are on the knife, and maybe she yelled a few threats on horseback—"

"Naked," Boone added between chews.

"Naked," I conceded. I smacked my lips together, catching every last morsel. "She'd had other breakups and didn't kill those guys." I took another bite. If I didn't finish off my sandwich, Boone would. I was sure of it because that's much how my divorce went. If I had something he and my dear ex wanted, they simply took it, except for Cherry House, and they would have gotten their grubby hands on that too if I hadn't found a killer and cheated Boone out of his lawyer fee.

"Maybe she suddenly felt it was time for a change," Boone said, his mouth stuffed. "She got messed over by one too many men and snapped."

We polished off the last of the sandwich and I squelched an appreciative burp. "How did you know I was here?"

"Saw KiKi's Beemer in the bushes, your purse on the

seat. I figured it was more likely you pinched your auntie's car and came snooping than that she'd taken a liking to that ugly purse you carry around and drive out here. You should keep in mind that this here is a crime scene and the police frown on nosy shop owners messing around on their designated turf."

"Percy Damon is Chantilly's lawyer; she needs all the messing around she can get. Too bad she can't afford you." The words were out of my mouth before I could bite them back.

"Chantilly's dad is retired police; I'm retired hood."

"Semiretired," I corrected.

Boone didn't argue the point and swiped his hand across his mouth to mop up. "We've had altercations, none lately." A slow grin spread across Boone's face, his teeth white against the dark night, a tiny dab of sauce on his chin. "I do believe you're paying me a compliment, Miss Summerside."

"I know how you work is all I'm saying. It isn't nice or pretty, but you win. I'm living proof of that particular point." I glanced back to the house. "Guess there's no getting in that place tonight with you already feeding and finessing the guard. You owe it to me to keep me in the loop."

"There is no loop. This case is closed. Thanks for the sandwich."

"Who asked you to snoop around?"

"No one in your social circle."

Meaning it was someone in Boone's circle, or was that *circles*? Boone rubbed shoulders with the mayor, the country club set, cops, drag queens, and boys in the hood. He rubbed considerably more than shoulders with a good portion of Savannah's female population, or so the gossips said.

I headed back to the Beemer, Boone watching me every step of the way. He'd done a lot of that during the divorce too, not because of my astounding good looks and sexy apparel but because a time or two I'd threatened to jump across his fancy expensive mahogany desk that Lee or Grant or, more than likely, Al Capone had once owned, and strangle Boone with my bare hands. Tonight he watched to make sure I left the premises without causing a problem. If I got caught snooping around, he'd get found out too and that's not how Boone operated.

THE NEXT MORNING I MADE CHURCH BY THE SKIN of my teeth. Afterward I passed on having hot coffee and grabbed toast and sweet tea, then scooped doggie kibble for BW. With no kitchen table or chairs, I hitched myself onto the yellow Formica counter with a chip on the left corner, feet dangling off the edge.

Just because I managed to hold on to Cherry House, which I single-handedly restored because Hollis didn't know a screwdriver from any other kind of screw except the kind he used on me when we divorced, didn't mean I could afford the place. To make ends meet, I'd stepped up my part-time job of escorting wide-eyed tourists around Savannah and pointing out historic homes, relaying deeds of heroes and scalawags, and giving slightly embellished accounts of ghosts and hauntings. This wasn't enough to pay for such luxuries as taxes, electricity, and water so I sold off furniture, and four months ago turned the first floor of Cherry House into a consignment shop. Chantilly helped me get started.

So how could I help her? How could I get Chantilly out of her current predicament? Who else wanted Simon dead? Forfeiting the privilege of being Mrs. Simon Ambrose didn't seem to bother Waynetta one lick. I spent the day sprucing up the Fox, adding displays, and thinking how to approach Waynetta about being my number-one suspect in who killed Simon until Hollis walked in big as you please and handsome as ever. Not that he got me all hot and excited. I got over hot and excited when I found him doing the horizontal hula with Cupcake while still married to me.

"Heard Chantilly served up her own version of wedded bliss yesterday," Hollis said in his best smooth-talking, I-want-something voice.

"You're here to chat about a wedding?"

"Things look kind of slow. Business not so good these days?" Hollis meandered around the shop as if he owned the place, then picked a scarf from the dining room table that I used for displays. "Be a downright rotten shame to lose the place to foreclosure after all the work you put into it."

If I wrestled him to the ground and strangled him with the scarf it would be bad for business . . . maybe. Hollis the Savannah Sleaze was known far and wide. "It's Sunday, Hollis. Things are always slow on Sunday."

"Heard they weren't much better the rest of the time."

"What do you want?"

"Just stopped in to say hello and . . ."

Wait for it. Wait for it. I knew something else was coming; it was the Hollis way.

"And to see if you wanted to sell Cherry House before you lose everything."

Bingo! "And you'd handle the sale, of course."

He grinned, his bleached teeth cutting a dazzling path across his tanned face. "Just because we're divorced doesn't mean we can't be friends. I can get a pretty penny for this place even in the condition it's in."

"And you'd get a hefty commission and I'd barely get enough to pay off the mortgage."

He held up his hands in surrender, except he wasn't surrendering anything—that would be me.

"Better than bankruptcy. I owe you for finding Cupcake's killer like you did and saving my behind."

"And this is how you repay me?" I pointed a stiff finger at the door. "Out!"

Hollis patted my cheek, put his business card and the scarf on the checkout counter, then sauntered to the door. "Think about it, Reagan."

"What I think is that you're total scum."

AT TEN SHARP ON MONDAY MORNING I OPENED THE front white paint-chipped door I loved, with original glass and brass hinges, and flipped the sign in the bay window from "Closed" to "Open." Today would be better, I told myself. Hollis was wrong saying I'd lose everything. August was a little off, is all. I had nice stuff and word would get out, except at the moment the only one who got that word was apparently Auntie KiKi, who was waltzing through the door.

"Thanks for loaning me the Beemer," I said as KiKi two-stepped her way into the Fox. When Auntie KiKi was born the angels chanted "cha-cha-cha" over her crib and turned her into Savannah's resident dance teacher, "Foxtrot" emblazoned on her license plate making it official. KiKi never actually walked anywhere but incorporated a bit of a bounce in her step, unless she had one too many martinis. She picked up a white straw hat with a pink sash from the checkout counter I'd fashioned from a pine door I found up in the attic.

KiKi perched the hat on her head, fluffed her humidity-influenced auburn hair, and studied her reflection in the hall mirror. "So where did you head off to last night? I heard the Beemer backing out of the drive. Putter had on his earphones and dozed off to *Sleeping Your Way Out of Sand Traps*. Lordy, this hat makes me look like a redheaded Hillary Clinton with a perm; your mother would have a heart attack."

KiKi tossed the hat back on the counter and picked up a blue straw bag. "Now this is more like it. Sold."

With no customers we sat at the dining room table between the display of costume jewelry and evening bags. On one side of the room, dresses hung from a dowel suspended between coat racks; blouses, jackets, and suits hung on the other side of the room. I'd draped pink, white, and tan skirts across the back of a Duncan Phyfe sofa on consignment and displayed shoes across a knickknack shelf salvaged from Mamma's attic.

"I drove out to Magnolia Plantation intending to talk to the guard and see if he knew anything about the murder. I even took along a Conquistador as a little enticement but Boone beat me to the punch with a black-eyed pea sandwich."

"From Matthews?"

"Is there anyplace else? I split the Conquistador with Boone and he grudgingly told me that Chantilly's fingerprints were on the cake knife, and she promised Simon she'd see him dead and in the grave."

"It's like Cher says, *Words are weapons, they do terrible damage.* On this particular occasion Chantilly went and did it all to herself."

Back in the day, Auntie KiKi was a roadie for Cher, never quite left the tour, and has been spouting Cher-isms to the rest of Savannah ever since. "Maybe Chantilly knocked off Simon for real?" KiKi went on. "You can't rule out the obvious, and heaven knows the man had it coming."

"Chantilly can't be the only person Simon messed over. Even Detective Ross noticed that Waynetta didn't seem overly distraught about Simon being among the dearly departed. With this being her wedding day she should have passed out cold right there on the floor. Fact is she was a lot more upset about the possibility of returning wedding presents, and did you notice her dress was falling right off? What was that all about?"

"I know for a fact that Doreen-the-wedding-planner considered murdering Simon a time or two, she told me so herself. She got all the blame when things didn't go right. The man was single-handedly ruining her reputation."

"And that's just what Simon has gone and done to me even from the grave," Chantilly whimpered as she shuffled through the front door in the very same clothes she'd had on Saturday. She leaned against the doorjamb, her hair limp and scraggly around her pale oval face, her uniform still smeared with icing and a UPS package in her hand.

"Oh, honey, I'm so glad you're out of jail." I gave Chantilly a hug and tried not to gag from the aroma of jail mixed with rancid icing. I led her to a chair next to KiKi. "Are you okay?"

"Mamma and Daddy put their condo up as collateral and posted bail for me this morning, bless their hearts. Percy was sort of clueless on that particular point of law since he's mostly into real estate law, but with Daddy being a retired policeman he knew the ropes and got Percy though it just fine and dandy. I went straight to work, didn't even bother to change. The police took my package delivery truck as part of their crime scene and now I have a loaner."

Chantilly handed me the package she brought in with her. "Neither rain or snow or gloom of incarceration keeps this carrier from her appointed rounds. A little UPS humor."

"Uh, this here package is for Reginald Sinclair over on West Gaston," I said to Chantilly. "Reginald is sixty, bald, and makes the pest pecan pies you ever put in your mouth."

"And yours are like sawdust." Chantilly grabbed back the package and burst into tears. She banged her forehead on the table. "This is it. I'm doomed. I'm fixing to get myself fired." She sobbed. "My boss is all upset with me putting a UPS truck in danger the way I did, and I have to pay Percy and I don't have much saved up, and my rent's due. "

I took Chantilly's hand. "Your friends will stick by you. We'll figure this out; you'll be okay."

"I don't have friends anymore." Chantilly sobbed harder. "When you ride a horse naked and make a few tequila-induced threats, your friends sort of fade into the wood-work."

"I'll help you any way I can, you know that. I'm here for you and so is KiKi."

Chantilly stopped crying and peered up at me through bloodshot eyes. "You really mean that?"

"Of course we do," KiKi offered in her best caring auntie voice while keeping an odor-buffer distance away. "Friends through thick and thin, that's what we are around here. Reagan will make you breakfast, some nice bacon and eggs will do you up just fine. I'll wash your uniform while you take a long, hot shower."

I started for the kitchen, hoping I had enough detergent to detox the uniform and something in my fridge other than hot dogs when Chantilly pulled me back down hard beside her. "I don't need breakfast," she said. "What I do need is someone to make my deliveries, fill in for me, and do the job right. If I screw up anything else, I'll wind up in the unemployment line for sure." Chantilly threw her arms around me in a bear hug. "You're the best."

Auntie KiKi gave me a supportive pat on the back. "I do declare that is a mighty fine idea. Everyone will get their rightful parcels like they should and be pleased as punch about it. You can do this, Reagan, honey. Right neighborly of you to offer."

"And Miss KiKi can go with you," Chantilly added, all

smiles. "She can look for addresses while you do the driving. All the packages are grouped together by zip codes and streets. You drop them off and get a signature for anything over a thousand bucks. Easy-peasy."

KiKi had the deer-in-headlights look about her now that the shoe was on the other foot. She waved a hand over the dining room. "Uh, someone needs to be here to mind the Fox. Besides, I look plum awful in brown, makes me look washed out and pasty like. I do much better in greens."

Chantilly took the cap with official UPS letters in gold lettering off her head and plopped it on mine. "Don't you fret one little bit about that, Miss KiKi. I only have one uniform with me right now." She looked down at the icing smears and gave a few futile swipes. "It's a bit of a mess at the moment, but that doesn't really matter much, now does it."

"It's kind of smelly," I said.

Chantilly waved away the criticism. "We'll perfume it, fix it up good as new." She shoved Reginald's package into KiKi's hand. "You all best be on your way. UPS runs a tight ship here in Savannah. I've seen the Abbott sisters fill in here at the Fox a time or two. I can go over and get them to help me with the store. They can teach me the ropes."

"What about Bruce Willis? I have a dog to take care of."

Chantilly scratched BW behind the ears. "We've bonded. I bring him hot dogs."

"Honey," KiKi said, desperation seeping into her voice, her arm around Chantilly mamma style. "Everyone will wonder where you are. You'll get reported for not showing up and having phony UPS wannabes filling in for you."

Chantilly swiped away the remaining tears, a little smile tipping the corners of her mouth. "No one pays any attention to a person in uniform, especially if all's going well. You could be from Mars with little green antennae sticking out of your head and no one would pay you any mind at all. As long as folks get their packages they don't much care who does the dropping off. I'm grateful to you all, I truly am." She kissed my cheek then KiKi's. "You'll look fine as can be in my uniform, Reagan. This is wonderful."

"THIS IS TERRIBLE," I SAID TO KIKI TEN MINUTES later while aiming the UPS truck, officially called a package car, up Abercorn. "I look like a log in flip-flops and smell like a French woman of ill repute."

"And you're in bad need of that fake tan stuff. Your legs are so white they could blind a person at twenty paces."

"Sun's bad for you."

"So is looking anemic like you're from New York City, God forbid." KiKi rolled her eyes to heaven and made the sign of the cross for mentioning a Yankee location. She'd parked herself on a big box next to me with the delivery information acquisition device thing clamped between her knees. I took a turn too fast and the packages in the back shifted, KiKi hanging on to the dashboard to keep from sliding out of the doorway.

"Sweet Jesus in heaven, you're going to kill us both," KiKi mumbled. "If not from your driving skills, then the smell coming off that there uniform. We have over a hundred packages to deliver. How are we ever going to manage such a thing? How are we going to breathe?"

"What's out first stop?"

KiKi studied the DIAD. "Says here River Street Sweets. Least I can get a few pralines to sustain life. All I had this morning was a cup of coffee with that artificial sweetener stuff. Putter says I need to watch my sugar intake of all things, but it's common knowledge that no one survives Savannah summer heat on one little old cup of coffee with fake sugar. Whoever thought of such stuff, bet it was a Yankee."

It took a half hour to hand off two packages because KiKi wanted extra hush puppies with her fried oysters to go at Tubby's, maintaining it would act like an air freshener in the truck. There was also a lengthy discussion about some foul odor creeping down the Savannah River and how the paper mill must be acting up again.

"Look at all these cupcakes," KiKi said as we walked into Cakery Bakery, customers sitting at wireframe sweetheart chairs with matching marble-top tables. A ceiling light of gingerbread cookies added to the delicious ambiance; a cupcake clock ticked off the minutes. I gained two pounds surveying the décor. KiKi handed the packages to me then elbowed two elderly ladies out of the way and pressed her nose against the display case of cakes, cupcakes, pies, and cookies. "So many goodies." She sighed. "So little time."

"Can I help you?" GracieAnn Harlow asked as she pranced out from the kitchen area, wiping her hands on her white frilly apron. She had a layer of flour dusted across her cheeks and a pencil with a cupcake eraser slid behind her ear. GracieAnn was midtwenties, green-eyed, cute as a pug puppy, and of the same proportions.

I eyed the raspberry supreme cupcakes with pink swirl icing and mumbled a quick Hail Mary to ward off temptation. "How are you doing today, GracieAnn?" I offered in usual Savannah greeting.

GracieAnn sniffed the air. "What is that gawd-awful odor? I do believe it came in here off the street." She waved her hand in front of her nose to clear the stench, her eyes watering. "What is this city coming to?"

"Sewer backup?" I offered and handed over the packages. "Top one's for you, the other for Miss Delta."

"She's in the back baking for the Wagner brunch tomorrow," GracieAnn said. "No matter what happens, it won't be holding a candle to the goings-on out there at the Waverly wedding. What started out as a mighty bad day wound up just peachy if you ask me."

GracieAnn tore into her package, cardboard and paper flying everywhere. "Wait till you see this." She pulled out a tan-and-pink purse and held it up. "It's big enough to carry all my stuff. I can even put a pair of shoes in here if need be. Got it on that Home Shopping Network. Watch it at night when I can't sleep. Spilled caramel topping over my last one. Don't you just love it?"

GracieAnn slung the purse over her shoulder and grabbed two trays of sugar cookies, one piped in white that looked a lot like the outline of a dead guy on the floor. The other tray held UPS trucks outlined in brown and gold. "Help yourselves, they're on the house. A little something for bringing me my bag."

"Practicing up for Halloween?" I selected one of the truck cookies. "It's not for another two months but these do look great."

"When I'm happy I bake myself into a stupor. I call this recipe Comeuppance."

The dead-man outline looked sort of familiar with chocolate swirls for curly hair, blue dots for eyes, and crosshatch for a goatee? There was no mistaking the UPS truck. KiKi and I exchanged looks. Holy mother in heaven! Simon and Chantilly!

Chapter Four

"SOME people just downright deserve what they get, don't you agree," GracieAnn said, passing around the cookies to customers, purse still on her shoulder. She picked up one of the Simon cookies and chomped it right in half, a smile on her lips, crumbs on her apron. "Simon got his just deserts and so did Chantilly since she went and stole Simon away from me."

Delta Longford hustled through the double swinging kitchen doors, spatula in hand. "GracieAnn, honey, those death-by-chocolate cupcakes you had cooling on the rack are ready to be put out if . . ." Delta stopped, crinkled her nose, and gagged. "What is that dreadful odor? Stinks like dead dog in here. How did that happen?"

"Sewer backup," GracieAnn offered.

"I do declare this just isn't my day. The repairman

called from the hospital. He went and fell off his own ladder this morning and won't be getting to fix my oven for weeks. How am I supposed to run a bakery with my main oven out of whack? All the repairmen around here are fixing air conditioners this time of year. I won't be able to get someone for weeks."

"If it gets over a hundred today, we can just bake things on the sidewalk." GracieAnn giggled, then skipped off into the kitchen like a schoolgirl. Delta eyed the cookies, then leaned over the counter and whispered, "At one time GracieAnn was all tore up over Simon. He treated her pitiful bad. Now she's sort of tickled to her toes the man's dead and gone. The rotten cuss left her for that UPS girl. 'Course then he left that UPS girl for Waynetta."

Delta looked me straight in the eye. "Honey, I declare that smell has attached itself to you like white on rice. Don't take this the wrong way now, but you smell plum terrible."

KiKi grabbed a cookie. "Did Simon date GracieAnn?"

Delta whispered under the din of customer chatter, her eyes narrowed. "GracieAnn used to work at that Wet Willies bar down on River Street. I wouldn't say that Simon ever exactly dated GracieAnn, but he sure led her on like there was something going on between them. The way I see it he cozied up to her for free drinks and eats and maybe even an occasional roll in the hay." Delta let out a weary sigh, then made the sign of the cross at the roll-in-the-hay part. "In the men's room he wrote *GracieAnn's a loose woman*, but it didn't say *loose woman*. He used the *w*-word. Can you imagine such a thing? If you ask me, he got exactly what he had coming to him treating women the way he did."

The bell over the entrance tinkled, announcing a new customer. "Hello and welcome," Delta greeted automatically, then stopped and growled deep in her throat. "Tipper!" she snarled, then snapped the spatula in two. "Why are you here? We're divorced, remember? Bad enough you showed up at the wedding. Go away."

Tipper Longford was five-ten in lifts, had a handlebar mustache, sideburns, and forever wore a gray Confederate soldier's hat. Sergeant Longford was totally immersed in reenactments out at Fort Pulaski or anyplace else in Savannah reminiscent of that fearful time of the unfortunate Northern occupation.

"It's a free country, I have a right to be here if I choose," Tipper huffed.

"And I'm the one who runs this place so I get to decide." Delta snatched a raspberry cupcake from behind the counter and flung it at Tipper, hitting him square in the forehead, pink cake and icing sliding down his nose and into his mustache. "Get out."

"That Waverly wedding cake was a disaster," Tipper said, scraping icing from his chin. "It was ugly, almost as ugly as you. The roses were all the wrong color and it leaned. Heard tell Waynetta's refusing to pay and it's your fault. I thought you should know."

"It's none of your business. I run the bakery. You're too busy fighting the Yankees and whoring around."

Tipper's face got all red and he shook his fist at Delta. "Divorcing you is the best thing that ever happened to me."

Sergeant Longford turned on his military boot heel and stomped out of the store leaving traces of raspberry cake in his path.

"Wow," KiKi whispered. Everyone else in the bakery was dead quiet, the only sound the hum of fluorescent lights overhead. "And here I thought UPS'ing was a boring job."

I eyed the cupcake clock, then snagged KiKi's hand. "We have to go," I said in a loud voice, propelling everyone back to normal. "Have a nice day now, you all."

KiKi and I took another dead-man cookie for the road and hoofed it out to the truck. KiKi said, "I knew the Delta/Tipper divorce was an ugly affair but it's even worse than I heard. Maybe that's why Delta's taken such a liking to GracieAnn. It gives her something else to think about other than Tipper."

"That and they both had bad guy experiences." I charged up Big Brown, the inside hot enough to strip paint. I could turn on the AC but then we'd be trapped inside with the smells from hell. KiKi claimed her spot on the box and covered her nose till I got the truck going and air circulating.

I headed across Broughton and KiKi rotated between gulping breaths of air out the door and studying the handy-dandy delivery information device. "Well, looky here, we have a few more stops to do then we go to the Pirate House. That brightens the day." KiKi tapped her finger to her lips. "You know, we could take a little time out for lunch and—"

"You just did fried oysters and cookies. You're going to explode."

"*We* just did oysters and cookies, and I have to keep up my strength for all this work."

The deliveries on Habersham and Price were foodless and quick-in/quick-out with keeping comments about smelly sewers to a minimum. Chantilly was right as rain in that no one noticed that a blue-eyed do-it-yourself blonde was delivering packages instead of tall, thin gal with brown eyes and hair. I hung a left onto East Broad and parked in front of the oldest restaurant in Savannah. "You figure out where we go from here," I said to KiKi while I grabbed the delivery. "I'm not trusting you anywhere near Pirate House pecan chicken and she-crab soup."

"Sourpuss."

The lunch crowd hadn't swarmed the place yet, only a few early stragglers wandering in. "There's a terrible sewer backup outside," I offered to the waitress with a blonde side ponytail and Cleopatra-blue eye shadow. I held out the package. "This is for your chef." When I didn't let go, the girl gave me a strange look and tugged to get it. "You were at the Waverly wedding," I added. "I ran into you. Suellen, right?"

"I wasn't at that there wedding and I have no idea who you ran into in that hallway." Suellen froze at the mention of hallway . . . which I hadn't mentioned. "Go away," she hissed. "Git out right now! I was supposed to be working here last night. You'll get me fired." A tear slid down her cheek. "How can Simon be dead? This is terrible."

"You knew him?"

"Of course I knew him. I mean, a lot of girls around here knew him. I gotta get back to work." She yanked the package out of my hands and ran off, her ponytail swinging side to side as she trotted down the hall.

I made my way back to the van and climbed in. "Simon's fan club continues to grow. This is all kind of strange," I said to KiKi.

"I'm sitting here in a UPS truck that's hotter than a ten-dollar pistol with my knees to my chin and my brain on meltdown. What strange are we talking about?"

I charged up the van. "Remember yesterday?"

"I'm trying to forget yesterday and I'm adding today to the list."

"Right before the Simon encounter in the dining room, I told you that I ran into a waitress in the hallway. That same waitress is at the Pirate House and all upset over Simon's demise. When we ran into each other at the wedding she said something about, *Now what am I going to do?* You think Simon had something going on with this gal, too?"

"I bet ponytail girl's cute, young, and sexy as all get-out. If that's the case, I'd say Simon was playing her and Lord only knows how many others. If bed-hopping was an Olympic sport, he'd take the gold."

"GracieAnn isn't what I'd call sexy."

"She was good for free eats and dessert, if you know what I mean. Simon kept all the girls on a string till he came across Waynetta, who is not cute or sexy but who's loaded, and that trumps everything." KiKi studied the delivery gizmo. "Jeez Louise. I got a fine idea on how we can make up some time. There's a package in back we should just lose. Say we couldn't find it. I figure that will save us a good twenty minutes."

I hung a right onto State, passing Oglethorpe Square with live oaks and Spanish moss and midmorning strollers hiding from the sun. "Is there a package for the police station back there? You think there's a law against impersonating a UPS driver?"

"We have a delivery for a Mr. Pillsbury over there on Seventeenth Street. I say we drop it at the corner, floor this here means of transportation, and go like the devil's after us." KiKi studied the delivery information. "Except the package is insured for over a thousand dollars and we need a signature. How do you feel about forgery?"

Seventeenth Street was the home of do-rags, not-so-concealed weapons, and a collection of Savannah badasses. I visited this location a few months ago and had no desire to repeat the experience. Taking my dearest auntie to this location was out of the question.

"Tell you what," I said, stopping for some wayward tourists who probably got one heck of a deal on hotel rooms this time of year. "We'll do the rest of the deliveries and then I'm dropping you at Clary's. You can get yourself a nice, cold chocolate milkshake. I'll make the delivery to Seventeenth Street, then swing by and pick you up."

Auntie KiKi gave me the slitty-eyed look, her lower lip in a pout. It was never good to get the slitty-eyed look and the lip. I was in for a lecture, and lectures were even worse than Cher-isms, especially in a hot truck. "Are you implying that I'm not up to the challenge?"

Here we go. "You're always up for the challenge."

"You think those bad boys can put one over on me? That I'm old?"

Oh, Lord have mercy, she's playing the old card. "No one can put anything over on you, honey."

"Don't you *honey* me, and I can darn well handle myself."

"Of course you can."

"We come from good stock. Don't you forget that our great-great granddaddy was General Beauregard Summerside of the Confederate States of America."

Yeah, and look how that turned out. "You know how golf is the great equalizer around here with everyone playing," I said, trying to come up with an excuse to keep KiKi from making the delivery. "What if the Seventeenth Street boys are into golf and meet up with Putter and they say they saw his wife, the dance teacher, down their way." Not that golf wasn't the equalizer. My guess was that the boys had more important things on their minds like street fights, gun deals, and the occasional carjacking to keep them occupied than how to birdie on the fourteenth hole.

I continued, "If Putter finds out you're frequenting Seventeenth Street, he'll have a conniption. Do you really want him huffing and puffing and stomping around the house muttering how you're a wild woman and whatever is he going to do with you?"

KiKi parked her hand on her hip, left brow arched. "What if someone from that particular area goes and tells your mamma where you've been hanging out? Then she'll be the one huffing and puffing around you."

"The boys of the hood do not voluntarily chat it up with judges. I'll be fine. Think of it this way, a UPS truck is neutral territory. It's like Switzerland. UPS doesn't choose sides, we just do our thing and all's well."

KiKi did a finger drum on the dashboard. "Cher says

you have to love spontaneity. It puts you in some strange and wonderful places in life. I should go with you."

"I don't think Cher was talking about Seventeenth Street."

We did the deliveries to the locksmith, then Fabrica, Book Lady Bookstore, Bohemian Gallery, and a raft of other places before I dropped KiKi at Clary's. When I drove off she had a double chocolate shake in her hand and a plate of fries. If I wasn't back in fifteen minutes, I knew she'd call the police and I'd be facing Detective Ross . . . again!

I took Oglethorpe and crossed Martin Luther King Drive. The street numbers got lower, the houses closer, yards smaller. Georgia red clay took the place of green lawns, ACs hummed in the windows, keeping the boys inside and the hood empty. Sweat slithered down my back. It had little to do with heat and everything to do with geography.

I killed the engine in front of a grayish clapboard bungalow with used-to-be green shutters, two red crape myrtle trees the Savannah Garden Club would salivate over, and a decent front porch. I hunted for the package, the contraption used for signing, and some guts. I figured this would take one minute, two tops. I knocked and the door that matched the shutters opened to see . . .

"Big Joey?"

My eyes widened; Big Joey's narrowed. He folded his thick ebony arms across his thicker chest. He gave me a smile sporting a new gold tooth. I considered complimenting his grill but he didn't look in a complimenting mood.

"White woman. You here again making trouble?"

Big Joey and I got acquainted some months ago, and

he helped me out a time or two, mostly when there was something in it for him. I rolled my eyes up to the official hat. "UPS."

"You got flip-flops. UPS don't allow no flip-flops. They run a tight operation."

"I have special dispensation." I held up the package. "I'm looking for Mr. Pillsbury."

"Bet your mamma don't know you're here." Big Joey pinched his nose. "What's that stink?"

"Sewer backup."

"Never happens in this part of town. I'm calling the sanitation department. What's this here city coming to?" Big Joey stepped aside, and a guy I hadn't had the pleasure of meeting before came out onto the porch. He stood a head taller than Big Joey, had a piggy bank tat on his left bicep, a dollar sign on his right, hair pulled back in a ponytail, and a yellow number 2 pencil behind his ear. J. P. Morgan on steroids?

"I'm Pillsbury," he said in a deep baritone vibrating through the porch floorboards. I held out the package. What could it be? Guns, ammo, body parts. I gave it a shake.

"Software." Pillsbury took the package and scribbled his name like he'd done this before. "Gives immediate visibility into our key performance indicators."

"Huh?"

"Sees where the boys pocket the Benjamins." Pillsbury tucked his thumbs in the waistband of his jeans looking like a stealth bomber ready for takeoff. "It tracks what pays, what don't. Joey says you have yourself a business? You need the cloud, girl. How you expect to stay in business without a data center?" Pillsbury tsked, he truly did. I swear it was just like KiKi. Hey, if three hundred pounds of living, breathing wrought iron wanted to tsk like a Savannah belle, it was fine and dandy by me. "Tells where you make the most dough."

"Pillsbury?" *Lightbulb moment.* "Money! You're the dough boy." I did the head-slap, duh thing. "That's really cute."

Pillsbury's eyes turned hard and cold and he looked nothing like the smiling pudgy guy on a roll of biscuits at the grocery store. "Or not so cute, but you do look sort of familiar. We've met?"

Pillsbury stood taller, adding another six inches to his immenseness, and I hustled back to the truck. If there was a list of things not to say in the hood, *cute* and *you look familiar* had top billing.

I picked up KiKi at Clary's and I relayed the story of Pillsbury as we chugged our way home through rush-hour traffic of heat and hydrocarbons. Chantilly reclaimed her truck and I begged AnnieFritz and Elsie to stay on for a few minutes so I could grab a shower and toss Chantilly's uniform in my old Maytag. I decided to keep the Fox open till eight, hoping to entice late-night customers. It never happened.

By August, everyone was tired of summer clothes, and shopping for fall sweaters, jackets, and suits in ninety-plus heat was not happening. Day business was no better, proven by the fact that AnnieFritz, Elsie, and Chantilly had time to leave me a pitcher of sweet tea in the fridge and a fresh-baked pan of corn bread.

While trying to figure out how to pay the taxes on Cherry House due next month, I locked up and stashed the meager daily take in a Ben & Jerry's container I kept in the freezer. Not exactly Bank of America, but unless a burglar had a hankering for Rocky Road I figured I was safe.

"Good thing you like hot dogs instead of steak," I said to Bruce Willis, who was sitting on my foot, both of us staring into the mostly deserted fridge. "How do you feel about peanut butter and jelly? It may come to that, you know. Times are tough."

"I hate peanut butter and jelly," a voice said behind me. "But the corn bread's mighty tasty."

Chapter Five

I JUMPED, yelped, and spun around to Walker Boone leaning against my kitchen counter eating my corn bread. BW jumped too, putting his front paws on Boone's shoulders and licking his face. Worst watchdog in three states. "How'd you get in here?"

"I can't tell if you're stupid or have a reoccurring death wish." Boone swiped his hand across his mouth, cleaning away corn bread crumbs. "What were you doing over on Seventeenth Street?"

"Men talk more than women ever thought about doing. Bet I wasn't even back in the UPS truck after making my delivery before the boys were texting you." Boone gave BW a chunk of bread and I snagged the pan away, knowing full well those two would kill off the rest given half a chance. "I was helping Chantilly with UPS deliveries, if you must know. She wasn't up to the task and I was helping out."

"Heard you went the wrong way down Drayton and nearly ran over a troop of Girl Scouts by the Juliette Gordon Low house. That's not good for tourism."

"We were looking for addresses. Do you know how difficult it is to find addresses in this city? Are you so bored with life you've taken to spying on me?" Boone had on a faded Crab Shack T-shirt, cutoffs, boat shoes, and a day's growth of beard most men didn't sport for a week.

"No need for spying. Did you realize Chantilly taught AnnieFritz and Elsie how to use Twitter? The kudzu vine just got kicked into the twenty-first century and word has it you're the guilty party who left the fearsome threesome together. Folks are mighty upset. I'd keep an eye out for voodoo dolls if I were you."

I racked my brain for the patron saints of tweets and dolls with pins. "They were supposed to be minding my store. Working."

"That's your job. You should stick to it. Pillsbury said you recognized him. Not good. He's more of a lay-low kind of guy, fades into the woodwork."

"I got news for you. At six-five and two-fifty-plus, the man's not fading anywhere."

"Seems you've made a day out of pissing people off."

I dropped the bread on the counter and glared at Boone. "Then you tell me what Pillsbury was doing at the Waverly wedding? I know he was there because I saw him with my own two eyes. He had on a suit that made him look shrink-wrapped and I'm willing to bet he wasn't on the guest list anymore than I was."

Boone's eyes darkened just a smidge. That meant he had to do something he didn't want to and right now that was tell me something. If he didn't, I'd keep poking around. "Pillsbury has a thing for Chantilly and figured she might cause trouble at the wedding like she did at the engagement party. He was looking out for her."

"Well, he didn't look hard enough, now did he; the girl's accused of murder." I broke off a chunk of corn bread and munched, trying to digest this latest piece of information of Chantilly and Pillsbury. "You really think Pillsbury killed Simon because he did Chantilly wrong?" I took another bite of corn bread and considered that. "That's kind of sweet."

Boone grinned. "Pillsbury's been called a lot of things but I doubt if sweet is one of them."

"What about cute?"

"You didn't."

"It may have slipped out."

Boone snagged the last chunk of bread from the pan and I gave him an evil look. "You know it'll go straight to your hips," he said. "Nothing more pitiful than a belle with big hips. You'll get the *Ain't she just precious* treatment."

Nothing puts the fear of God into a Southern woman more than the precious treatment. *Ain't she just precious* is what people say about you when there's nothing much good to say at all. At present I was divorced, over thirty without a man, and couldn't cook to save my life. If I got big hips, I'd definitely be in the *precious* category. I dropped my corn bread back in the pan and Boone grabbed it up.

"You played me."

"I'm hungry."

Tired to the bone, I hitched myself up onto the yellow counter and tucked one leg under the other, trying to get comfortable. "Sweet or not, Pillsbury wielding a cake knife doesn't compute. A man that size appreciates food—he'd never harm a raspberry layer cake—and my guess is the boys have more effective ways of disposing of a body than in the middle of a wedding."

Boone pulled out the pitcher of sweet tea. He poured a glass, took a drink, then poured tea into a bowl, setting it on the floor for BW. The pecking order of man, dog, Reagan.

"Caffeine *and* sugar? Really?" I groused. "BW will be up all night driving me crazy."

"Who else is on your radar of suspects?" Boone gave me a sideways glance. "I'm just helping Pillsbury and he's on Chantilly's side."

I swiped the glass from Boone and took a long drink. "I've never even heard Chantilly mention Pillsbury. Secret relationship?"

"So secret she doesn't know. He's from the hood, her daddy's a retired cop. Some things aren't meant to be. About those suspects?"

Meaning he told me about Pillsbury and Chantilly so now it was my turn to cough up information. "GracieAnn's baking dead-guy cookies over at Cakery Bakery. They look an awful lot like Simon. Waynetta Waverly is more concerned about keeping her wedding gifts than her almost-husband facedown in fondant and buttercream. Neither seems all that upset that Simon's taking up permanent residence out at Bonaventure Cemetery." I considered mentioning Suellen from the Pirate House as a suspect but decided she was more of an upset waitress who saw a dead guy in a cake. Then again, there was that mumbling about *Now what am I going to do.* "Who do you think killed Simon?"

Boone snagged back the sweet tea, drank, and shrugged. "GracieAnn had motive. She was at the wedding and knows her way around a cake knife." Boone put down his glass. He turned to me and tucked a strand of hair behind my ear. A caring gesture not like Boone at all and there was a glint of devilment in his eyes. Boone was trouble enough without the devil thrown in. He said, "Last time you went snooping for a murderer you nearly wound up dead in your own shop. This time I might not be around to save you, Blondie."

I parked one hand on my still-somewhat-narrow hip and poked Boone in the forehead with my index finger. "Don't call me Blondie, and your memory is a touch foggy because *I* saved you."

Boone arched his left eyebrow, then headed for the kitchen door. I threw the pan at his head, missing by a mile. The canine vacuum cleaner gobbled the corn bread and I watched through my back window as Boone disappeared down the walk to the street. "I *did* save your sorry, miserable hide, and right now I'm wondering why I went and did such a dumb thing."

AT TEN THE NEXT MORNING, I OPENED THE PRISSY Fox. The heat index hovered near sweltering and by noon would reach sizzling. "You got to do something right quick." Auntie KiKi bustled through the back door in yellow slippers and a matching housecoat billowing out behind her. Her hair was done up in big yellow rollers all over her head and the cucumber mask gave her the look of a green raccoon hiding out in a banana. "I've been on the phone for an hour," she panted, pulling sweet tea from the fridge. Horror stricken, I watched as she gulped straight from the pitcher. Sweet mother in heaven! No belle old or young ever gulped from a pitcher. All Savannah was in desperate need of ice skates because hell had just frozen over.

"Chantilly's out making rounds this morning," KiKi hurried on. "She dropped off Henrietta Duncan's prenatal vitamins to Sister Donovan over there at St. John's Church. Father Gleason saw the whole thing and is lighting candles and saying novenas as we speak. I'm not quite sure what that's all about but it doesn't look one smidgeon good for either of them."

Auntie KiKi took another swig and wiped her mouth with the sleeve of her robe. "You ought to be calling Chantilly right this very minute and tell her you'll do the delivering again today." KiKi held the pitcher high looking a bit like the statue of liberty in hair rollers. "If General Beauregard Summerside took up the cause to save our fair city from harm and devastation, you need to be doing the same." KiKi held out her iPhone. "Call."

"I have a shop to run and there's something about a cloud and profits I need to look into and I'm tired."

"I tell you Chantilly's more distraught than a hen in a hurricane with all that's going on and making more mistakes than this city can tolerate. Besides, you don't have yourself any profits and there's not one single cloud in the sky today so you can't be looking at that. We all know the reason you're tired is you're taking up with that Walker Boone person." Auntie KiKi folded her arms and tapped her left foot. "I saw him swaggering out of here last night big as you please."

"He's trying to prove Chantilly innocent, is all, and came over to see what I knew, which isn't much. I can't believe you had yourself such a good time yesterday that you're up for round two of UPS for beginners."

"Oh, honey, not me. I can't be going with you today. I have a dance lesson with Bernard Thayer. Missing a lesson with him just wouldn't be right. He pays double and in advance. You're flying solo today."

Dancing with Bernard was like driving a Mack truck with bad breath. "You're a chicken, you know that."

KiKi patted my cheek. "Cher would call it inspirationally resourceful. And there's more."

"I don't want more. I don't want any. I want to go back to bed till September."

"Chantilly's on her way out to the Waverly Farms this very minute to pick up a UPS package. She told Sister Donovan all about it when dropping off the pills. Chantilly intends to give Waynetta a piece of her mind about getting what she deserved in stealing Simon the way she did, then him dying on her right there at the wedding."

"UPS sent Chantilly to the Waverly Farms?"

"UPS isn't all that plugged into the Savannah kudzu vine." Auntie KiKi put the phone in my hand. "You got to get a hold of Chantilly and talk sense into her right now before she gets to Waynetta or there's going to be a catfight out there like no other."

"If Chantilly's intent on ranting and raving, she's not going to pay one bit of attention to a phone call."

"That's just what I'm thinking." Kiki reached into her robe and pulled out the Beemer keys. "Go get her."

FIVE MINUTES LATER I WAS BARRELING OUT OF town—or as much as anyone barreled in Savannah on a hot summer morning—heading for Whitemarsh Island and Waverly Farms. Not that I wanted to do this. The front hall of Cherry House was mouse gray and in desperate need of new paint if I could beg KiKi's leftovers from redoing her kitchen, and somehow I had to come up with ideas on how to get more customers. Hollis's threat of foreclosure and no business was more real than I'd ever tell him. Then there was the cloud issue. Scary thought that the moneyman for the hood knew one heck of a lot more about running a business than I did. I considered his cash flow and mine and decided he had reason to know more.

The Beemer could overtake a UPS truck any day of the week but Chantilly had a good start on me. I hoped she had a few more deliveries before meeting up with Waynetta to give me a little time. My second hope was that she didn't cause too much mayhem in town while making those deliveries or her job was history.

I got onto East Victory and did a quick stop at Sisters of the New South to pick up a bag of delicious temptation.

If your mamma and grandma didn't keep a jar for drippings on the stove, then Sisters was not the place for you. It was pure Southern eating and near Bonaventure Cemetery, a convenient location for those who frequented the sisters a little too often.

I crossed over the Wilmington River, sparkling like diamonds in the sunlight as it meandered its way out to sea, then took the second right off the main drag. Wild oats and marsh grasses hugged the road, a UPS truck lumbering along just ahead. Honking, I got up next to Chantilly and pointed to the side for her to pull over.

Chantilly must have guessed that I was here to head her off before she reached Waynetta because she hit the gas, leaving me in a cloud of exhaust. Poking her head out the window, she did a hand gesture that would make her mamma faint dead away then threw her head back and let out a cackle I could hear even over the roar of engines.

Chantilly was in serious need of therapy. I wasn't sure how much I wanted to catch up with her in this state but I couldn't let her run around town in a UPS truck either. I punched the Beemer and launched forward, sea grasses whizzing by, KiKi's fancy car neck and neck with the truck. If someone came in the opposite direction the Beemer was toast and my favorite auntie would kill me dead. Planning ahead for this very thing, I gripped the steering wheel with one hand and held the Sisters green-and-orange bag over the roof of the car. I made the bag do a little dance to get Chantilly's attention, and sure enough the UPS truck slowed and coasted to a stop.

"What do you think you're doing?" I slammed the car door and stomped my way toward the truck.

Chantilly looked like a crazed porcupine with curls, her hair sticking out in all directions from under her UPS hat. She made a grab for the Sisters bag, but I yanked it out of her reach. Her brow wrinkled and her lips thinned. "Bet you got fried chicken, yams, cabbage, and corn bread in that bag. The sisters make to-die-for corn bread."

"And smothered pork chops and you only get it if I'm the one picking up the package at Waverly Farms."

"That there's blackmail pure and simple. Your mamma would have a stroke if she knew you were into blackmail. Besides, I'm fine as can be. Guess I could do with a dough-nut."

"You'll have to get your own doughnut. Honey, you're not yourself these days. You got everyone over at St. John's Church in a tizzy, phones are ringing off the hook, Twitters are tweeting and it's not even noon. If you meet up with Waynetta, you'll fight like dogs over a bone, and your bail might get revoked and you'll wind up in jail looking guilt-ier than ever."

Chantilly eyed the bag and licked her lips. "I'm not sure I like you right now."

"Give me the keys to the truck so I can pick up the package at Waverly Farms, I'll give you the bag. No eating in the Beemer or KiKi will have a conniption." I held the bag high. Chantilly squared her shoulders and did likewise with the truck keys. "On the count of three we swap," I suggested.

Chantilly nodded; I counted and on *three* grabbed the keys and Chantilly grabbed the food. "You also have a pickup over at Icy's fish house down by the docks," Chantilly said around a mouthful of smothered pork chop, gravy coating her fingers. "Don't mess it up," she said between licks. "I'll get fired for sure. My boss is on his last nerve with me."

"Gee, imagine that." I peeled Chantilly's hat off her head deciding that since I had on a brown Gap T-shirt, the hat was all the UPS uniform I really needed. Gap, UPS— letters were letters, no one paid attention. I climbed in the truck and took off.

Sitting on a log and munching corn bread, Chantilly waved a bye-bye pork chop at me, then faded into the distance. Waverly Farms forked left and I followed the painted plank fence to the big white house, fountain splashing in the front. I killed the engine and jumped off the truck just like a real UPS person as Reese Waverly shouldered his rifle and took aim. Holy mother-of-pearl! And here I thought everyone loved UPS!

I considered diving under the truck to take cover but

realized Mr. Got-bucks wasn't aiming at me but a life-size cutout of Simon propped against the fence. A shot rang out, leaving a hole right smack in the middle of Simon's forehead. There was dead and real dead. What did Simon do to have Reese Waverly taking potshots at him when he was already at the morgue?

"Pickup is around back," Waynetta said from behind, making me jump. Gunshots will do that to a person. Waynetta had on a yellow cotton skirt, white blouse, pearls, and the tiara she'd won as Miss Peaches-and-Cream some years ago. I figured that her self-esteem must be in need a little boost after the wedding from hell, but this wasn't exactly a picture of a grieving bride.

"I'll get the package and be on my way," I said.

Waynetta gave me the *I can do anything better than you* look that she did so well. It was the have and have-nots of the tiara world and a UPS driver clearly had not. "There's more than one package," Waynetta ordered. "Fact is I have a whole living room full. I'm returning all my wedding gifts. My fiancé was murdered; you probably read about it in the papers. Bessy May has done packed up all my gifts, took her a full day, and I do declare I'm plum worn out from the experience."

"I'm so sorry for your loss."

"That's mighty neighborly of you." Waynetta offered a wobbly smile, then sniffed and swiped at a nonexistent tear. "There was a truly lovely silver tea service I'll miss something awful."

I was referring to Simon dead as a bedpost down at

Savannah's House of Heavenly Slumber. Another shot rang out, the cutout of Simon swaying from the impact. "I take it your daddy wasn't all that fond of Simon."

The *I can do anything better* look turned to an *eat dirt and die* look. "I'll have you know Daddy loved Simon. They were pals, he treated Simon like a son, and the reason Daddy's shooting at his likeness is that he's so mad at Simon for getting himself done in that he has to let off steam." Waynetta's eyes got all watery again but the wishing-me-dead part lingered.

Waynetta didn't mourn the death of her almost husband and was doing her best to convince me that her daddy liked Simon when obviously he didn't. Savannah-style mourning consisted of rounds of forty-year-old bourbon, Havana cigars, and a deviled egg or two, but not bullets in the head.

I waited for Waynetta to go inside but instead of heading for the back of the house to get the packages, I strolled out to Reese Waverly. Something was going on out at Waverly Farms and it wasn't a lot of crying and carrying on.

"What?" Reese asked, not taking his eyes from the target.

I held up my handy-dandy DIAD signature thing. "I just need for you to sign that I'm picking up packages. I'm sorry for your loss." That line got Waynetta talking and I hoped it would do the same thing now. "Yeah, some loss." Reese neutered Simon with one pull of the trigger.

"Waynetta doesn't seem all that upset," I ventured.

Reese snarled, "She's plenty upset. Cried and carried on something fierce all night long. She keeps her feelings to herself with strangers is all." He scribbled on the little machine. "Packages are around back. Go collect them and be on you way." This time Reese put a bullet clean through Simon's heart.

Taking the hint, I scampered back to the truck, put it in gear, and headed for the rear entrance just as a red '57 Chevy convertible crunched its way down the crushed-oyster-shell drive. Walker Boone? No one else I knew had that car. It wasn't exactly a silver SUV like the rest of the country drove. What was that man doing here? The Waverly horse farm was third-generation Southern sophistication; Walker Boone was first-generation legit and at times even that was questionable. Boone had his share of snobby friends and even belonged to the country club, but he and Reese Waverly didn't run in the same circles. They barely lived on the same planet. Yet here they were.

If Boone can drop in on me, I can eavesdrop on him, right? I got the truck out of sight, killed the engine, then wiggled between the magnolia tress in front to catch a peek. Boone shook Dead-eye's hand, but it was more businesslike than good-old-boy friendly.

"You are some kind of busybody," Waynetta said from behind me again. "I'm calling your supervisor right this very minute."

"Thought I dropped something out of the truck is all. Thought it rolled into the bushes and I was looking for it."

"Why are you spying on my daddy?" she hissed. "Are you spying on me, too?" She eyed my T-shirt. "Gap is not UPS. I know you. You're that Summerside person. Your mamma's running for city council and you own a consignment shop and got divorced from Hollis Beaumont. I should call the police; I bet you're here trying to run off with all my stuff to sell at your place. You're nothing but a thief and up to no good and causing me more problems than I already have."

I pointed to Big Brown. "I *am* UPS and I don't need any of your stuff to sell," I lied on both accounts. I was faux UPS, Waynetta had first-rate stuff, and it would sell like hotcakes at the Fox. Since I was already busted I decided to push on. "You don't seem all that upset about Simon being dead and I'm wondering why."

"I most certainly am upset." Waynetta put the back of her hand to her forehead drama-queen style, knocking her tiara kittywhumpus. "I'm in such a sorry state by all this nonsense and it's frightful hot out here. I'm going inside and you better leave if you know what's good for you, or else."

With sweat sliding between my boobs and my hair stuck to my scalp, I loaded the truck. When I left a half hour later Boone's car was still parked out front. Maybe he was doing some legal work for Waverly Farms, but Reese for sure had his own band of legal eagles, so what was with Boone?

I hung a left onto the two-lane. Whoever assigned the UPS delivery routes was determined to keep Chantilly out of town and doing pickups more than deliveries. Guess they figured that was one way to minimize problems. I took Lighthouse Road down to the weathered docks stretching far out into the river to accommodate tides. I parked Big

Brown next to the clapboard sun-bleached building with "Icy's Fish and Shrimp" scripted in faded blue on the side.

Two shrimp boats with huge black nets hanging loose bobbed at the end of the pier. Men who looked as if they did more than lift a pencil or peck a keyboard for a living hosed off decks and scrubbed. In May when the ocean was cool, shrimpers stayed out twelve days at a stretch to get their quota. Now that the water was warm they shrimped a few hours in the morning or late at night. Come fall they'd be back to long weeks onboard. It wasn't that I knew so much about shrimp boats but I knew plenty about fresh shrimp stuffed with crab and wrapped in bacon.

Inside the building, refrigeration hummed and a man stood behind a display case, his back to me as he packed shrimp in ice. A chalkboard reading "Catch of the Day" sat to one side, and the smells of ocean hung heavy in the air. "UPS for a pickup," I called out.

The man turned, his once-white apron wet and dirty. He was late fortyish, thinning hair, no smile, no shave, no bath, and built like a backhoe. He pulled five brown paper packages out of the display case. "Packed in dry ice. Don't put 'em in the sun."

I handed over the signature gizmo that looked lost in his huge hands and would smell like shrimp for a week. "You were at the Waverly wedding," I said, making a little innocent conversation as he wrote. "I saw your truck. That sure was some affair. Have people talking for months. Bet you did the shrimp for the shrimp cocktail. Bet it was great."

Shrimp shoved back the gizmo along with a look cold as the dead fish in the case. "Best mind your own business."

I snapped up the packages and headed for the truck. What happened to my innocent conversation? First Pillsbury didn't want to be recognized at the wedding and that I understood. But now Icy Graham—that was the name he scribbled on the DIAD device—had a nasty reaction to the situation. Why? Bad shrimp? Did he overcharge the bride? Maybe he ripped off the caterer? He could have knocked off the groom except I couldn't imagine Icy in a peach bridesmaid dress or running with the likes of pretty-boy Simon. Then again, I didn't know Simon very well and Icy could have had a female accomplice.

The DIAD was equipped with GPS but the back roads on Whitemarsh meandered all over the place like a drunken snake. I had a better chance of not getting lost if I headed back toward Waverly Farms and drove to town from there. The sun hovered at a blinding four o'clock angle, making me do the how-could-I-forget-my-sunglasses squint. The air smelled hot, still, swampy, and stagnant. Sea oats and grasses stood tall, not a puff of breeze anywhere.

I was tired and hungry and needed to have a little heart-to-heart with Chantilly. I couldn't do this every day; I had a shop to run and keep out of Hollis's money-grubbing clutches and a hall to paint and—

Something smacked the truck from behind, snapping my head forward and lurching the truck to the side. I fought the steering wheel, Big Brown swaying back and forth across the road, packages sliding everywhere, stuff crashing to the floor. I was hit again harder, this time packages flying through the air. The tires caught the side berm, dragging the truck off the road. I gripped the wheel for all I was worth, bracing myself, heading toward the water, cattails and oats smacking the windshield as I sank down, down, down into the murky, smelly Savannah swamp.

Chapter Six

THE engine sputtered and died. Water rushed in the open doorway, trapping me inside, inching up my legs, covering my knees, making me wish I was six-two for a little more breathing room instead of five-five. *Lord, get me out of this one and I'll do something really nice,* I bargained. Not that God needed a bargain from me but I figured He was always up for a good laugh.

Big Brown settled onto the bottom, dropping into the primal goo, leaving me dry as a bone from the waist up. I made the sign of the cross and rolled my eyes skyward. "I thank you kindly, Sir, I truly do."

Marsh bugs chirped, the stillness of the swamp closing in around me as if nothing life-threatening happened at all. Packages bobbed about like toys in a bathtub; a silver teapot swirled by, then dropped into the murkiness. A turtle swam by, then climbed onto one of the packages from Icy, the little flotilla drifting out the door into the marsh.

"Is everything okay down there?" bellowed a voice from the road.

"Just peachy," I yelled back, not wanting anyone to see me in such a state. I was still shaking, I smelled like *sweat eau de swamp*, and my clothes stuck to me, showing off things best not exposed by accident and only by choice. A swamp encounter was not by choice. I scooched off my driving perch, the water creeping to just below the Gap on my shirt. Cautiously I stepped into the squishy bottom, now wet up to my boobs and instantly losing my flip-flops in the goosh. Pushing aside a growth of cattails I took a few steps, the muck sliding up between my toes. Something slithered against my leg and I bit back a screech. If it was a snake, the Lord himself would not be the only one walking on water.

I wiggled between more grasses, caught sight of the road, breathed a sigh of relief until I gazed up at a red Chevy convertible and Walker Boone beside it fit, trim, and perfect.

"Reagan?" Boone's brows arched over his aviator sunglasses. He slid them off to get a better look no doubt, a smirky smile making its way across his lips. "I should have guessed."

I poked my head around a clump of weedy things, keeping the rest of my transparency out of view. "No, you shouldn't have guessed it was me out here. I don't usually drive a UPS truck into a swamp."

"But you wind up in some mighty fine messes and this time you outdid yourself. I came around the bend and saw the truck take a header into the water. What happened? Too used to driving KiKi's Beemer?"

"I can drive a truck just fine, thank you very much."

"Uh, Reagan, you got to get out of there."

"So you can see my clothes stuck to me and give me a lecture on getting in shape and not eating junk food." I parked my hands on my soggy hips. "I'll tell you what, I happen to like junk food. It makes me happy, a lot happier than I am right now. I'm all about Snickers and doughnuts and I hate tofu. It's like eating sponge. It's gross."

"Gator."

"I hate alligator meat, too."

"It's not mutual. Alligator behind you. Run . . . or maybe swim."

"Gator?"

"Now, Reagan."

"My feet are stuck. It's like quicksand in here." I was so scared I couldn't have moved anyway. I forced myself to look back at the alligator, is tail swaying gracefully back and forth, propelling his long, dark green sleek body toward me at a nice, steady pace. He sized me up, I could tell, thinking *one bite or two*, his mouth of seventy-five teeth opening. Seventy-five? Where did that come from? Amazing what you remember when facing the jaws of death.

Boone turned for his car.

"You're leaving me! You can't leave me. I'll haunt you every night, I swear I will."

He reached into the backseat, then jumped into the marsh, dropping to waist-high water, baseball bat in hand. He slogged toward me. "A bat!" I yelled. "You're from the hood and you're packing a bat? Where's the gun, the heat? The AK-47." I didn't know what an AK-47 was, but it sounded powerful and mean and right now that was a good thing.

"I don't shoot gators."

"Just people?"

"On occasion."

"For crying in a bucket, Boone, he wants to eat me!"

"Had that feeling a time or two myself." Boone grabbed my arm, yanking me out of the goop like a toy, and whacked the gator on the snout. The gator arched up, flung his tail and looked pissed as all get-out. He opened his mouth wider and snapped at Boone, chasing us backward.

"Good God, you're making him mad."

"You got a better idea, Blondie?"

"He's Southern. He's a foodie." I tore open one of Icy's packages floating by and flung fistfuls of shrimp at the gator. He chomped at the food, all those teeth coming together in one loud ferocious bite after another.

"Well, I'll be," I said in complete astonishment. "It worked."

Boone snagged me around the waist like a football and propelled us through the cattails to the bank. We stumbled up the muddy side, across sand and rocks, and scrambled into the car. Gators were fast as greased lightning on land but they couldn't open car doors for diddly . . . yet. You never knew for sure about gators.

"Why aren't you in your shop?" Boone said between pants, his shirt glued to finely sculpted six-pack abs. Bet the gator was female; no wonder she went after Boone. If she'd been screwed over by him in a divorce, she'd know better.

"Don't call me Blondie, and why were you out at Waverly Farms?"

Boone plucked up a strand of my scraggly hair and slowly gave it a twirl, his breathing settling back to normal. "But you are blonde. On occasion that is. And you act blonde."

I folded my arms over my chest hoping for a dollop of modesty with things poking out of a wet T-shirt that shouldn't be poking. "Don't you stereotype me, Walker Boone. You can get sued for that, you know, and you're just trying to change the subject and get me ticked off. What about Reese? What are you up to?"

"Right now, saving your bacon."

"Hey, I'm the one who threw the shrimp. That makes me saving *your* bacon, again, I might add." I caught a glimpse of Big Brown all forlorn in the swamp and felt a huge tug of sadness. "Guess this means Chantilly will get fired for sure."

Boone started the car but instead of speeding off down the road he turned to me and swiped a smear of mud from my chin. He touched a sore spot on my forehead and gave me a strange sort of look. "Are you okay? I mean are you really okay?"

Boone concerned about me? What? How'd that happen? After two years of torture and anguish this was sort of . . . sweet. "I'm okay; are you okay?" I picked a glob of weed from his shoulder and flung it back into the swamp.

"Been though worse." My gaze met Boone's for a split second, something dark and mysterious lurking there. He cleared his throat, then hit the gas. "Try not to drip on my seats, okay."

I held up a wet arm. "What am I supposed to do? Will myself dry?"

"Sit on the floor. You smell like a swamp."

"You're no rose garden yourself." And here we were leaving *sweet* in the dust and back to scum-sucking lawyer in less then thirty seconds flat.

"WELL, IT'S OFFICIAL," CHANTILLY WHINED AS SHE shuffled into the Prissy Fox the next morning munching a doughnut, coffee in the other hand.

I had the door open enjoying the morning cool before the city turned into a blast furnace. I happened to be in the midst of changing the display in the front bay window from a yellow cropped jacket and green capris to fall colors of denim and khaki and cute ankle boots. I needed something to get people thinking about fall and a new wardrobe. If I could figure out a way to get the temperature out of the nineties and into the seventies, that would help a ton.

Chantilly scratched Bruce Willis behind the ears, fed

him a chunk of pastry, then plopped down on the little green stool. She parked her chin in her palm, elbow resting on the old door serving as a counter. She broke off a section of doughnut for me, then polished off the rest. "UPS fired my sorry behind and it's all because of a few broken dishes and packages of shrimp. Everything was insured; I don't know what all the fuss is about." She licked the glaze from her fingers one by one. "How could this happen? Where's the understanding, the compassion? I'm an overwrought woman here."

"Their package truck and delivery acquisition information device is in the middle of a swamp."

"There is that. I suppose I'll just have to work here at the Fox." When I didn't reply in the affirmative, Chantilly peered at me out of the corner of her eyes. "You owe me, you know. You were the one who drove into the water."

"I was rammed off that road from behind," I offered in my own defense and added a navy jacket to the display.

"Well, *I* never get run into a swamp and neither does any other driver I know. A flat tire now and then and maybe a parking ticket but never this. What did you go and do?"

"I picked up packages, period." I made a cross over my heart in promise style and left off the part about interrogating Reese, infuriating Waynetta, and ticking off Icy, all pretty much Reagan style.

"Well, Lord be praised!" Auntie KiKi hurried through the front door. She threw her arms around my neck. "You could have been eaten by a gator. Thank the saints in heaven Walker Boone came along when he did and saved you. I got a tweet this morning from Elsie Abbott."

"Since when do you tweet?"

"Couldn't let the Abbott sisters outdo me now, could I. I'd be kicked off the kudzu vine as a has-been." Kiki pulled out her iPhone, touched the screen, and read, *"FTW. Reagan in Gray's Creek with gator and Boone. Delish. Who to eat what."*

"What were the Abbotts doing on Whitemarsh? And for your information Boone did not save me. And what in the world is *FTW.*"

KiKi and Chantilly exchanged exasperated looks. *"For the win,* honey," KiKi said as if teaching me how to conjugate verbs like she did in the fourth grade. "It's my tweet kicks your tweet right in the patoot."

"You started all this." I glared at Chantilly, shaking my finger at her. "No one's going to get away with anything with this tweet stuff going on."

"Like you and Boone together?" Chantilly grinned.

"He insisted I sit on the floor so I wouldn't drip all over his car and he said I smelled. Guess the sisters missed that part." I didn't have a phone. My mode of transportation when I wasn't mooching KiKi's Beemer was the Chatham Area Transit system and the only tweets I got were from birds outside my window.

KiKi continued, "My guess is the sisters were out at Bonaventure for a wake since August seems to be a right popular month for people dying. My guess is folks are just plum tired of the heat around here and want to escape any way they can. Elsie and AnnieFritz went over to Basil's Deli out that way for one of those margarita wraps. They probably got lost in the back roads, they usually do that too, and happened to see Boone rescuing you in the swamp."

I started to protest the rescue bit again but got distracted by Percy Damon standing outside on my sidewalk. He had on a blue suit with high-water pants, white starched shirt, red tie, and sweat slithering down his cheek. By noon he'd look like a drowned flag. He'd talk to my would-be customers. They'd listen, then run off as if chased by evil spirits. I said to Chantilly, "What's going on out there?"

Chantilly's gaze followed my pointing. She closed her eyes for a moment and massaged her forehead. "Percy said if he has to question every single person in Savannah to prove I'm innocent, he'd do that very thing. He's really into my case. I mentioned I was working here and he figured the real killer might show up to find out what I know. That he'd return to the scene of the crime."

"The Fox isn't the scene of any crime, and I have few enough customers as it is without Percy scaring people off with murder questions. No one's going to give up vital information out there in the open air on a sidewalk. They could be implicated, and if they do know anything, they'll clam up all the more so as not to get involved. What is he thinking?"

"He's trying to be helpful."

Another lady in a nice dress with a Coach bag over her shoulder hightailed it back down my sidewalk. A scream inched up my throat but that wouldn't do much to attract customers either. "What I want to know is why on earth did you get Percy as your lawyer in the first place? He's a nice kid and all but has no experience. UPS pays fine. You should have savings enough to find better representation."

"I'll have you know that my hiring Percy has been good for his self-esteem. He wasn't the most liked kid in school with his classmates teasing him about his name, his red hair, and being short. He worked his way through law school doing odd jobs and it took him three tries to pass the bar."

"You hired him because you feel sorry for him?" KiKi said. "Honey, invite him to dinner or sit next to him at church or fix him up with a hot date for Saturday night. Don't put your life in his hands."

Chantilly rolled her shoulders in defeat. "I'm sort of broke after the cruise and the down payment on the condo. Percy's right cheap. I'm afraid he'll have to do."

Auntie KiKi handed me a khaki skirt with ruffles at the hemline to add to my display and said to Chantilly, "Get a second mortgage. You must have equity in the condo or you wouldn't have been able to buy it. Banks are right cranky these days about who they lend money to. A year or so ago Delta Longford over at the bakery tried to expand the place. The banks refused outright. Then she and Tipper got divorced and she gave up the idea."

"I didn't have enough of a down payment for the condo so Simon lent me money." Chantilly looked all dreamy-eyed and clasped her hands to her bosom. "Fact is that's how we met. I was having a beer down at Wet Willies and telling GracieAnn about my financial state of affairs. She told me about Simon and that he might be able to lend me the money I needed. I don't think she considered the possibility that Simon and I would get on like we did. GracieAnn and I had a falling out over Simon and that's a pity, but I just couldn't help myself. Simon was some kind of handsome and dressed fine as can be and then got that canary yellow Audi sports car he drove all over the place."

KiKi studied my display and did a thumbs-up. "Well, I hope that cruise was worth it."

"I'm here to tell you it was worth it and then some. Mamma and Daddy had the best time. They even got to have dinner with the captain himself right there at his table."

"You sent your parents on the cruise?" And here I gave myself a big pat on the back when I took Mamma to lunch once in a while.

"Mamma and Daddy were so down in the mouth after Daddy got shot in that drug bust last year they needed cheering up so I sent them on the cruise. Then this condo came up for sale not far from my apartment and Simon knew the owner. He got a fine deal on it for me. Daddy can't keep up the house anymore and after doctor bills there wasn't much equity. Simon was such a great boyfriend, for a while." Chantilly sniffed. "And now he's gone."

Chantilly was one fine daughter and here was Simon taking advantage of her and she didn't even realize it. I thought of Simon dumping GracieAnn for Chantilly and then Chantilly for Waynetta. Dear dead Simon was working his way up the financial food chain and finally hit the silver tuna at the top with Waynetta. "What interest rate did Simon charge you?" I asked Chantilly.

"Interest rate?" Chantilly had a wide-eyed oblivious look about her. Love wasn't blind, it was just plain old stupid. I knew that firsthand from my prenup experience with Hollis. Too bad Chantilly suffered from the same affliction. "Does Percy know about this loan?"

"Why would any of that matter?"

KiKi patted Chantilly's hand. "Honey, you owed Simon thousands and now he's dead." We all made the sign of the cross for the dead. "It's called motive for wanting Simon gone and out of your life."

"But I didn't want him gone or out of my life," Chantilly protested, her eyes misting. "I loved Simon. I know he treated me badly but that wasn't the whole story."

"When you figure out the interest rate he was charging you, you'll probably spit on his grave." I made a display of scarves on the counter.

"I would never do such a thing."

"Give it time, honey. You will when you realize how much you were going to pay him over the years. I wonder where he got the cash to lend to you. His mother is a server at the Pink House and he's a junior officer at the bank. Money had to be coming in from somewhere if he was lending it out."

Chantilly folded her arms, her lower lip in a stubborn pout. "Simon had nice things, a condo in the Oglethorpe

Building, corner unit that faces York Street and gets the morning sun and not the cheap ground floor. He gave me a big old diamond I truly loved when we got engaged. 'Course he took it back, but this all goes to prove the man had some business sense about him. He was even named Employee of the Year over there at the bank and has the trophy to prove it."

"How does somebody get their hands on serious money?" I said aloud, trying to put the pieces together.

"They inherit it, work for it, steal it, marry it, make it," KiKi said in an offhanded manner as someone who knew a lot more about big bucks than I did. She added a shoulder bag and brown belt to the scarves.

"If he was printing money in his attic, he'd be caught by now, and if he was skimming from the bank, he'd be in the slammer for sure. Marrying money was next on his list. That leaves stealing." I slapped my hands on the counter making my dear auntie, Chantilly, and BW jump a foot. "Look around here. What do you see?"

KiKi gave the Fox a once-over. "I see a lot of clothes you want to sell and not doing very well at it."

"I don't sell a sweater, then pay off the person who consigned that particular sweater with that same money. I have other consigners and pay the next one who comes in with that money. My guess is that's what Simon did."

"Oh my stars and garters," KiKi said in a drawn-out voice of understanding. "There were others!"

"Other women?" Chantilly wailed. "Where did the man get the stamina for carrying on like he did?"

"Others in that he lent money to others," I soothed. "They paid him a hefty interest each month just like you did. He kept some of the money and lent the rest to generate more income. Simon Ambrose was a big, fat loan shark, but lending money for a condo is a lot of cash. How many others did he have on the hook? If GracieAnn sent you to Simon to borrow money, I bet she sent others and if they couldn't pay, that's a good motive for murder. I need to talk to GracieAnn."

"But he said the loan was just for me. That I was special to him and he wanted to do me a favor." I could tell from the look in Chantilly's eyes she was a step closer to spitting on Simon's grave and a step further away from *Simon, the love of my life*.

"I'm coming with you to the bakery," KiKi said, heading toward the back door. "I'm having company for supper tonight and could do with a nice peach pie and some yeast rolls. I have to put on my face and grab my pocketbook. Give me a minute or two," KiKi's voice trailed off, then the back door slammed shut, the quiet of the Fox now deafening, my brain fixated on the peach pie.

"Do you really think Simon was a loan shark?" The desolation in Chantilly's voice snapped me away from pie. "How could he do that to me? And it seems sort of risky. If someone couldn't pay, they'd just turn Simon into the police."

"Not if they were into something illegal or it made them look stupid to their family and friends. My guess is Simon would take something if they didn't pay up."

"He was a repo man?" Chantilly's eyes widened. "He'd

take something like a yellow sports car or even Mamma and Daddy's condo right out from under them?" Chantilly's eyes got beady. "Simon was nothing more than a big, fat, no-good rat!"

Chapter Seven

I HITCHED up Bruce Willis and met KiKi outside her back door. We waved to Percy, then KiKi, BW, and I took off. "Who are you having over for supper?" I asked KiKi as we hung a right onto Drayton, walking on the inside of the sidewalk under the oaks and keeping out of the sun. "One of Putter's golf friends?"

"He's a really nice man that Putter met at one of those medical conferences. He's in town and—"

"No way." I stopped right there on the sidewalk, alarm bells bonging so loud in my head my eyes crossed. "Don't you even think about such a thing."

"I have no idea what you're talking about," KiKi said with a lilt in her voice that said she was guilty of just what I thought she was guilty of. She took my arm and pulled me on. "I'm simply having a friend of my husband's for supper is all. Perfectly innocent."

"You don't have an innocent bone in your body when it comes to blind dates. What you're cooking up amounts to another doctor-for-Reagan event and luring me in with peach pie. I hate when you do this." I hated more that it worked. I was a sucker for peach pie. "Remember Dr. Fat-and-bald you tried to fix me up with in the spring? He wasn't even nice. He called BW an *m-u-t-t*!"

"But the guy was rich and you could do with a little doctor money in your life," Kiki persisted.

"I'm not marrying for money!"

"It was just a thought; not many customers in the Fox this morning even without Percy." KiKi was right about that. I could feel Hollis's presence like a black vulture hovering over me.

We passed Forsyth Park with the big white fountain spraying skyward, water droplets dancing in the sun. "Besides, this guy's different. He's a crackerjack surgeon and tall and handsome with blue eyes and young and a real hunk and—"

"Divorced three times with alimony payments that match the national debt and a bunch of bratty spoiled kids."

"No kids, no divorce, and if you don't come, he and Putter will talk doctorese and I'll have to listen to recounts of a triple bypass over rare roast beef. Last time that happened I couldn't eat meat for three months. Have pity on me. Be nice, help me out here."

Nice. I thought of the promise I made out in the swamp.

Considering it had involved Boone that was a bit of a dirty trick on God's part. "Okay, I'll do it."

"Okay?" KiKi blinked twice and gave me a round-eyed stare of disbelief. "That's it? No argument, no begging, no reminding that I'm your favorite auntie and the guy truly is a hunk."

"You're my only auntie and I don't care if he's a hunk, and can I borrow the Beemer tomorrow?"

"So you can go to Simon's funeral?"

I stopped dead. "Tomorrow's the funeral?"

"Unless you know someone else who's croaked recently." We made the sign of the cross at *croaked*. "Ten o'clock," KiKi went on. "It's the layout and then straight off to the cemetery and into the ground all in one fell swoop. My guess is Simon's mamma wanted to drag things out and milk the occasion, but Reese Waverly's paying for the whole shebang down to the headstone and the Abbott sisters and their weeping hankies. Reese wanted fast, so fast it is."

"We should go," I said. "It'll be a big social event."

"We?"

"Then we need to go check out a truck."

"We?"

"When the UPS truck got hit from behind, I was so busy trying to keep Big Brown on the road I didn't catch who did it. My last pickup was from Icy Graham and I know he has a truck because I saw it at Waynetta's wedding. Icy's seafood store isn't too far from Bonaventure and out on Lighthouse Road. Icy wasn't thrilled I mentioned he was at Waynetta's wedding, like he was trying to hide something and not wanting to own up to it. There was no mention of *Gee, what do you think about the groom winding up with a cake knife in his back.* Seems that might be expected idle conversation, don't you think? You can buy shrimp and crab and keep Icy busy while I take a look around his place. Someone doesn't like me asking questions and right now Icy has top billing with the swamp being so close to his place."

"You think whoever shoved you off the road killed Simon?"

"I'm thinking maybe Icy borrowed money from Simon. Late summer is a tough time of year for shrimpers. Maybe Icy fell behind in his payments and did in Simon so Simon wouldn't repossess his business. No one would suspect the shrimp guy as the murderer at a wedding. With a bunch of other people running around he kind of faded into the background."

"Like Cher says, *Someone has to pay for the frog and dancing fairies,* except for Simon it was cars and condos." KiKi pulled a sour face. "Well, here we go again. I'm your distraction, your snooping-around beard. I try and come up with stuff to keep people busy. That isn't much fun you know."

"Neither is triple-bypass chitchat over rare prime rib."

"There is that."

The closer we got to the bakery, the faster BW pulled me on. I had a sweet tooth or two, but BW had a whole mouthful. The bakery was at midmorning lull between early breakfast folks on their way to work and the idle rich or retired senior brunch set. KiKi was in a quandary over a strawberry Danish or an éclair; I got a doughnut with sprinkles. I'm a sucker for sprinkles and they're cheap. Reagan cuisine.

"Can I talk to you for a minute?" I asked GracieAnn when I paid for my doughnut at the old brass register, where the prices flipped up in the little window on top and a bell rang when the drawer slid open. GracieAnn's apron was smeared with pink icing and a dab of something chocolate. GracieAnn's apron looked delicious.

She hitched her head to the side counter and I followed her around, KiKi in tow. GracieAnn took an order over the phone with her cupcake pencil, then held out a tray of dead-guy cookies to us. "I got another batch cooling," she said. "Delta's in the back decorating them for me while trying not to have a stroke now that one of the mixers won't work. I tell you, we're running this place in the ground. Heard you ran the UPS truck into the swamp and Walker Boone had to rescue you."

GracieAnn fanned herself with a pink order pad, her plump rosy cheeks taking on a deep blush. "That man is mighty handsome, I tell you. Prime grade-A beefcake. He can come and rescue me anytime, night or day. Preferably at night, if you get my drift. I wonder if he knows how to fix a mixer?"

I leaned across the counter. "What do you know about Simon?"

GracieAnn formed a pucker as if sucking on a lemon. "Other than he was a rotten, no-good dirtbag, what else is there? You sure you don't want another cookie?"

"What was he like as a banker, and I'm not talking

about his job at Savannah Bank and Trust. I mean his other banking attributes as a self-employed entrepreneur. Did you know his other clients? You sent Chantilly to Simon."

"Biggest regret of my life."

"Did you send anyone else?" KiKi said with a mouthful of Danish.

"No one else matters. I made those UPS cookies for a reason, you know. Chantilly got what she deserved. She stole Simon from me and now she's a prime suspect in his murder and I couldn't be happier about the whole situation."

"But she's innocent," I added, trying for a bit of compassion and some information.

"Not to me she isn't. She's guilty of boyfriend-napping." GracieAnn studied me for a second. I could almost see the little gears churning away behind her emerald eyes. She leaned across the marble counter, her nose nearly toughing mine. "Chantilly's your friend, that's what you were doing in that UPS truck. You were helping her out because she's fretting over getting arrested and messing up her job. She's been mucking up deliveries. I hear stuff, you know. I bet you're trying to get Chantilly off the guilty list and that's why you're asking me all these dreadful questions."

The gears churned again. "You want to blame Simon's demise on someone else who he lent money to instead of Chantilly? Well, it's not going to work, sugar." GracieAnn stood tall and parked her hands on her well-endowed hips. "Chantilly's guilty as all get-out, pure and simple, and now she gets to pay the price."

"I'm helping Walker Boone. He's working on her case."

Oh, Lordy, did I really just say that? I must have because KiKi kicked me in the shins.

"Walker Boone is helping Chantilly?" GracieAnn looked impressed. Heck, I was impressed I came up with that award-winning lie right there on the spot.

"Who would have thought?" GracieAnn said, a little breathless.

I crossed my fingers behind my back. "Bet I could get him to come around and talk to you for a bit about the case."

That warranted another KiKi shin-kicking but GracieAnn beamed. "I bet I could tell him a few things he'd like to know about this here case. Stuff he never suspected."

"You could tell me and I could tell him. He'd be mighty grateful."

"Now why would I do a thing like that if Walker Boone's showing up at my door? I'm here to tell you that sure would make my day." GracieAnn fluffed her voluminous hair held in place by a net. "Someone like Walker Boone is a million times better than Simon. That man's the icing on my cake."

GracieAnn nodded, a sensual glint in her eyes. KiKi grabbed my arm, hauling me across the wood floor, Bruce Willis following, lapping dropped pastry crumbs along the way.

"What are you doing?" Auntie KiKi growled between barely moving lips when we got outside and sat at one of the little white wrought-iron tables for coffee and goodies alfresco. "The icing on the cake! Boone is not going to appreciate you feeding him to GracieAnn like that."

"It wasn't a full-out feed, more like a necessary nibble," I whispered back. "I had to come up with something to get her talking. I bet dollars to doughnuts that GracieAnn sent other financially distressed clients to Simon, and I have to keep her on my side so she'll tell me who they are."

"Honey, she's not going to tell you beans, and when she finds out you fibbed about Boone she's gong to have a hissy. This is the woman who bakes dead-people cookies. Did you ever see that *Sweeney Todd* picture? Bet GracieAnn could be another Sweeney Todd given half a chance. She's not someone you want to tick off. Think *Reagan* cookies with blonde icing hair and flip-flops. I'm going back in that store and get my baked goods for tonight, then stop over at Dan's Flora and Fauna for some of those sunflowers in his window that are bigger than a roasted turkey. Then I'm taking a cab home. Don't be late for dinner, and wear something presentable. A little lipstick wouldn't hurt either."

"I can go with you," I said, thinking another sprinkle doughnut might be in order. "I bet Percy's still out front of the Fox, so I don't have any customers. How am I ever going to get rid of him?"

"Worry about that later. You have bigger fish to fry. Confession's good for the soul, and this time it might save your hide, least with Boone. You best go tell him that GracieAnn might be looking for him. If she shows up on his doorstep and says you sent her, Boone will hunt you down. With GracieAnn you best watch your back, literally."

Auntie KiKi took my hand, her look pained. "Honey,

you got a particular way of getting yourself in deep doo-doo these days. Someone ran you into the swamp and now you might very well get baked up into cookies. How does this keep happening?"

I watched KiKi go inside. GracieAnn had information I could use. I should watch her, see whom she was friendly with and maybe catch a conversation or two. That made me a stalker, and part of the Sweeney Todd conversation replayed in my head. I needed one of those bug things to plant in the bakery. Right, I couldn't even afford a phone.

Chatting it up with Boone was not on my wish list at the moment. He'd fold his arms, shake his head, and proceed with a *what were you thinking* lecture. I wasn't in a lecture-by-Boone mood. When I got back to the Fox there was no sign of Percy on my sidewalk. Things were looking up till I went inside to find my AC unit in bits and pieces all over the dining room hardwood floor. Percy had his jacket off, red tie loose and limp at his neck, a smear of grease on his right ear, a toolbox at his side. He sat on one of my dining room chairs digging around in the metal AC case wedged in the window. Central air was not a luxury of old homes with radiator heating and money-challenged owners.

"What's going on?" I asked Chantilly, a few customers in the shop trying to act as if having machine pieces on the floor were a common occurrence.

Chantilly nodded at the mess. "Your AC was making weird noises."

"If you were as old as that unit, you'd be making weird noises, too."

Chantilly crooked her finger at me and I leaned across the checkout counter. "It may be a little warm in the Fox, but Percy isn't harassing customers either. He chased off a whole busload of Red Hat ladies from the First Baptist Church over there on Bull Street who came to shop. You know how those gals in the red hats spend money. I remembered Percy did repair work to earn his way though college and told him about the AC. When he gets that done maybe we can break something else around here to keep him busy and off the streets so to speak."

"He looks happy. I think he's humming."

" 'Oh, What a Beautiful Mornin' from *Oklahoma*. At it for an hour now."

I went into the dining room and, without looking up, Percy said, "I'll have this baby up and running for you in no time. One summer I helped my uncle Chicken. He's a repairman over there in Garden City. Can you hand me that Phillips head screwdriver out of my toolbox? Always keep my toolbox in my car just in case something like this happens. Got to be prepared, that's what Uncle Chicken says."

I handed off the screwdriver, then retrieved a denim jacket out of the display for a customer. Chantilly was busy at the checkout. Well, shut my mouth and call me a clam. I was actually making money. I glanced back to my AC unit and Percy reconnecting hoses and metal parts like he actually knew where they belonged. He attached the front cover of the unit and flipped the switch to *on*. When nothing happened Percy gave the unit a smart whack with the flat of his hand and the unit hummed to life, sounding better than ever. He grinned like a kid at Christmas. "I still have the touch."

"What do you know about mixers?" I asked, a plot brewing in my desperate brain, the fear of no customers gnawing at my insides.

"Uncle Chicken says I have the Damon Gift. I'm the Superman of the motor world. But right now I have a case to work on." He looked back at Chantilly and lowered his voice. "She's counting on me, she truly is. I have to come through for her. I know she's innocent, I just have to prove it."

I whispered back. "GracieAnn over at Cakery Bakery was involved with Simon. He was a loan shark and GracieAnn sent him business."

"No." Percy gasped, his eyes wide.

"Yes," I gasped back, hoping to add a bit of drama and excitement to my plan. I pulled Percy to the corner. "And if we can find the other people GracieAnn sent to Simon to borrow money, we can maybe pin the murder on one of them."

"Others?"

"Chantilly borrowed money from Simon, and GracieAnn won't talk to anyone like me who is trying to get Chantilly off. She believes Chantilly stole Simon from her and she's out for revenge. Nothing would make her happier than Chantilly behind bars permanently. What we need is to watch GracieAnn, listen in on her conversations, and see who she meets with. What we need is for someone to go undercover." I draped my arm around Percy and drew his head close to mine. "The mixer and the oven at the Cakery Bakery conked out; you can fix them like you did my AC and keep your eyes and ears open. You can be our undercover guy."

"They know I'm Chantilly's lawyer. Won't they recognize me and wonder what I'm doing as a repairman?"

"Put on a brown uniform. If there's one thing I've learned from my UPS days, it's that no one pays attention to who you are if you have on a brown uniform. Bring your toolbox and you're in."

"But I have to prepare Chantilly's defense."

I grabbed the front of Percy's shirt and ground out, "Right now we have no defense. We have Chantilly the sobbing, jilted ex-fiancée who rode a horse naked, borrowed money from the murdered guy, and ate his wedding cake when he was marrying someone else. Things aren't looking good here."

"And if I find someone suspicious at the bakery, I follow them and get the goods on the killer like they do on *Law and Order*?"

Good God in heaven, I created a monster! "No getting the goods. Undercover means you keep your mouth shut and ears open." I looked Percy straight in the eyes to add some stern to my words. "This is not a TV show; there's a real killer out there. He murdered once and wouldn't blink at doing it again." *Especially if you're humming show tunes.*

The last thing I wanted to do was put Percy in harm's way. I just wanted him out of *my* way. If he stumbled onto some information we could use, so much the better. "If anything looks suspicious, bring it to me and we'll talk it over."

Percy nodded with a smile. "This is a really good plan, but I just can't walk into the bakery with my uniform and toolbox, they'll think I'm up to something. Everyone knows there's not a repairman to be had in Savannah in August with all the old AC units on the fritz."

"Delta's the owner and my bet is she's called so many people to fix the mixer and oven she's lost count. Tell her you had a cancellation. She'll be tickled to see you and won't think about asking questions. Hey, you'll get free doughnuts."

Percy rubbed his hands together, a little grin playing at the corners of his mouth. "I do have a brown work uniform from Chicken-On-The-Run. That's Uncle Chicken's shop. I love cinnamon doughnuts. I do believe I could make this work." Percy wiped his hands on a T-shirt that I'd never be able to sell now. Considering my customer flow I probably wouldn't have sold it period.

Flipping his coat over his shoulder James Bond style, Percy picked up his toolbox, gave Chantilly a reassuring smile, then swaggered out the door not stopping to question the next customer. So far so good and maybe things would get even better tomorrow at the funeral. Not that I had a particular liking for funerals, but my guess was whoever killed Simon would show up. Dropping Simon's cold sorry butt in the ground was the cherry on the sundae for the person wanting Simon dead.

But that was for later. Right now I had to fulfill my *nice* promise to God and Auntie KiKi. Reneging on a promise to either was never a good idea so I was off to dinner with a little coronary bypass chitchat to keep things lively.

"NO, YOU CAN'T GO TO THE FUNERAL," I SAID TO Chantilly as I opened the door at ten sharp the next morning. I had on my one-and-only little black dress and heels that pinched my big toe and turned it black-and-blue. I could wear something from the Fox, but in my present state of financial difficulties I couldn't afford the Fox.

Chantilly stood in the hallway, arms folded, lower lip extended. BW gave her a quick once-over. Not finding any readily available treats, he wandered outside to greet the day and water the grass and weeds. BW was an indiscriminate waterer.

"Simon's *my* boyfriend. *Was* my boyfriend," Chantilly amended. "This is a free country; I have a right to be going to his funeral if I want to and I really want to."

"You'll cause a ruckus. You'll meet up with Waynetta and she'll pitch a fit. It'll get ugly and you'll look guiltier than ever. You have on a red dress for crying out loud!"

"I want to say a proper good-bye."

"I'll put a rose on his casket for you."

"I was thinking more like taking Daddy's shotgun and blasting Simon's casket to smithereens. Simon wasn't in love with me, he was in love with money, other people's money, *my* money. Last night I did the math and Simon was charging me a blooming fortune in interest just for the down payment on Mamma and Daddy's place like you said. How could he go and do such a thing to me? We were engaged. I'm glad he's—" I slapped my hand over Chantilly's mouth before she could say the *d*-word, especially after the shotgun comment and with early-bird customers coming up the walk.

"You're in enough trouble," I whispered, flipping the "Closed" sign in the bay window. "Stay here. Mind the store."

"Simon Ambrose was a first-rate jackass and I want to tell him that in no uncertain terms. I never got the chance when he was alive. I was stupid and in love, or at least thought I was in love. Mostly I was just stupid."

Been there, done that. I pulled Chantilly behind the door/counter as two ladies strolled in. I lowered my voice. "We'll go back to the cemetery this afternoon. You can dance all over his grave if you want. We'll bring champagne, make a toast. Just not now!"

A horn blast cut through the morning calm, meaning KiKi wanted me in the Beemer ASAP. I headed for the door. "Watch BW. Don't let him get overheated. Only one hot dog for lunch and don't let him wheedle two. He's a great wheedler. If you need anything, call KiKi's cell. Number's in the Godiva box." Translation: cash box. Ben & Jerry guarded my wealth at night; Godiva did the same by day. Did I have good taste or what?

"We're going to be late," KiKi huffed, barreling down East Gaston. "What will people think if we're late to a funeral. Lord have mercy, we'll be Twittered about and did you and Dr. Hunk have a good time last night? I noticed he walked you home."

"And I noticed how you just slipped that last part in there all casual like I wouldn't notice. I live next door. Doc Hunky wanted to meet BW."

"You could do with a little hunk in your life, you know."

"No zing."

"Zing?"

"Chemistry, attraction, animal magnetism that makes you all hot and sweaty."

"It's August, there's enough sweat going around. Besides, look what happened with you and Hollis, the king of zing. And what about kids?"

"Sweet mother, how did kids get into this?"

"You're thirty-two with no prospects."

"I have a dog."

KiKi gave me the Southern auntie tsk, then hunkered down and drove Savannah style, keeping one eye on the speedometer, the other on the lookout for ticket-happy police wanting to replenish city coffers. I never talked when KiKi drove like this, the g-forces scaring the talk right out of me. She got on the Truman Parkway, officially Harry S. Truman Parkway. No one ever called it that, of course, being that Harry S. was one of those frightful northern Democrats. What his parkway was doing here in Savannah was a mystery to us all.

"Chantilly wanted to come to the funeral," I said to KiKi when she got to our exit and laid rubber screeching onto the two-lane. I had to change the subject fast before she brought up Dr. Hunky again.

"No doubt Chantilly wanted to come naked and on a horse. Saints preserve us. How did you talk her out of it?"

"Told her we'd come back later on today. She finally realizes Simon was using her. You wouldn't happen to have a spare bottle of champagne lying around, would you?"

"Bet Simon used a lot of people and took their savings, thanks to Miss GracieAnn and her referrals. I wonder why he ditched that girl to take up with the likes of Chantilly? That never did make much sense to me."

"Think of Chantilly-the-lovely in her pre-breakup months. Now think of GracieAnn any month."

"But she was Simon's money machine. Eventually he hooked up with Waynetta but that was later on down the road and not even on the horizon when he and GracieAnn were doing business. Fact is, about the time Simon ditched GracieAnn, Waynetta was engaged to Sugar-Ray and they were getting ready for that wedding. Of course when she found Sugar-Ray doing the unmentionable with Robert Carter she fainted dead away, went to some chichi spa in Alabama to recover, then took up with the first thing that came along and Simon made sure it was him."

I stared at KiKi slack jawed. "Robert Carter and Sugar . . . Sugar . . ." My head started to spin, little dots dancing before my eyes.

"All very hush-hush," KiKi went on. "Waynetta not wanting to admit she was engaged to a gay guy and Sugar-Ray not all that interested in coming out of the closet, so to speak, with him being a marriage counselor and all. Cher says, *Men aren't necessities, they're luxuries*, and Waynetta always has been hell-bent on having her share of luxury."

"But that's crazy. Why did Sugar-Ray go into marriage counseling of all things?"

"I figure he got into that particular business, then realized he was so not suited for that particular business, if you get my drift. By that time he had a decent reputation and was pulling in money. Coming out isn't as easy as people think. Customers would have second thoughts on taking advice from someone who leaned in a different direction. I'm not saying it's right, but it is what it is."

"How . . . How do you know these things?"

KiKi did a wicked little laugh. "Oh, honey, the dance teacher hears all. When you hold someone's hand and his arm is around your back, you form your own little world. Things just sort of come out." Someone needs to tell those CIA guys never to take dance lessons. We pulled up behind a string of cars respectfully parading under massive trees draped in gossamer moss and through the heavy black iron gates of Bonaventure Cemetery. No place did cemetery better than Bonaventure. The line curled past family plots first populated over a hundred and fifty years ago and cordoned off by rusting fences and aging markers. Some headstones were tilted, weathered, and forgotten. Other markers were brand-spanking-new and bedecked with baskets and bouquets of fresh flowers. We drove past Wilmington River on the left then to Marguerite Laveau's tombstone surrounded by candy, cigars, white rum, and money.

Marguerite was the resident voodoo queen who knew her stuff even from beyond the grave. If you wanted help with romance and finance, you came to Marguerite. Word had it that someone once stole five dollars from her grave and dropped dead before he reached the gates, his body withered clear through to the bone right there on the spot. No one messed with Marguerite before or after her residence at Bonaventure.

The cars stopped, and KiKi killed the engine. Quiet settled around the procession following the casket to the shaded grave draped with a green cloth to hide the fact that there was a big six-foot-deep hole soon to be occupied.

"See anyone who doesn't belong here?" I whispered to KiKi, pulling her to the back of the procession.

Kiki gave me the *shhh-mind-you-manners* stare that aunties do so well. There were a lot of people gathered around what looked like a really expensive bronze coffin. Not that I was some expert on such things, but my guess was Reese Waverly had spared no expense. Did he do it out of fondness for Simon like Waynetta insisted or because Reese Waverly was happy as a pig in mud to be rid of the guy and it gave Reese great pleasure to do it up in style? Turning Simon's likeness to Swiss cheese with a Remington long-barrel indicated the latter. The question was, why?

Vidallia Ambrose sat in the front row place of honor, but it was the Abbott sisters sniffing and crying and carrying on something fearful that drowned out Reverend Weatherman. I surmised that they were trying desperately hard to make up for the total lack of sniffing and crying and carrying on by everyone else, except for Vidallia.

I caught sight of Icy Graham across from me and

standing next to Pillsbury in the back of the crowd. Icy had on a rumpled brown suit two sizes too small; Pillsbury's suit was not the one he wore at the wedding when impersonating a bouncer but a suit that cost what I made at the Fox in a month. Okay, two months, but I was trying right hard to drum up business. Why was Icy here? Why did Pillsbury show up? And what in the world was Walker Boone doing here?

Delta and GracieAnn looked almost happy with barely contained smiles. They stood next to Suellen, the waitress, her eyes red, a soggy hankie wadded in her fist. Doreen-the-wedding-planner looked a lot cheerier at Simon's funeral than she had at his wedding. Waynetta was emaciated, bored, and in a pout like always. With her funeral black hat perched on her head and lower lip sticking out, if she turned sideways, she'd look like a swizzle stick. Reverend Weatherman coaxed the last *Amen* from the congregation. Close friends and relatives put white roses on the casket. There weren't many roses. When I looked back to where I'd seen Boone before, he was gone.

KiKi and I started for the Beemer, others offering condolences to Vidallia and Waynetta. KiKi whispered, "That was a mighty strange funeral if you ask me. You'd think people would be more distraught with someone so young dead and all."

"I think it depends who the someone is that happens to be dead." I cut my eyes to Icy climbing into an old blue Pontiac. "That's the guy we're going to see. His market was the last stop I had in the UPS truck before Swamp Adventures with Boone. I have no idea how Icy Graham knows Simon, but he's here for some good reason." I glanced around, soaking up the serenity. "To tell you the truth I was hoping for a little more drama at this thing. Elsie and AnnieFritz won best of show hands down."

I opened the car door and heard shouting by the gravesite. Waynetta shoved the bridesmaid who'd lost her dress at the wedding onto the pricey casket, scattering white roses everywhere and knocking the casket off its brass perch, Simon landing half in, half out of his six-foot hole.

"You're nothing but a common old two-bit whore," Waynetta screeched, waving her arms. "You screwed Simon the very day he was to marry me and I know all about it. I saw your bridesmaid dress on the floor of your room and the bowtie on the bed and heard all that commotion coming from inside the closet. I knew what you were up to in there. How stupid do you think I am!"

"Simon was marrying you for your money," Bridesmaid screeched back, scrambling to her feet. "He sure didn't love you."

Vidallia burst into tears, Suellen sobbed, Delta gave the casket a good shove, sending it nose-down into the hole with a solid thud, and GracieAnn pulled a dead-man cookie from her purse and bit off the head. Bridesmaid continued, "He never intended to be faithful to the likes of you, he told me so himself that very day. I was going to be his mistress."

"He'd tell you anything to get into your pants." Waynetta yanked off her little black hat and threw it at Bridesmaid. "You and Simon deserve each other. If I had my way you'd be dead too and lying right next to his sorry self in that coffin; it's what you both deserve."

KiKi gave me a little poke in the ribs and whispered, "I do declare, you got your wish and then some, honey. This here is drama with a capital *D*, and if I'm not mistaken, we have ourselves another prime murder suspect or two."

Chapter Eight

"Turn here," I said to KiKi and pointed at the sign for Lighthouse Road. The Beemer slowed, tires crunching over the gravel leading to the docks.

"I don't see any big old truck that could have knocked you into the soup," KiKi said, pulling to a stop by the sun-bleached fish market house. "There's no one here, not a single car in the lot. Maybe we should forget this. Icy didn't appear to be all that pleasant, and whatever in the world am I going to talk to the man about anyway to try and keep him occupied?"

"Shrimp." I got out of the car just as a young woman came around the corner of the building, toddler in her arms.

"Can I help you?" The girl was young, midtwenties, with short blonde hair and bright blue eyes.

"What a cute little boy," KiKi said, giving me a *this is what I'm talking about* look. "Children are a true blessing." Subtlety was not Auntie KiKi's strong suit.

"They are indeed." The girl cradled the toddler and blew raspberries on his tummy. He giggled and squirmed, his dark eyes laughing, his black curly hair shining in the sunlight. "If you all are looking for shrimp, we're sold out for today. My father had a funeral and didn't get a chance to go out in the boat this morning. He gave the crew the day off—too hot on the water to catch much right now anyway, especially midday.

"Funerals are so sad," I ventured, trying to get some information as to why Icy was out at Bonaventure. "Hope it wasn't anyone close."

"Oh, Lordy, no. Just some no-count, troublesome piece of scum I got mixed up with and who we're all better off without." The girl kissed the top of the toddler's head. "Isn't that right, doodlebug." The girl looked so serious and protective, cuddling her baby close in spite of the heat. "I think Daddy wanted to make sure the bastard was gone for good and out of our lives. Things will be better now, I'm sure of it," she said to herself as much as to us. "So much the better. I know that sounds mighty terrible, speaking ill of the dead and all, but this person was the devil incarnate and then some." She nodded at the market. "I have some nice flounder inside."

"Flounder," I repeated tying to digest what I just heard.

"Fresh fish? Isn't that what you're looking for?" The girl asked.

"Right," KiKi said. "Fresh fish, of course. We sort of

had out hearts set on the shrimp. We'll be back tomorrow." She tugged me toward the car. "Take care of that baby now, you hear."

"Oh, I will. His granddaddy would skin me alive if I didn't."

KiKi and I got in the car and exchanged wide-eyed looks. We waved to the girl and she waved back, her little boy doing the baby bye-bye thing. "Holy Moses and sweet Jesus above," KiKi whispered as we headed up Lighthouse Road and turned onto a country lane. "Are you thinking the same thing I'm thinking?"

"That if we gave that baby a goatee and added on thirty years, we'd have Simon Ambrose reincarnated?"

KiKi pulled off onto a sandy shoulder, careful not to do Swamp Adventures part two. "Icy Graham wasn't into Simon for borrowing money. Icy wanted Simon out of his grandson's life."

"That's what I thought too, but it just doesn't add up if you think about it. I mean instead of Icy wanting to get rid of Simon, why didn't the girl blackmail Simon. She could have threatened to tell Waynetta that Simon had a child. Waynetta would have hated that and ditched Simon in a heartbeat. Simon sure didn't want that to happen. He would have paid her plenty to keep quiet, don't you think."

KiKi shook her head. "That's not the way that little girl thinks. She loves that baby. He's her whole life and my guess is he's Icy Graham's life too. Simon was all about money, anything for a buck, and now Icy Graham and his daughter are glad he's dead. There was money in this for Simon somehow. He was working an angle."

"What if Simon the jackass made threats about wanting to claim the child as his own. Maybe he said he wanted the baby and so did Waynetta. Icy and his daughter don't travel in the same circles as the Waverlys. They don't know Waynetta like we do, that someone else's child is the last thing on earth she'd tolerate. Icy paid Simon to stay away from his daughter and grandson. Simon being Simon wanted more money. A man like Icy wasn't about to have his life ruined by Simon Ambrose, so Icy killed him." I considered the possibility of what we just put together. "Then again that sounds a little extreme, if you ask me."

"Oh, honey, I think that's it," KiKi said, heading down the road. "It's not extreme at all. When you're a mamma or grandparent or auntie, what matters is that child, the love of your life. Icy knew the Waverlys would bring in expensive lawyers and take his grandson away. That's all he could see and he wasn't about to take the chance."

"Icy wanted Simon and Waynetta to go away and it had to happen before the marriage or Waynetta might have a legal claim on Simon's child." I looked at KiKi. "It fits. We need to get into Simon's house and look around. I bet there's a birth certificate or other papers that connect Simon to Icy or the daughter or baby. I wonder what else that sleaze was up to? If he was willing to go after the mother of his baby, the man has no limits."

KiKi bit at her bottom lip. "But what if Icy did indeed kill Simon?"

"We give him a medal and bring in a marching band?"

"We can't put a grandfather in jail for protecting his daughter and grandson. And if we don't, Chantilly could go to prison . . . or worse." KiKi shook her head. "We need to get into Simon's place soon. We'll bring vodka, lots of vodka to numb the ickiness of touching things Simon-ized."

"Tomorrow we'll go," I lied in agreement. I couldn't involve my dear aunt in B and E, vodka or not. "But right now I've got to get home and get Chantilly to Bonaventure. There was talk of making use of her daddy's shotgun, and I don't want her taking aim at me for not keeping my promise."

"I DON'T BELIEVE THIS," CHANTILLY WHINED, THE two of us standing in front of Bonaventure Cemetery, the massive wrought-iron gates padlocked together. I stepped closer and read the little plaque dangling from the chain. "Summer hours. The place closes early in August."

"Since when do dead people get summer hours? They're dead. They have no hours. This is crazy." Chantilly grabbed the gates and gave a hard shake that did no good at all except to make a lot of racket. "I knew we should have come earlier." Chantilly stepped back, parking her hands on her hip, staring at the high stone wall surrounding the place.

"I had customers," I offered in my own defense. "It's real-estate tax month." *And Hollis is ready to pounce,* I added to myself. "I couldn't shoo out potential sales."

"They didn't even buy anything, and I need to see Simon now. He might still think I'm sweet on him, and I need to set the record straight."

"He's dead, honey. What more do you want?"

I got the beady-eyed stare. "You promised."

I switched the heavy picnic basket holding KiKi's donated bottle of champagne to my other hand and hitched Old Yeller up on my shoulder. "All right, all right. We'll sneak in. I know a way, but first off we need to park the car out of sight so no one knows we're breaking into a cemetery. Not as uncommon as one might think."

"You really sneaked into Bonaventure?" Chantilly said, brows raised after we found a spot for the Jeep on a side street. "You're the goody-two-shoes judge's daughter."

"I was desperate. Come on, we got to get a move on, it's getting late." We hoofed it to the rock wall surrounding the cemetery, then followed the sidewalk beside it to the river. The walk ended and we stepped into the grass, heading for the sandy riverbank under a line of birch trees. I pointed to a break in the wall where the water came in. "The river's low in late summer. We'll go around the end and get in that way. Sometimes in the spring you have to swim."

Chantilly grabbed the strap of my purse, eyes huge, feet planted firmly in the dirt. "There're water moccasins in that there river."

I was tired and cranky and out of patience, moccasins or not. "Do you want to see Simon?"

"What had you so desperate to swim with snakes? It must have been a doozy of a reason."

We were never getting to Simon at this rate. "I wanted a date for junior prom. If I didn't come up with one Auntie KiKi was going to fix me up with the kid who cut her grass. He was two years younger and kept his clipped fingernails in a mayonnaise jar. I saw it with my own two eyes. Now let's get going."

Chantilly grinned as I pulled her along. "You devil. You sneaked in to see Marguerite."

"Cost me fifty bucks, forty for Marguerite and ten to the kid who told me how to get in here."

"I heard the going rate was a hundred. So who did Marguerite fix you with for a measly forty bucks?"

I took a deep breath. "Sugar-Ray Dunlap." I kicked off my flip-flops, offered up a quick prayer for no snakes, then stepped into the river, the cool water swirling around my ankles. I could hear Chantilly breathing hard behind me. "Simon's grave isn't far," I said to keep our minds off snakes. I threw in the events of Waynetta, Bridesmaid, and the casket for added distraction.

"And you made me miss out on all that today," Chantilly said when we got to the other side of the wall. "I should have been there."

"Along with the police in riot gear."

"There is that."

Now I understood why there was a procession to bury the dead—a crowd made a cemetery a whole lot less creepy. Two lone souls on a deserted gravel road with an overcast sky was not a procession or a crowd.

"You know," Chantilly said, edging close to me, or maybe it was me edging close to her. "Did you ever think that Waynetta killed Simon? She had a mighty good motive if she knew he was doing the slippery-slide with Bridesmaid on her wedding day in the closet. Maybe Waynetta took Bridesmaid's dress when she saw it on the floor, then stabbed Simon to frame Bridesmaid. Do them both in at once, so to speak."

I nodded up ahead to the grave freshly covered with a mound of dirt, a backhoe parked off to the side. "There's your boy. You dance, and I'll pop the champagne. Make it quick; I think a storm's rolling in off the ocean."

I braced for a deluge of grief. Chantilly wanted to take her time, savor the moment, dance her heart out. She cut her eyes side-to-side looking around and said, "I sort of thought this would be more fun." She shivered then babystepped her way to Simon's grave. She paused, then touched the tip of her toe to the fresh dirt and shivered again.

I sat on the edge of a tombstone that declared Mildred Snyder was indeed beloved, missed, a devoted wife and mother, and a member of the Savannah Garden Club. Chantilly did some wild gyrations that made me want to give her a few complimentary lessons with Auntie KiKi. I twisted the wire cage off the top of the champagne bottle, pried up the cork, and—

"This here ain't no dance club and hoochy-coochy bar," a voice said behind me, making me jump, scream, pop champagne, fall backward over Mildred, and instantly turn forty all in two seconds flat. I looked up at a guy right out of the grave complete with a shovel in his left hand. I figured he was about two hundred years old, shirt and pants ripped and muddy, face and hair caked with dust and sand.

"Help?" I stammered, Chantilly running over to assess the damage.

"I'm the caretaker, grave digger, and whatever else needs doing around here. What's wrong with you people? Doesn't anyone know how to read these days? We're closed up and what's with all the interest in that there grave over yonder anyway?" Graveyard guy pointed his shovel to Simon then peered down his nose at me. "You don't have a dead chicken or cat in that there basket do you? Folks are always hauling in dead chickens and cats. Do you know what it's like to clean up—"

"No!" My heart ricocheted around in my chest like a BB in a box. "I have no idea what it's like." And I didn't want a blow-by-blow description.

"Even found a human toe once," Graveyard guy went on undaunted. "I don't mind a little chicken blood now and then as long as they keep it off the tombstones so it doesn't leave a stain. Blood stains something awful and is the dickens to get out. People got to do what they got to do, but we have to keep things clean and not be dripping—"

"What kind of interest in that new grave are we talking about?" I asked, forcing my brain to work and forget about big toes, dead animals, and bloodstains.

"Well now, another gal was here earlier crying something awful. Felt right bad for her at first, but then she got all mad and cursed like a sailor. Haven't heard the likes of it since my navy days. I take it that there is that Simon's grave. She sure did call him a bunch of unflattering names. A bit later a man came along and spit on the grave."

"What did they look like?"

"Just saw them from behind. Got another grave to dig before noon tomorrow over yonder." Graveyard guy pointed through the trees. "It's August, people are dropping like files. To escape the heat is my guess." He nodded back to Simon. "Love and hate, that's what makes the world go round, but you need to be doing it when the place is open, not now. I'm going off to eat some supper. You can get out through my caretaker shack by the front. I'll be back to lock up and I best not find you here, if you get my meaning. It's fixin' to rain. You don't want to be locked up in here at night in the rain. Gets kind of peculiar if you don't mind me saying so."

He tossed his shovel onto the backhoe with a loud clank, charged up the engine, and took off in a growl of exhaust, the locals not too concerned about their daily intake of hydrocarbons.

Chantilly grabbed the champagne bottle off the ground and took a long swig, the drone of the backhoe fading. "Lordy, I needed that." She squelched a burp, hiccupped, then swiped her hand across her mouth. "We got to get out of here. That guy is creepy."

"What's he going to do to us?" I asked trying to add a bit of sanity to our situation.

"Girl, this is a man partial to chicken blood and finding hacked-off extremities. You want to hang around here and find out?"

I finished the last of the champagne, which didn't amount to much, Mildred and Chantilly getting the lion's share. I dropped the bottle back in the basket next to the glasses that didn't get used and followed Chantilly. We power-walked without saying a word, disrespectfully cutting in and out of grave plots. Angry clouds blocked the sun. Wind whipped through the trees and tumbled leaves and twigs over tombstones. If a zombie popped out, I wouldn't have been one bit surprised.

We rounded a marble crypt and spied someone by Marguerite's grave, someone who obviously didn't want to be seen or they would have obeyed the little plaque out front. I grabbed Chantilly's arm and we ducked behind a tombstone that looked like a mini Washington Monument.

Who is it? Chantilly mouthed to me. I hunched my shoulders in *I don't know.* We crawled over behind a big iron flower basket, taking us close enough to hear bits and pieces of a chant between gusts of wind, something about money and Waverly and Simon. Holy mother-of-pearl! The person chanting and throwing money was Sugar-Ray. I figured it was one of those déjà vu things where you go years without seeing or even thinking about someone, then you mention their name once and suddenly they're there.

Thunder rumbled over the ocean. Sugar-Ray did another lap around the grave, bowed three times, took a swig from a bottle that I assumed was white rum, that being the drink of choice with Marguerite. He dropped a wad of cash on the base of the tombstone. I leaned to the side to get a better view. Old Yeller heavy against my side threw me off balance and I fell against the basket, the empty champagne bottle clinking against the glasses.

Sugar-Ray yanked a gun from his pocket. Beady-eyed, he gazed around, not looking at all like the Sugar-Ray I had danced with when I was sixteen and who refused to kiss me good night, giving me a kissing complex for months. Then Ronnie Bowler took me to a drive-in, and by the time Indiana Jones found the ark I was cured.

I didn't move. Chantilly froze beside me. If someone was packing heat to a graveyard, they meant business, and this being off-hours, it was private business. Sugar-Ray slid the gun back in his pocket and my heart started up again. He screwed the lid on the bottle of rum, put it on the tombstone, then hurried off toward the river, probably leaving the way Chantilly and I got in.

"Oh my stars and garters," Chantilly whispered. "He had a gun, did you see that! I don't remember Sugar-Ray being a gun-toting kind of person, and did you catch the part about Waynetta and money? Simon wasn't the only one with dollar signs on the brain."

We stood and I grabbed the basket. "Why did Sugar-Ray and Waynetta break up?" Chantilly asked as we started off. "Whatever the reason, the man's none too happy about it."

"Irreconcilable differences, I have it on good authority." I picked up the pace, my flip-flops slapping against my feet, the sound comforting, knowing each step took me closer to getting out of this eerie place.

"I bet he wants to get back with her," Chantilly huffed, keeping up. Headstones cast dark shadows across our path, the cemetery falling into shades of black and gray. "I heard his marriage counseling business is going straight to the dogs since his engagement to Waynetta fell apart. I mean if you can't manage your own relationship, it sort of puts a big old damper on your expertise in that particular field. Maybe that's why he came to see Marguerite? He needs money and sees Waynetta as the way to get it and toss in a little romance to boot. Waynetta might very well go right back to him since Simon bit the dust. She's desperate for a man. I know her."

"Honey, believe me when I say she isn't that desperate." We reached the caretakers shack in a full-out run. The place held a lot more cutting and chopping apparatuses than I wanted to see right now. The door to the outside opened and I couldn't have been happier if Saint Peter himself let me though the Pearly Gates. Chantilly felt pretty much the same way because she knelt right down and kissed the sidewalk.

"WELL, DID CHANTILLY GIVE SIMON A PROPER send-off," Auntie KiKi asked that night, sitting beside me on the front porch and handing me a double martini, two olives. Usually I considered a double a bit on the lethal side, but taking into account the day I had at Bonaventure Cemetery not once but twice, it looked like heaven in a glass. I took a sip, the cool trickling down my throat, my brain shifting into relax mode.

Moonlight spilled through the cherry tree and BW did his nightly routine of sniffing and sprinkling. After the storm, humidity had turned Savannah into one giant communal steam bath, the whole city sweating together. I suppose it made more sense to sit inside with the AC and chat, but gossip never flowed quite as freely inside as it did on a front porch or over a fence. My guess was that whereas Twitter dished the dirt fast and furious it would never take the place of real gossip. There was simply no room on the information superhighway for such things as *Lord have mercy, now ain't she just precious,* and *I do declare.*

"Chantilly did the hokey-pokey over Simon and we came across Sugar-Ray shelling out money and drinking white rum over with Marguerite."

"The best Chantilly could muster up after all Simon's put her though is the hokey-pokey?"

"Maybe Sugar-Ray knocked off Simon."

KiKi snagged the martini right out of my hand. "You're zonked after one tiny sip. Not everyone's a murder suspect, you know."

I snagged back my martini. "Sugar-Ray was chanting something about Waverly, money, and Simon so I say the odds are better than even I can add him to our stick-it-to-Simon list. Breaking up with Waynetta ruined his business. He borrowed money from Simon to stay afloat and when he couldn't pay it back Sugar-Ray did the old boy in. I bet that was double sweet for him since Simon was the one who took Sugar-Ray's place with Waynetta. That ties things together pretty neat in my book, and there's the added fact that Sugar-Ray's a slender guy; he'd fit right into that brides-maid dress if he didn't zip up. And he was packing a gun."

"Just one?" KiKi tsked. "Never did understand the just-one concept of gun toting. What if it got misplaced, then where would you be?" She swirled her olives around in her glass while I considered what in the world my auntie had stashed in her purse.

"Killing Simon at the wedding," KiKi said in a thought-ful tone, "was a desperate last-ditch effort to stop the wed-ding, and that wedding didn't matter diddly to Sugar-Ray. Waynetta's completely off his radar. There's no connection there.

"Except," KiKi said, her blue eyes dancing in a blast of divine revelation, or closer to the truth, martini revelation. Sometimes in Savannah it was hard to tell which. "Waynetta isn't the only Waverly. Reese is a Waverly and you said he was blasting holes in Simon's picture that day you went out to his place for the packages. Reese is a shrewd business-man. He wouldn't buy a company without digging around and he wouldn't let his daughter marry someone without making sure everything was on the up-and-up."

"Boone was out at Waverly Farms, I saw him. Maybe Reese hired Boone and Boone found out that Simon was doing Bridesmaid and into loan-sharking. Reese pays Sugar-Ray to do in Simon before he gets his grubby hands on Waynetta and the Waverly money. But then why would Sugar-Ray be at Marguerite's now? It's sort of after the fact."

"It could have been a thank-you visit for a job that went off without a hitch. Simon's dead, Chantilly's the prime suspect, Sugar-Ray's off the hook, Waverly money's safe and sound, Waynetta's back man-hunting." KiKi clinked her glass to mine. "It's like Cher says, *If you can't go straight ahead, you go around the corner.* Sugar-Ray was Reese's way of going around the corner to things done right. That makes perfect sense especially with Sugar-Ray des-perate for money the way he is."

I finished off my last olive. "Yeah, but there are a lot of other possibilities that make sense too, like Waynetta her-self wanting Simon dead because she caught him messing with Bridesmaid, GracieAnn wanting Simon dead for dumping her for Chantilly, Icy wanting Simon dead for his grandson's sake, and Pillsbury wanting Simon dead because he hurt Chantilly, the secret love of his life."

"Didn't know about Chantilly and Pillsbury."

"Boone told me and considering Pillsbury's connections I'd say we keep that bit of information to ourselves. Do you think Bridesmaid could have polished off Simon because she was afraid Waynetta would find out about the two of them having a hot fling? You saw Waynetta at the cemetery. She's not a *forgive and forget* kind of woman, she's an *I'm going to get you if it's the last thing I do* kind of woman. I bet Bridesmaid's name is getting permanently and forever removed from all social Savannah events even as we speak. The Waverlys have that kind of clout and all because of a roll in the hay, or in this case the closet, which had to be downright uncomfortable if you ask me."

KiKi sipped at her martini, gaze fixed, brain stewing. "I bet when we go to Simon's condo we'll find more people who couldn't stand the man. You don't get yourself into this much trouble without leaving a trail of some sort."

"I suppose you don't have any idea on how we're going to get in that condo?"

"Thought I'd leave that up to you, sweet pea." KiKi snagged my glass and polished off the last gulp. "Tomorrow I have a dance lesson at eight, you have a belly-dancing class at nine, and the Daughters of the Confederacy are having a late luncheon over at the Pirate House. I think they're wanting to put yet another cannon down there on the riverfront. Tipper Longford and his band of merry men are doing a reenactment over at Emmet Park for us so that pretty well shoots the day, literally speaking I might add. We'll just have to visit Simon's domicile tomorrow night."

I was a little numb between the ears but not that numb. "Me? Belly-dancing? Since when? I just did dinner with Doc Hunky for you."

"Oh, honey, Doc Hunky was for *you* and my belly does considerably more flopping and dropping than dancing these days. I'm fiftyish and I do like my dessert."

I couldn't afford dessert. "But I'll have to wear one of those jingly skirts with little bells, my midriff and navel haven't seen the light of day for years, and I don't have enough boobs to keep a tied-on blouse up. I have a business to run, you know."

"The Silver Spoon Girls want to get in shape for their annual trip to Italy. If they lose a few pounds now, it's more red wine and pasta in Tuscany, not to mention firmer tushies to get pinched by all those fine I-talian men. They send their offspring to me for cotillion dance lessons every year. They're repeat customers. I can't disappoint, now can I?"

One teenage summer I was plump, pimply, and depressed with no friends. After three months of dance lessons with Auntie KiKi I lost weight and was pretty much the hit at any party. That was the good side of dancing. The bad side was I could teach belly dancing. "No way."

"Ten gals at fifteen bucks a pop for one hour's work."

"See you at nine."

KiKi saluted me with the two empty glasses and did a little swing step all the way back to Rose Gate, the house named after the roses twined into the wrought-iron framework of the garden gate designed by Colonel Bubba

Vanderpool himself. I brought BW inside, gave him his daily hot dog and favorite blankie, then slung my purse over my shoulder. I set off for Simon's place, the clock at St. John's bonging out ten. KiKi would have a hissy I went to the condo without her but I'd rather face Auntie KiKi in a snit than put her in danger. Not that I expected anything bad to happen at Simon's; it wasn't even the crime scene. But there were a few glitches to consider, like breaking and entering being against the law, a murderer running around town, and a bunch of people jubilant that Simon was six feet under at Bonaventure who didn't want their names connected with the situation.

Sticking my nose where it didn't belong was never healthy under such circumstances. I knew that from personal experience.

Chapter Nine

WHATEVER Simon Ambrose was into, he did a first-rate job of it. His place was located in a restored red brick 1890s Romanesque building facing Wright Square. The square was named after the last British governor of Savannah. Honoring Wright made as much sense as Harry S. and his parkway, but the fact remained that anything facing one of the twenty-three squares in Savannah, no matter whom they were named after, cost more money than I'd see in a lifetime.

I sat on a wood bench in the square, sweating, shooing away palmetto bugs big as my foot. I watched Simon's building and the people going in and out. There was a code on a sophisticated-looking pad at the main door, meaning decent security. If I'd known that, I could have asked Chantilly how to gain access. A '57 red Chevy convertible motored down Whittaker, Boone and a chickie obviously out for the night. Where did Boone take his chickies? Someplace swanky, then to bed no doubt. The man probably notched his headboard to keep count, the thing having so many notches by now it was in serious risk of collapse. Not that I cared.

A young guy went to the door of the building, pulled out his keys and his iPhone. He punched around on the phone, then plugged in the code. Bingo. A newbie. A guy newbie who hadn't memorized the entrance code yet and kept it stored on his phone. I'd lip-gloss my way into Simon's condo. I rooted around in Old Yeller and came up with a few things from my pre-divorce days. Amazing what gets lost in a big purse. I gooped up my eyes, ratted my hair, added two shades of lipstick and eye shadow, and opened my blouse, letting my pink bra show. Tacky. Guys loved tacky.

I crossed the street and found the intercom and the name printed in dark black not yet having time to fade from the sun. Beau Delong Jr. Sweet mother, it was like taking candy from a baby. I hit Beau's doorbell, smiled into the camera saying that I had the condo on the other side, just moved in, couldn't think of that silly old code thing to save my life and if he could just buzz me on in I'd be mighty grateful indeed.

Like I said, taking candy from a baby. He buzzed me straight in.

Chantilly had mentioned previously that Simon had the corner condo, second floor. I looked over the doorframe for a spare key and under a little table in the hallway with a fake ficus beside it. In desperation I tried the door handle and it turned. A burglary? I peeked inside to a TV that rivaled a movie theater. No burglary, but there was an ADT pad by the door blinking green. Thank the Lord it wasn't blinking red. Seemed to me like the anxious groom was in such a hurry on his wedding day that he didn't bother to lock up or he just didn't care about what was left. My chances of unearthing anything important were slim to none.

Simon's black leather couch was soft as a baby's bottom. I know because I tried it out. I resisted the temptation to check HBO with the remote sitting right there on the end table next to his Employee of the Year trophy. A floor light on a timer lit up the place. One of those tall contemporary open bookcases with shelves crisscrossed on the diagonal separated the living and dining areas and, from the looks of it, Simon was not a great reader. The place had original hardwood floors, the dining room table from Pottery Barn, same as the chairs. I could picture Simon moving easily around his pad, doing his thing, chatting with one of his babes on his iPhone.

I wandered into the kitchen, putting off the bedroom. Lord only knew what I'd find there, but the kitchen was great, with granite countertops, new appliances, and one of those fancy-dancy coffeemakers that used little individual cups and churned out flavors like Mudslide, French Vanilla Bean, and Double Mocha Latte. I had a sudden attack of kitchen envy. Not that I was a great cook, I wasn't even a good cook, but everything here was new and shiny and under warranty. The warranty on my appliances had fizzled out around 1980.

I opened drawers to mostly emptiness, cupboards the same except for five glasses, two plates, a pack of those coffee pods, and a plastic container of chocolate chip cookies from Cakery Bakery. Now that was interesting. Simon stayed in contact with GracieAnn?

A six-pack of Moon River sat alone in the fridge, a half gallon of Rocky Road in the freezer. I closed the freezer door, then opened it again, staring at the big lonely ice cream container. Not a pint for a bachelor needing a Rocky Road fix at midnight but a big old half-gallon. I figured I had about as much in common with Simon Ambrose as I did with Lady Gaga. However I thought an ice cream container made a good hiding place so maybe . . . I took out the container, pried up the end flaps to find a brown spiral notebook wedged inside. I so needed a new place to hide my cash.

I put the carton back and headed for the front door, book in hand, my feet not touching the floor. Was I good or what! This was Sherlock Holmes good, Hercule Poirot good, Nancy—Out of the corner of my eye I caught sight of the bookcase coming right at me . . . falling? Holy cow, it *was* falling! I dropped the book and put out my hands to stop the impact. Not moving fast enough it flattened me to the floor, the bookcase landing with a thud on my back. I couldn't talk, the wind knocked out of me. Thank the Lord Simon wasn't into Tolstoy and Dostoyevsky. I blinked a few times fast to get my eyes to focus. The lamp went out and a beam from a flashlight danced around the floor. Footsteps came closer, then stopped. I was pinned down and could only make out shadows from the outside streetlights. There was some movement and rummaging around. The steps retreated, the front door opened, then closed. *Note to self, unlocked door means someone is inside.*

My head throbbed, my back ached. This is why I hated little places. It was hard to get out of little places. Nowhere to move. Nowhere to turn. Little prickles of panic danced up my back. It was hard to breathe. If I didn't do something, I could rot here. I couldn't rot. I had a dog to feed, a shop to open, a belly-dancing class to teach. Amazing how much I wanted to teach that class. Tinkling bells and bare feet sounded pretty good right now. Maybe if I wedged my hands under my body and pushed, I could raise the bookshelf up on my shoulders and try to squirm my way out. The door opened again and the lights came on. "Reagan, are you in here?"

"Boone?"

"Where are you?"

"Where do you think I am?"

There was a string of curse words right off Seventeenth Street. "What happened this time?" Boone hoisted the bookcase upright, books and knickknacks littering the floor around me.

"This time? What do you mean, this time?"

Boone hunkered down beside me on the floor. "Are you okay? Can you move? You're bleeding." More cursing. "I'm calling an ambulance."

"No!" I flipped myself over onto my back, landed fish style, staring at the ceiling, pain shooting up my arms and legs as all my bones realigned. "I'm not in here by invitation and Mamma's running for city council." I tried to sit but Boone held me down, running his hands on my legs. What in the world?

"Can you feel that?"

"Y . . . Yeah."

An intent look on his face, he rubbed my arms. "How about that."

Oh, yeah, I could feel that just fine. "You could have hit your head." Boone ran his fingers through my hair. They were warm and gentle and caring. I felt safe and secure and . . . and . . . What was I thinking? Boone was a big pain in the butt and had been for two years straight, I reminded myself.

I shoved his hands away and bolted straight up, pain shooting everywhere. "I'm okay, I swear on my mother's grave I'm okay."

A slow grin played across Boone's mouth and he sat cross-legged like we were at camp around a fire ready to toast marshmallows. His white shirt lay open at the neck, sleeves rolled up, well-worn jeans. Nice package in front. Not that I cared about any packages, just an observation is all.

"Your mother's still alive." Boone took a handkerchief from his pocket and pressed it to my forehead. I flinched at the pain. "Did you black out? If you did, you really need to go to the hospital, cops or no cops."

"Just winded. Need to catch my breath. Thanks for getting the bookcase off me. I owe you." And I did, no matter how much I didn't want to.

"Any idea who did this?"

"I think I smelled vanilla."

Boone pointed to a toppled candle. "Simon the romantic."

"You should know that GracieAnn from Cakery Bakery may be stopping by your house. I sort of told her you were helping me with Chantilly's case. She called you a beefcake."

Boone closed his eyes and massaged the bridge of his nose. "Why me?"

"I was trying for information, and you were my ace. There, I told you and now we're even. You lifted the book-case and I warned you about GracieAnn. Done."

"We're not even. You're the one who sicced GracieAnn on me in the first place."

"How'd you get in here?"

"I saw you sitting on the bench when I drove by. I sur-mised you weren't outside Simon's condo enjoying the night air. The light to Simon's condo was on then. It's on every night. When I came back it was off and you were gone. I figured you went in but why would you turn off the light? Didn't add up, and with your knack of winding up in places you shouldn't be I thought I'd check it out."

"How'd you get past the code by the front door?"

"I know a woman on the first floor."

"Well, of course you know a woman on the first floor. You know a woman on every floor, in every building."

Boone smoothed down my hair. "She does my taxes." He plucked at the sliver of pink bra showing. "I bet I know how you got in."

I blushed. I could feel the heat clear up to the roots of my hair that needed another dye job bad. Enough comparing sex appeal for one night, especially since I'd lose. "Can we get out of here?"

Boone put his arm around my back and helped me onto the couch. "Why are you being nice to me?" I asked him. "You weren't nice in my divorce."

"You were stupid in your divorce. Though coming in here wasn't an act of genius. There's a killer running around, remember? Why are you here anyway? What the heck are you looking for?"

I was all ticked off at the *stupid* comment until the *looking for* comment came along and jarred my brain. "Oh, no!" In the throws of near death and contemplating rotting away, I forgot about the notebook. I glanced around the floor. "It's gone. That's what he was after."

"What's gone? Who's after what?"

This was always the great dilemma with me and Boone. How much to tell him? He never leveled with me. Oh, he'd give up smidges of information to try to cajole more information out of me, but he never did the full-disclosure thing. Yet here he was lifting bookcases off me and getting tagged as beefcake because I opened my big mouth. I wobbled to my feet and took a few deep breaths to steady myself. "Simon was into loan-sharking and womanizing, not that I'm telling you anything you don't already know. I was looking for something that would point to his killer." I headed for the door.

"What did you find?" Boone snagged Old Yeller from the floor and turned the door handle. We stepped into the hall and Boone reset the lock. Neighbors had big ears so we didn't say anything till we got outside and started down

Whittaker. "I found a notebook in Simon's freezer," I said figuring I owed Boone something and this I could tell him because the notebook was gone. "It probably had a list of people who owed Simon money and my guess is someone on that list killed him. Either they owned him money they couldn't pay or there was information that needed to be kept quiet for some reason."

Interest flickered in Boone's eyes. Usually his eyes gave nothing away, calm and cool and dark. So dark. "How did you know to look in the freezer?" he asked.

"Hey, don't knock the freezer. It's a darn good place to hide stuff, so I've heard." I stopped by Boone's convertible, my brain starting to function beyond life and death and ice cream. "That's how you knew about the light that's always on. You've been to Simon's condo before. You were looking for stuff on Simon too. Why did you go see Reese Waverly? How does he play into all this mess?"

Boone opened the passenger side for me. "I can't say."

I sank down into the cushy white upholstery and Boone took the driver's side. "Sugar-Ray was sharing a bottle of white rum with Marguerite today out at Bonaventure," I said to Boone. "He was chanting something about the Waverlys and money and Simon. I think Sugar-Ray killed Simon and Reese paid him to do it so Simon couldn't marry Waynetta. Simon was scum and Reese knew it. Maybe you're the one who gave him a heads-up on the guy?"

A half smile pulled at Boone's mouth. "Now that's a new one." Boone put the car in gear and eased into the light traffic. He circled the square with the rest of the one-way traffic, old iron lamplights casting the city in a warm golden glow. At night the city was made for romance and lovers and here I was with a bump on my head, essential evidence gone, and Walker Boone.

We headed down Abercorn toward the Victorian district and Boone said, "You're right in that Sugar-Ray's not the namby-pamby most people think he is."

"What about Icy Graham and Pillsbury?"

"You got a list of some pretty mean dudes there, Blondie."

"So what do I do about it? Go back to managing my shop and let Chantilly take the fall for something she didn't do because these guys don't play nice?"

"I'll look into it."

"Like that's going to happen. You're bought and paid for by Reese Waverly." I knew that wasn't true before I opened my mouth. No one owned Walker Boone. I folded my arms and sat back. "I just said that 'cause I'm mad about the bookcase and not having any solid leads. Chantilly's a friend of mine and you think she's guilty."

Boone pulled up in front my house, motor running. He turned sideways in his seat and leveled me a cold, hard stare. "I think Chantilly didn't mean to be guilty. She was mad, furious mad and jealous. Bad combination and there was a knife right there on the table. It just happened."

I got out of the car. "There's a bunch of people with as much motive to kill off Simon as Chantilly. One of them did it, not her." A caught a glint in Boone's eyes. It was almost unnoticeable, just a flicker, but I'd been around Boone a lot, a lot more than I wanted to be. "You talk a mean game, but you don't think Chantilly's guilty either.

You're lying to me to get me to back off. You really think I'd do that?"

Boone put the car in gear. "I should have left you under that bookcase. You'd be a heck of a lot safer."

"I'm not backing down, Boone. You know something."

"I know plenty and I'm not going to help you wind up next to Simon at Bonaventure. You're out of your league on this one. It'll work out, just leave it alone."

"In case you haven't noticed I'm always out of my league." I watched Boone take off, leaving behind a quiet summer night. Usually I liked the quiet but now with Boone gone and being attacked by a bookshelf I felt alone and a little scared. I hated being scared but until Simon's killer was behind bars and I wasn't poking into everyone's business and stirring up trouble, scared would pretty much be a way of life.

THE NEXT MORNING I HURT IN PLACES I DIDN'T know I had and gyrating my hips and torso and shoulders to *Bellydance Overdrive* was not helping one bit. The Silver Spoon Girls seemed to be having a good time. I had my back to them at the moment, the soft jingle of bells and tinkle of finger symbols filling Auntie KiKi's oversized parlor. I rotated and swayed and did a double twitch of my hips but didn't hear any more tingling and jingling. I turned around to make sure the girls got that last move but they didn't get it at all. They didn't get anything. They stood perfectly still, frozen in place, bleary-eyed, not breathing, and staring at . . . "Boone?"

He didn't say anything, his gaze glued to me. Sweet mother, now what? Maybe he realized Reese Waverly was guilty like I said? Maybe Chantilly was guilty and he found proof positive and hated to tell me? Maybe he had indigestion? "That's all for today," I said to the ladies.

The girls drifted past Boone in various stages of salivating. "Are you okay?" I asked him after the last Silver Spoon Girl closed the door behind her.

"What was that?" Boone's voice sounded weird and his voice never sounded weird. Condescending from time to time when berating me and always superior, but that was about it.

I checked my skirt and blouse tied in the middle to make sure something hadn't slipped out that needed tucking in. Not that I had much to tuck nor would it be of much interest; it sure wasn't to dear old Hollis. "It's a dance lesson," I said. "What are you doing here?"

"I don't know."

"Boone?" I waved my hand in font of his eyes. "Are you having a stroke or something?"

He peered down at me, his black eyes darker than ever. "I came to see if you were okay. Obviously you . . . are. Dang, girl." Boone turned and walked away hunched over like he had a hernia. He opened the front door and Auntie KiKi came in as Boone left without so much as *How are you these days, Miss KiKi, and how is Doctor Putter?*

"What's wrong with Boone?" KiKi asked, both of us staring at the door.

"Who knows? He's a man; there's no figuring them, I swear. I used to think they were just like women but unshaved." I grabbed my flip-flops off the floor. "I have to go. It's ten and I might have customers."

"Hope springs eternal, honey," KiKi called after me as I hurried out the door. I ran across the grass, thinking maybe I should call Dinky, Boone's secretary to have her keep an eye on him. Dinky and I bonded during my divorce. I cried on her shoulder, she asked me to be a bridesmaid. She'd want to know if her boss was losing his marbles.

By noon the mailman had delivered an electric bill so exorbitant I immediately turned off the AC. There was also a postcard saying the Daughters of the Confederacy were having an ice cream social out at Forsyth Park on Friday night to raise money for the new cannon. Must be one heck of a cannon. There was also an envelope, my name and address scribbled menacingly across the front. The paper inside read, *Next time the alligator wins. Mind your own business.*

The little dots were back dancing before my eyes. I sat down on the stool, sucking air to keep from passing out. I was a shopgirl and dabbled in house rehabbing. Death threats in the morning mail was not the usual bill of fare. Whoever knocked me into that swamp meant business. Visions of my sorry self floating facedown in Gray's Creek surrounded by hungry alligators flashed before my eyes. I sucked in more air. Maybe I should back off Chantilly's case, let Detective Ross settle this. Except Ross's idea of settling was Chantilly behind bars for the rest of her natural life.

For the next three hours the mailman along with one obnoxious woman accounted for my entire customer list, giving me plenty of time to think about the letter and Hollis's threat to sell Cherry House. I looked down at BW lying on my left foot, both of us behind the counter in the hall. "How do you feel about being an orphan?"

BW put his paw over his eyes as Chantilly came in the front door. "I'm flat broke," she whined. "With no job at UPS and paying Percy, I'm going to have to vacate my apartment and move in with my parents. Do you have any idea what that'll be like? They'll want to know where I am, who I'm seeing, did I brush my teeth and have my yearly mammogram. Can I move in here?"

"I can't afford AC and BW and I share a bed, but you're welcome to the floor."

"My life sucks." Chantilly banged her head on the checkout counter. "Tell me good news about something, anything. I'm desperate here, Reagan."

In her present state of forlorn I didn't have the heart to tell Chantilly I lost the notebook that could very well have helped her case and that I was getting death threats so I went with shallow and mundane. "Know that ugly brown sweater you and I both hated? It's sold so we don't have to look at it any more."

"Wonderful." Chantilly brightened. "That's a good start. What else did you sell?"

"The sweater's the start and the finish. In a month from now everyone will be clamoring to freshen up their wardrobe, sell the stuff in their closets, and looking for fall deals. But that's at the end of September when it's cooler. It's not doing me one lick of good now at ninety-two in the shade and I owe Savannah Electric and Power a bunch of money. Maybe you could send out another tweet talking about the bargains here. It worked last time."

"Being arrested for murder, I've been unfriended and unfollowed by everyone except your auntie and Reverend Weatherman." Chantilly hoisted herself onto the checkout counter, feet dangling off the edge. She picked up the ice cream social postcard, the nasty-gram right beside it. Casually I plucked the nasty-gram from the pile and slid it under the Godiva chocolate box/cash box. No need to upset Chantilly any more than necessary. One of us upset was enough.

Chantilly waved the ice cream card. "Too bad you're not a charity. You know how folks in Savannah rally around a good cause. You need some rallying."

"KiKi's at a luncheon with the Daughters of the Confederacy as we speak to raise money for that cannon they want to put down on River Street. Tipper Longford and his boys are doing a reenactment. I suppose it's practice in case the Yankees get rambunctious again."

"That's it!" Chantilly hopped down and did a little Snoopy dance right there in the hallway that still needed painting.

"Honey, I know there are those who think otherwise and always will, but the war is indeed over . . . really. I have the tax returns to prove it."

"Not that, you need to be a charity."

"The one thing I do not need is a cannon."

"But the Daughters of the Confederacy do and they're having all sorts of events to get money for it. Tell them the Prissy Fox will donate a percentage of its sales for the next month to their cause. You know how the daughters are all gossip queens; they'll get the word out that shopping at the Fox benefits their cannon and we'll have tons of customers in no time and bring in new ones." Chantilly pushed me toward the door. "Go get 'em, girl."

"You want me to talk to the daughters now?"

Chantilly swept her hand over the empty store. "Times a-wasting and things are not improving here."

"I don't even have my purse."

"There's nothing in there but junk." She slammed the door in my face, leaving me alone on my own front porch staring at my white peeling paint and bay window. I loved my peeling paint and window. Rumor had it that Robert E. Lee himself once came calling to Cherry House. I had no idea if that was true but it made for a great story and if I didn't do something quick and bring in more cash, I'd go belly-up like Hollis said and that mighty good story would be someone else's to tell.

I started off for the Pirate House as a navy Jaguar purred up to the curb beside me. Another lost tourist I imagined. A rich lost tourist. Except it wasn't a tourist at all but Doc Hunky. He was tall and gorgeous and flashed me his hundred-kilowatt smile.

"I realize this is short notice," he said after powering down the window. "But if you'd happen to be free this evening, I'd love to take you to dinner. I was thinking the Olde Pink House? I hear they do a mighty fine shrimp and grits and their bread pudding is divine. I tried to phone but I must have the wrong number." The smile kicked up a few more kilowatts. "I ran over here between surgeries hoping I'd catch you, and here you are lovely as ever."

And the bait was free food, really great free food of shrimp and grits, and a big dose of flattery. I could live with that. "Why, thank you kindly," I said throwing in a bit of Southern belle-ese, feeling a bit belle-like at the moment. Doc Hunky could do that to a girl. "I'd simply love to have dinner with you."

His eyes danced. Don't think I ever had that effect on a guy before except in tenth grade where Simon Castor and I dissected a frog together and I spilled the formaldehyde.

"I'll pick you up at seven." Doc Hunky winked and motored off and I didn't care if he did talk triple bypass all night. I hadn't been to the Pink House in ages, and did I mention the part about the free food?

Chapter Ten

"HONEY, that's called a date and it means the age of miracles is not dead and gone after all," KiKi gushed when I caught up with her in the Captain's Room at the Pirate House. I'd just finished making my little presentation to the Daughters of the Confederacy as they forked down plates of blueberry buckle with vanilla ice cream. Hard to compete with blueberries and ice cream but I think they got the point that shopping the Fox meant money for the cannon. The girls were now headed across the street to Emmet Park to watch Tipper save Savannah while KiKi and I lingered in the AC.

"It's not a date," I insisted as the busboys cleared the tables. "Think of it as free food; that's what I'm going on."

KiKi hitched the blue straw purse she got at the Fox onto her shoulder, then pulled me out into the hall. "You can't use the man like that. It's downright indecent. He's a fine person and intelligent and not your meal ticket. You need to think of this as your first venture back out into the world of dating since the Hollis fiasco."

"I hate dating, look what I wound up with the last time. I'm really bad at dating. I think I married Hollis so I didn't have to date anymore. This is just dinner." But KiKi was right about the meal ticket. For a minute there my empty fridge overrode good manners. "All right, all right, I'll dress nice and engage in scintillating conversation and compliment his shoes."

"And do something with that hair of yours. You got yourself two inches of roots showing and for crying in a bucket put on some color and stick out your boobs."

I was trying to decide if free food was worth all this effort and maybe a dinner of Cheerios wasn't so bad after all when the daughters filed back inside the restaurant. They dabbed perspiration with their grandma's laced hankies and declared it much too hot to do battle in Savannah in August and if the Yankees wanted Savannah in this heat, they were welcome to it. The daughters passed around glasses of sweet tea to revive themselves from the ordeal; the soldiers, in full wool Confederate uniforms and sweating like field hands, headed for the rum cellar below.

Legend had it that tunnels led from the cellar to the Savannah River and pirates plied men with rum, then kidnapped them aboard their boats to get crews. The tunnels were haunted with ghosts of those who resisted . . . or so I told everyone on my tours to fuel the hype that Savannah was indeed the most haunted city in the U.S.

I was getting ready to hitch a ride home with KiKi until I caught a glimpse of Suellen the waitress, her arm hooked around Tipper Longford, or in this case Captain Longford. Tipper laughed at something Suellen said and together they took the steps down into the cellar. The last time I'd seen Tipper he was doing battle royal with Delta at the Cakery Bakery, fists clenched and the little blood vessels in his eyes ready to pop. This was Tipper in happy mode. Go Tipper!

A waitress balancing a tray of beers wobbled at the top of the steps. I grabbed an edge of the tray to steady it and set it on table. "I can help with a few of those if you like."

"Oh, sugar, you are an angel sent from above, I do declare. These here mugs get so heavy and I hate doing these steps more times than I have to. 'Course if Suellen had taken her share instead of being all goo-goo-eyed over a certain someone, I wouldn't have to do all the work myself, now would I."

I grabbed an extra tray, and we divvied up the mugs. "Not that this is the first time," she went on. "With Suellen and men it's like bees to honey. She sure couldn't afford one of those new town houses over on East Taylor with a waitress salary, now could she? Had herself some help, if you ask me. Man kind of help."

The rum room had an old stone foundation, wood barrels and cargo nets lining the walls, scarred wood tables and chairs in the middle. Brass nautical lamps lit the room, a dartboard to the side. Tipper sat at a table, Suellen on his lap, his captain's hat perched on her head. That hat on someone else's head was sort of unnerving, like seeing Auntie

KiKi swinging Uncle Putter's golf club around, not that such a thing would ever happen in the Vanderpool household. Suellen pulled a fancy pink-jeweled iPhone from her pocket, held it up in front of her and Tipper, and clicked a picture of the them laughing together.

"This goes right on my Facebook page," she said, all smiles. "Thank you for giving it to me; you are so sweet." Suellen kissed Tipper on the cheek and he blushed all the way back to his ears. I couldn't remember seeing Tipper and Delta laughing together like this ever.

I put the beers on the table, one soldier handing me five bucks as a tip. Maybe if I moonlighted at the Pirate House I could afford a phone. I gave the money to the waitress, then hurried back upstairs before KiKi left me and I had to hoof it back home on my own two feet or wait an eternity for an afternoon bus.

"Where in the world have you been?" KiKi drew up beside me. "I've looked my eyeballs out for you. You've got to get ready for tonight." She peered at me with critical auntie glint in her eye and sucked in a quick breath. "It's going to take a while, a long while."

"Did you happen to see that waitress Suellen with Tipper Longford?" I asked KiKi as we headed for the Beemer parked in the side lot. "I thought she was into Simon?"

"My guess is when Suellen isn't near the man she loves she loves the man she's near. The girl's moving on, is all, something you need to do."

"Seems kind of fast don't you think? I mean we just hauled dear old Simon out to Bonaventure."

KiKi shoved me in the passenger side. "Maybe she was in need of a little variety in her life and doing Simon-the-younger and Tipper-the-elder at the same time. We'll visit Simon's place tomorrow instead of tonight and try to piece things together." KiKi patted me on the head like I was five. "Because tonight you're going on a date."

"It's not a date."

I LOCKED UP THE FOX AT SIX AND SNAGGED A BLUE dress with a white jacket off a display ladder I had painted yellow and rigged up in the hallway for display. I stuffed an IOU for the dress and sling-back shoes in the Rocky Road container so I wouldn't forget to pay the consigner then headed for the shower. The problem was the hair. There was no time to dye it, and if I cut off the blonde part I'd have two inches of brown spiking out. When in doubt, curl!

"You look lovely," Doc Hunky said as I stepped out onto the front porch at seven sharp.

"You look lovely, too." He laughed, but I was dead serious. I was starved and he was going to feed me. Then I remembered my promise to KiKi to be scintillating. "Nice shoes."

THE PINK HOUSE WAS DELICIOUS AS ALWAYS, DOC Hunky charming and sophisticated and a connoisseur of wines that didn't have a screw lid. There was no unsettling talk of anything bypass-related. It was only ten when

Hunky dropped me off, needing a good night's sleep to save more hearts on the morrow.

"I had a great time," he said, his eyes blue and dreamy. "I'm attending a conference in Atlanta with your uncle, but when I get back maybe we can get together again?"

Visions of the Pirate House danced through my brain. I tried to squelch it, I really did, but the lure of pecan chicken is hard to ignore. "I'd like that," I said with true sincerity even though the motive was questionable.

Hunky did the bright-smile thing and kissed me good night. The kiss was okay, but truth be told I'd gotten better from Bruce Willis. The best part of it all was I got a doggie bag!

I waved as the navy Jag pulled away from the curb, then skipped back onto the porch. I kicked off the sling-backs and pried open the crunch of aluminum foil shaped like a swan. BW peered inside with me, out heads together over the goodies, his tail in overdrive. "How would you like a nice piece of pecan chicken? I already took out the bones for you."

"No thanks, I've already eaten."

I jumped up, turned, and faced Boone leaning against one of the porch posts, moonlight in his hair, paint flakes on his black shirt, a glint of humor in his eyes. That didn't happen very often. "What was that all about?" he asked.

"Leftovers? And why do you keep sneaking up on me?"

"It's more fun that way. Who's the guy? The Jag?"

"Oh, Doc Hunky." My head started to clear from the one-too-many glasses of very fine wine. I felt a blush creep up my neck. "Heart surgeon."

Slurping sounded behind me and I spun around to BW's snout buried in the foil. "That was tomorrow's dinner for both of us, you know. Ever hear of sharing?" I looked back to Boone, my head clearing a bit more. "What are *you* doing here?"

"There was a car with out-of-state plates and Reagan Summerside riding shotgun."

"You're following me!"

"I was at Abe's on Lincoln doing Snake Bites with Pillsbury. I noticed."

Snake Bites are half hard cider, half Guinness and taste like burnt tar. After a few of those I don't know how anyone noticed anything. "I don't need a keeper."

That got me a *you wanna bet* look.

"I can take care of myself."

"I'll remember that the next time you're in a swamp or trapped under a bookcase and, for the record, I hope Hunky's a better surgeon than he is a kisser."

"Bet he's better than you are." *Open mouth, insert foot.* Boone's kisses were legendary, the stuff women talked about in hushed voices late at night after finishing off a pitcher of margaritas. "I don't need you critiquing my love life."

"Blondie, you have no love life."

"Out!" I pointed a stiff finger toward the sidewalk before I said anything else stupid.

A slow sort of grin spread across Boone's lips and he trotted down the steps and headed for the Chevy parked in the shadows across the street. I watched Boone drive off, then stomped around the porch in my bare feet wondering if I had two functioning brain cells left in my whole head. Boone used to tick me off regularly during the divorce but I thought the days of him getting to me were over. Well, think again!

It was too early and too hot to sleep and I was still mad at Boone and even madder at myself for saying dumb stuff. I slid on flip-flops, then hitched up BW. We headed for the park. Couples strolled hand in hand by Forsyth Fountain along with late-night joggers squeezing in some exercise time. Not all that long ago walking in this particular area at night implied you had a death wish. Then the historic district of downtown Savannah got way overpriced and the Victorian district blossomed with scaffolds and saws and fresh coats of paint, bringing the place back to the splendor it had once possessed.

At East Harris I caught sight of Bridesmaid coming out of Pinkie Master's, one of the oldest watering holes in Savannah, proven by the layer of dust collected over the yellow neon Miller sign behind the bar. The place was frequented by all who loved cheap PBR tallboys and Tabasco popcorn. That meant everyone in town, including Jimmy Carter once upon a time. Long live the Jimmy!

"Hi," I said to Bridesmaid, wondering if she would remember me especially in her present state of alcoholic bliss. She gave me one of those *do I know you* looks.

"I was at the wedding."

"Well, I for one am glad that bastard's dead and gone." Bridesmaid swayed, her blonde hair flopping in her face. I sat her down at one of the tables in front of the bar. Bridesmaid knew a lot more about that wedding than I did and maybe she'd be willing to share her thoughts on the subject now with a few drinks in her.

"Do you have any idea who'd want to kill Simon?" I asked, sitting down beside her.

"Me!" Bridesmaid waved her hand in the air, nearly falling off the chair. "That dipstick lied to me. He told me stuff he didn't mean one bit. Said he wanted me instead of Waynetta all along and I believed him. I should have known better than to make whoopie at the wedding but I was a little woozy from the champagne." She stopped and rolled her shoulders. "Actually I was drunk as a skunk." Bridesmaid dropped her voice. "What Simon really wanted was *s-e-x*. I know that now." She gave me a glassy-eyed stare. "I didn't just imagine it, did I? Simon really is dead?"

"As a doornail. Were you afraid Simon would tell Waynetta about your encounter?"

"Nope." Bridesmaid shook her head. "I knew he wouldn't do a dumb thing like that. Simon had a whole lot more to lose than I did if Waynetta found out we were together. Waynetta's not much into sharing. She's more a get-even kind of girl. When I couldn't find my dress I went looking for it. I knew if it didn't turn up, I'd ruin the wedding and Waynetta would kill me." Bridesmaid hiccupped and rested her forehead against the palm of her hand. "But she found out anyway, then took my dress, put it on, and killed Simon herself."

My heart stopped. "You saw her?"

"Didn't have to. I know Waynetta. Mess her over and you're dead." Bridesmaid held her arms wide open. "She might as well have killed me, too. I don't have any friends.

No one will talk to me. That's why I'm here. I have to meet some new people. I'll never land myself a proper husband after all this." A tear slid down her cheek, smearing her mascara.

Waynetta may have been frothing at the mouth over Simon doing Bridesmaid in the closet, but murder him because of it? Scratch his eyes out maybe but out-and-out stabbing?

I put my arm around Bridesmaid and BW parked his big head in her lap offering doggie sympathy. I needed to get Bridesmaid some coffee and a cab. "Waynetta doesn't control all of Savannah, you know," I said in consolation. "There are those out there who don't give a flying fig what she thinks." I considered Bridesmaid's social circle and realized my last statement was a complete lie. "You'll find someone."

"A janitor no doubt."

"I bet he'll be a really nice janitor."

"PECAN CHICKEN, GRITS, BAD KISSER," I MUMBLED to Auntie KiKi at the crack of dawn the next morning. She was standing over my bed shaking me awake.

KiKi plopped down beside me. "How did you know I was going to ask about your date?"

I pulled the sheet over my head. "You're obsessed about Doc Hunky and you know where I hide my spare key."

"Well, don't fret about the kissing part. I'm willing to bet he's a right fast learner. Is he going to ask you out again? I bet he is. Look at you, you're lovely. Well, not now of course, you look like something trapped in the woods."

I heard KiKi pacing the floor. "Call him. You need to call him today, tell him you had a great time. Ask him over for dinner. No! You're a lousy cook, no dinner. Wash his car, men love it when you take care of them. Send him flowers. Do women send men flowers?"

I peeled back the sheet and propped myself up on one elbow, the alarm clock reading six A.M. BW was still fast asleep. My dog had a better life than I did. "How many cups of coffee this morning?"

"Three, four, maybe five . . . and a half. Putter's off to a conference in Atlanta and was up early to make the drive with Doc Hunky. So now I'm awake and so should you be." Meaning if KiKi was awake, the whole world was awake especially if they happened to be on a date the night before. She had on a pink housecoat, a hint of floral nightgown underneath, matching slippers, and pink rollers in her hair. Auntie KiKi color coordinated in sleep and beyond.

"Did he hold your hand?" KiKi grinned, pupils dilated. "Bet he's a great hand-holder, being a surgeon and all."

The only way to get out of a blow-by-blow recounting of my date with a doctor was to offer up something better. "Why don't we head on down to Cakery Bakery for out-of-the-oven doughnuts, hmm? They open at six. They start baking at four thirty. Everything will be fresh. We'll be one of the first in line. Can't you just see the glaze melting off the warm doughnuts, white icing dripping down the sides, the aroma of things cooling on big racks?"

"I'm supposed to be on a diet of sorts. Then again, I did use skim milk in my coffee."

"Well, there you go." And fifteen minutes later we were in the Beemer, because walking was not near fast enough with the promise of fresh pastries at the other end of the journey. As we drove, the city stirred to life, hazy morning gray surrendering to full sunlight. People with dogs and cups of coffee in hand took to the sidewalks while others snatched newspapers off the front porch or headed for work.

"So, did you wear something nice? Show some cleavage? Maybe that kept his eyes off your roots."

Even doughnuts couldn't save me. "We had good food and wine and split bread pudding for dessert. That was my low-fat concession for dating a heart guy."

"Thought I saw Walker Boone's car parked out front."

"Must have been another '57 red convertible. Look, the lights are on in the bakery. We're just in time."

KiKi parked and locked up. "I've never been here just when they pull the first batch from the oven," she said, taking off in a fast trot.

"And with a little luck it'll never happen again." I opened the green door with a cupcake stenciled on the window as Hollis came out. Every bleached hair in place, teeth buffed to a high gloss. As far as I knew the man never got out of bed before ten.

"What are you doing up at his hour?" he asked me, a sarcastic edge in his voice. "Making a doughnut run?" His eyes drifted to my middle, brow arching in disapproval.

"I have an early meeting with the mayor," he said, his usual I-am-God attitude firmly in place. "Thought I'd bring some doughnuts for the office. Selling some property to the city. Going to make a nice commission." Hollis folded his arms. "Are you ready to let me sell Cherry House? Bankruptcy isn't pretty, Reagan."

"When I'm ready to sell, you'll be the last to know." I pushed past Hollis before I lost my appetite completely and met up with KiKi at the display case, the sight of fresh gooey things reviving my spirits.

"What did Hollis want?" KiKi asked, a touch of doughnut drool at the corner of her mouth.

"To drive me nuts, and he's succeeding. I should have let him rot in jail."

"But then you would have lost Cherry House."

"There is that."

Early-bird pastry lovers trooped in, Delta and two other counter gals all smiles and greeting people. The way I figured it, Savannah was divided into two parts, the morning people and the night people. Sometimes the parts ran into each other, like when the morning people got up extra early or the night people got in extra late or there were extenuating circumstances like a buttinsky auntie throwing everything out of whack.

Most of the bakery orders were takeout for offices and people on the go. Only a few customers occupied the tables. GracieAnn and repairman Percy, toolbox at his side, sat by the window sharing a strawberry Danish. GracieAnn smiled at Percy and fed him a dollop of filling that he licked off her finger. She squeezed his hand, then pushed back her chair and headed for the counter to help Delta wait on customers. Either Percy was a natural at undercover work or something else was going on. I left KiKi to memorize the display case and wandered over to Percy, keeping my back to GracieAnn. "How are things?" I asked Percy in a near whisper. "Any news I might be interested in?"

"Oh my goodness, yes." Percy didn't look up at me but stared straight ahead toward the counter. "Isn't she the most wonderful girl in the world?"

I glanced back to GracieAnn to make sure that's who Percy had in his sights. Yep, it was GracieAnn all right.

"I'm in love, I truly am." Percy blushed, his usually pale cheeks the color of his hair. "I'm a man smitten."

I sat down in the chair GracieAnn had just vacated and looked Percy straight in the eyes. "Chantilly? Murder? Any of this sound familiar? We're trying to find a killer here, remember? Someone GracieAnn knows may have offed Simon. Any leads? I need leads, Percy. I'm a desperate woman here. Focus, man, focus."

"GracieAnn wouldn't know a killer. She's sweet and kind and loving and she always smells like warm cookies. We're good together. GracieAnn keeps breaking things in the bakery so I have to stay around here to repair them. Isn't that the most romantic thing you every heard? Today I'm fixing the deep fryer for the doughnuts. She cut the electric wires just for me. What a girl."

"What happens when she finds out you're Chantilly's lawyer?"

Percy gasped, then put his finger over his lips. "I can't tell her that," he said under his fingers. "She hates Chantilly. She loves me, she truly does." Percy let out a deep sigh, the dopey smile back. He propped his elbow on the table, his chin in his palm gazing at the woman of his dreams.

I met up with KiKi, balancing two doughnuts on a plate and two cups. I snagged the cups. "Any more caffeine and you can flap your arms and fly back to East Gaston."

"Decaf, honey, just decaf and the doughnuts are baked, not the glazed. I figure that puts me about fifty calories to the good and it's only six thirty. I like this diet." I followed KiKi outside to the tables and selected the doughnut with sprinkles. "So what's Percy found out?" KiKi asked.

"That he's in love with GracieAnn."

KiKi's eyes rounded over her chocolate doughnut with chocolate icing. "Now that proves beyond a shadow of a doubt that God does indeed work in mysterious ways. How'd that happen?"

"Maybe God had a little help and GracieAnn recognized Percy as Chantilly's lawyer and she's making a play for him. She could be protecting the real killer by keeping Percy occupied and not concentrating on the case."

"Maybe she's guilty and keeping the heat off herself. Anyone who bakes dead-guy cookies has my vote." KiKi took a bite and closed her eyes to savor the moment, the first taste always the best with the little flavor buds on your tongue alive and happy. "We'll get into Simon's place today," KiKi said around a mouthful. "I bet he has a list of people he lent money to. The thing is, that list will make our list of killers even longer. We don't need longer. Did anyone like that guy besides his mamma?"

My doughnut suddenly tasted like glue. "Uh, I sort of already had a look around Simon's place. There's this guy Beau that I know." I did sort of know Beau . . . now. "He lives in Simon's building and he let me in. I couldn't pass up a great opportunity like that, now could I?"

KiKi placed her unfinished doughnut back on the plate and folded her hands on the table like she was praying in church. Auntie KiKi not finishing her one and only doughnut allotment for the day was not a good sign. Folded hands meant drama was on the way. "You cut me out of the loop."

"No loop cutting, it just happened. It was a dead end anyway. I didn't find anything that would help." I couldn't tell her I found the book and it got stolen. She'd have a fit saying it would never have happened if we'd both been there. Truth is we would have both wound up under the bookcase.

KiKi stirred her coffee, deep in thought. Either she was mentally cutting me out of the will or she had an idea. She said, "These days everyone keeps information on a computer or iPhone, but Simon would have a hard copy of vital information stashed somewhere. He was mean and conniving and heartless and a swindler and a two-timing rodent, but he wasn't stupid."

Lord be praised, she bought the Beau explanation! I was off the hook.

"Computers crash, iPhones get dropped in toilets and other watery places," she went on. "I bet Simon used one of those flash-drive things for backup." KiKi kept stirring her coffee, brain cells fully caffeinated. "His mamma said he was moving out to Waverly Farms right after the honeymoon. I bet a lot of his things are out there right now."

"He wouldn't leave incriminating information out in

plain sight for anyone to pick up, especially out there at Waverly Farms."

"It wouldn't be all that obvious. Everyone has flash drives, dime a dozen, just another piece of plastic lying around. If you didn't find anything at the condo, then Waverly Farms is the next place for us to look for Simon's backup information. Its two days since the funeral and without a proper wake I should be paying a call out there. I do believe a covered dish is in order now that I think about it. It's the neighborly thing to do."

"The Waverlys have two cooks and three maids. I think they're covered."

"They don't have KiKi Vanderpool's deviled eggs, now do they, and everyone knows mine are even better than Paula's. Here's what we'll do, you chat it up with Waynetta and I'll snoop around the place and see what I can find out."

I dropped my doughnut in my coffee, splashing it everywhere. What happened to off the hook? "No way. Waynetta barely knows me, hates what she does know about me, and you can't go wandering all over the Waverly house pawing through things."

"Honey, Waynetta hates everyone unless they're rich or famous. If that catfight out at Bonaventure was any indication how things are out at Waverly Farms, my guess is Waynetta has Simon's belongings packed up somewhere and ready to dump them at his mamma's or just the nearest swamp. Besides, it's my turn to snoop. You got to do the condo with Beau, remember." She tipped her chin. "Or do you think I'm too old to snoop around?"

"What if you get caught? It could be downright embarrassing."

"It's a big house. I'll say I'm lost."

I was trapped and it was all for nothing. There was no flash drive or book because I already found the blasted book at the condo and had it stolen right out from under me. Not that I could tell KiKi that. I'd be admitting that I lied and indeed cut her out of the action. At least Waverly Farms wasn't someplace dangerous to be roaming around. It wasn't the middle of the hood at midnight. How much trouble could KiKi get into? "Okay, I'm in."

"I knew you'd see things my way." KiKi scarfed down the last bit of doughnut. "Chantilly can mind the Fox till noon. We should go to the Waverlys first thing this morning. Everyone will be bringing out a covered dish today and we want to beat the crowd with me snooping around the place. It is a pity we can't do this later on in the day. Reese Waverly makes a mighty fine martini and I do so hate to miss it. I'll put on the eggs as soon as we're home and use Grandma Vanderpool's Old Country Roses bone china deviled egg plate. Things always taste better on a nice china plate, don't you think."

What I thought was, *This is how God gets you when you lie to your auntie.*

Chapter Eleven

"**Y**ou!" Waynetta snarled at me when she opened the front door. "There're no more packages to pick up here. Go away."

Undaunted, Auntie KiKi held out the Old Country Rose plate. "Oh, honey, we were wondering how you're getting on these days?"

"You brought me eggs?" Waynetta stared, her lip curling at the corner. Waynetta Waverly, the soul of gratitude and good manners.

"We are mighty sorry for all that you and your dear daddy have suffered and wanted to pay our respects," KiKi gushed, ignoring the curl and patting Waynetta's cheek.

Paying respects is one of those phrases that gets you automatic entry to any house in Savannah. Waynetta stepped aside and I followed Auntie KiKi into the living room. Summer curtains filtered the blasting sun's rays to a soft glow, sparing the antiques and Oriental rug. I sat on the blue davenport, KiKi beside me, Waynetta in a chair with a gilded back and brocade seat that looked remarkably like a throne.

"It's been such a long ride," Auntie KiKi said to Waynetta after she summoned Bessy May for tea. "Hot as the dickens even at this hour. I'd like to freshen up a bit if you don't mind."

Waynetta gave directions. I racked my brain for something to talk about as KiKi disappeared down the hall. At least Simon and I had Rocky Road in common.

"How are you?" I asked Waynetta. I did feel bad for her and all her troubles. She may sit on a throne, but she was a perfect example of how money can't buy happiness.

"To tell you the truth, I'm not well at all." Waynetta dabbed her tearing eyes. "Daddy told me the most dreadful news this morning and I just don't know if I can bear it. I'm supposed to be in mourning for a year, a whole twelve months, can you imagine such a thing! That means no parties or social events till next August. Whatever will I do with myself? How will I survive? I'm in charge of the Christmas Cotillion, for heaven's sake. Who made up this stupid mourning rule, anyway? Sounds like something out of the Dark Ages if you ask me."

"Well, you weren't actually married to Simon; maybe six months would be long enough?"

"You think so?" Waynetta's eyes sparkled. "Maybe even

three months since Simon was cheating on me. That should count for something. What a great idea, thank you kindly." Waynetta gave me a quick once-over. "How did you resign yourself to your plight?"

"Plight?"

"After your divorce did it get easier to accept the fact that you'll wind up a spinster? You are just precious, you know."

"Spinster?" *Precious?* I was still getting over plight.

"You don't have to take care of yourself any longer and that has to be a relief. You can just let yourself go, be free as a bird. I must say earthy is a fine look for you. Flip-flops, khaki pants, recycled blouse, mousy brown hair coming in nice and bushy. Next week I'm off to Atlanta for a new wardrobe. Now where can Bessy May be with that tea? All these problems have me parched as desert cactus. And where is Miss KiKi?"

A crash sounded from upstairs followed by a scream. For a second I thought the scream came from me. After *plight*, *spinster*, and *precious* followed by *earthy* I had a right. A maid ran into the room wringing her hands. "You best come quick, Miss Waynetta. That dance teacher lady passed right out in the upstairs hallway."

According to Cher via Auntie KiKi *there aren't many scripts floating around for fifty-year-old chicks* but my guess was KiKi just invented one. I took the steps behind Waynetta and found Reese Waverly helping KiKi to sit up.

"I came around the corner," Reese said, looking trim and rich in a hundred-dollar haircut and two-hundred-dollar slacks. "And there KiKi was in the hallway. She just sort of slowly sank to the floor right in front of me." Reese looked to me. "Should I call the ambulance? Did she have a stroke? Has she been ill?"

"Are you all right?" I asked KiKi, kneeling down beside her, patting her cheek.

"Well, I do declare," she said, eyes fluttering open, a little wink added for my benefit. "I think the heat got to me and then I was disoriented and flustered in this big, beautiful house. It was simply too much to take in. I'm fine as can be now. Maybe a martini to revive my spirits."

I gave KiKi the bug-eyed look and she added, "Or a glass of water would be fine, too."

The doorbell sounded downstairs and Waynetta let out a long-suffering sign. "Holy Moses and blessed Saint Mary, this place is busier than a stump full of ants. Must be more visitors, no doubt. I swear if I could kill Simon Ambrose all over again for what he's put me though, I'd do it in a New York minute."

Kiki gulped some water the maid gave her then Reese assisted her down the steps. A contingency from the Daughters of the Confederacy filed into the living room, covered china dishes in hand. We all exchanged greetings then I charged up the Beemer and KiKi and I headed down the gravel drive.

"Did you hear that?" I said to KiKi not having the patience to wait till we got off the property. "Waynetta said she wanted to kill Simon *again*, meaning she could have very well caused his demise the first time around. And there's something else, last night I ran into Bridesmaid and she seemed to think Waynetta was more than capable of killing off Simon. What's going on around here?"

"Oh, honey, you bet your sweet tomato a lot's going on but I'm not sure it has anything to do with Waynetta." KiKi fished around in her cleavage as if she had a bad case of poison ivy in that most inconvenient spot. "Looky what I found in Reese Waverly's office."

KiKi pulled out a black flash drive and held it up like she'd won first prize. "This here is why I had to faint like I did. I didn't want Reese to suspect I filched this little old thing right off his computer, and you should see the man's office. He must have just had it redone. Maybe I can get Putter up there for some ideas. His office needs an updating and—"

I jammed on the breaks, leaving skid marks. "You stole that thing out of Reese's office!"

"Borrowed for an extended period of time."

"How do you know it has anything to do with Simon?"

"*SA* written right here." KiKi pointed to the letters on the flat side in red marker. "Simon Ambrose. I bet Reese found this in Simon's stuff when packing it up. It had to be important for him to still have it connected to his computer like it was."

"KiKi, honey, think about this. You were upstairs by his office. Reese is going to know you took the flash drive. Simon could have died because of that information. Reese has guns, lots of guns, big guns and knows how to use them. I've seen him in action. This is not good."

KiKi tsked and waved her hand in the air. "I'm the little old dance teacher who goes around quoting Cher. No one will suspect me of anything. I'm harmless."

"You're the dance teacher who gets into everyone's knickers!"

"There's going to be people in and out of that there house all day long. Reese will think someone else took it. I'm telling you we're home free."

Except I didn't feel free, I felt like there was a big old bull's-eye on my back and now one on KiKi's back as well. I should have leveled with her about the stolen notebook, but I swear on a stack of Bibles I thought going out to Waverly Farms was safe as going to a church picnic.

It was noon when I pulled into KiKi's driveway. A few cars I didn't recognize lined the curb out front of our houses along with one sweet-looking Harley. KiKi said she'd bring over her computer and the flash drive later on, but right now she had another dance lesson with Bernard Thayer. He'd been Mr. Weather on WSAV more years than I'd been alive and was determined to get on *Dancing with the Stars* or die trying. KiKi was close to granting him the latter option.

The Fox was hopping with customers sorting through dresses and jackets and trying on shoes. A rack of newly consigned clothes hung off to the side ready to be tagged and put out. I savored the moment and stifled the *yippee alleluia* squeal of joy creeping up my throat. Chantilly had great instincts when it came to business but not so much when it came to men. Not only did she hook up with Simon the sleaze of Savannah but next to her behind the checkout at this very moment was Mr. Pillsbury of Seventeenth Street fame and fortune.

He had on True Religion jeans that had nothing to do with church on Sunday and everything to do with costing plenty. Only a hint of the piggy bank and dollar-sign tattoos on his biceps peeked out from the sleeve of a navy T-shirt. The customers didn't seem to mind a little eye candy behind the counter. Fact is, every woman loves the bad boy and Pillsbury would never ever be taken for anything but.

He gave Chantilly a friendly kiss on the cheek, BW a pat on the head, nodded to me, then sauntered out the front door and down the steps. The roar of his bike vibrated into the Fox. I wrote up a sale for a denim jacket and brown leather bag, then asked Chantilly, "Have you lost your ever-loving mind!"

She giggled like a schoolgirl and turned red. "I do believe I have. He likes me."

I gripped her shoulders and looked into her starry eyes. "This is one of those times to think about what you're doing. Your daddy's retired police. Pillsbury's working hood. Things could get messy."

"Look at me, Reagan. My life's nothing but messy. I can trust Pillsbury, I know I can. He'd never hurt me like Simon did. He'd never betray me."

Oddly enough I agreed. The Seventeenth Street gang had issues to be sure. Ask anyone who'd had their car stolen, house broken into, was in need of untraceable firepower, bookie, or dealer for whatever purpose, but word had it the boys kept drugs, guns, and other nasty things away from schools, parks, and churches, which was a big chunk of

Savannah real estate and something the cops never could pull off.

"He gave me a present."

"A Mercedes with the VIN filed off?"

Chantilly held out her hand sporting a lovely gold ring with a small sapphire. "It was his mamma's. He wanted me to have it. We got to be friendly when I made UPS deliveries. I can't help how I feel."

"Guess that's not the worst I've heard today. Percy's fallen for GracieAnn and she bakes dead-people cookies."

"Must be a full moon."

CHANTILLY LEFT AND BY SIX I HAD MOST OF THE newly consigned clothes priced and put out on the racks. I had better sales than all the previous week combined. I subtracted 10 percent for the cannon, wrote a check to the daughters that would go out in the morning mail, then stuffed the cash in the freezer. I turned around to KiKi coming through the back door, a jar of plump green olives balanced on her laptop, a sweaty pitcher of ice-cold martinis in her hand. Sometimes KiKi's visits were a lot more enjoyable than others.

"Figure we needed a little libation," she said, kicking off her shoes. "My big toe barely survived Bernard and you've been entertaining the boys from the hood. The kudzu vine knows all."

"Chantilly has no man sense."

"Honey, when it comes to men, at one time or another

none of us has any sense." We shoved aside a display of jewelry on the dining room table and KiKi flipped open her laptop. We sat down, poured out the martinis, then plugged in the flash drive.

"A golf course?" KiKi said, both of us staring at an architect's drawing on the screen. "I don't recognize the clubhouse and I've probably visited every single one of those things in the area with Putter for some benefit or another. Maybe this course is in the planning stage."

"Why would Simon be interested in a golf course? Was he into loan-sharking to build it?"

KiKi sat back and sipped. "This sort of thing is way out of Simon's league. Golf courses cost millions, they have investors and backers and sponsors and endorsements. Maybe Simon wanted to get Reese involved, get money from him to invest in it." KiKi sat up, eyes wide. "Maybe Simon was out to swindle Reese and that's how he wound up dead."

"He was going to marry Waynetta. Why double-cross her father?" I said to KiKi.

"We've been assuming all along that Simon would fall into tons of money when he married Waynetta but what if he signed a prenup? If Simon did, he'd get nothing when Waynetta got tired of him and as we all know, Waynetta gets tired of everyone but herself sooner or later. This golf course hoax was one way for Simon to walk off with a chunk of Reese's cash. That also explains why Simon kept Icy on the string too and others like Chantilly. He wasn't going to be as well off as we thought, marrying Waynetta.

He planned on marrying her to get to her daddy. Also, if Simon signed a prenup he looked all the more trustworthy to Reese and then could rope him in for the kill on the golf course."

"Except the kill part backfired. So you mean the golf course isn't for real?" I said, trying to put this together from Simon's viewpoint. "Reese Waverly then finds out he's been taken to the cleaners by Simon and gets Sugar-Ray to kill him. No one scams Reese Waverly and gets away with it and Sugar-Ray needed the money." I chewed an olive. "But there's still the fact that Reese would get his attorneys to investigate the golf course before he laid out money."

"Simon worked at the bank." KiKi added. "Setting up dummy accounts and making things look legit is something he knew how to do. That guy was one smooth operator and he was into the scam business. He told Reese this was a sweet deal he'd come across and Reese needed to get in on it right quick before it was too late."

I flipped through a few more screens on the computer. "It looks like a terrific country club. Best I can tell it's supposed to be someplace between Savannah and Bluffton. It can draw from both locations and the Hilton Head group. No wonder Reese fell for it. Says here they have a five-star chef lined up from Atlanta for the restaurant and some golf pro guy from Florida. Look at the mockups for the décor. If I could afford it, I'd invest. It's gorgeous. This is a lot of work just to scam Reese Waverly."

"Reese is no dummy. It had to look good. If we knew

for sure that Simon signed a prenup, that would make our speculation about the scam and Reese wanting him dead a lot more believable. Right now we're just guessing." KiKi took a drink and looked at me out of the corner of her eyes. "Walker Boone would know."

"You'll have to ask him. He never tells me anything."

"Bet if you showed up in that belly-dancing outfit, he'd tell you whatever you wanted to hear."

I put down the empty glass, my thinking powers severely compromised. "What does that mean?"

"I'm just saying it had some effect on the old boy, is all."

KiKi headed back home for an evening of bachelorette bliss of chick-flick movies that Putter would hate and a tub of low-fat popcorn, taking the lose-a-few-pounds idea to heart. After a dinner of Cheerios I leashed up BW. Humidity hovered around 150 percent, making everyone a little shiny and coated with a fine layer of Savannah sweat.

Going to see Boone was probably a big waste of time but he was my best shot on finding out if Simon had indeed signed a prenup other than asking Reese outright. That didn't seem like a great idea if indeed Reese killed Simon or more accurately had him killed. Boone and Reese were in cahoots over something and a prenup with a conniving future son-in-law had to have come up at sometime.

Not that Boone would tell me what was going on, but over the last few years I had learned to sort of read him. When I was way off base about something Boone was ready with a sarcastic comment. If he yawned, then sat back and looked bored I was getting closer to the truth, and if he had his blank lawyer face in place and said nothing, I'd hit pay dirt.

Trying to ignore Kiki's belly-dancing comment, I knew the powers of Angel's pulled pork sandwich with Voodoo sauce and a side of mac and cheese. Boone would need the mac and cheese to put out the fire from the Voodoo sauce.

Chapter Twelve

A NGEL'S was up on West Oglethorpe, a long trot from East Gaston, but Bruce Willis seemed to be in a walking kind of mood and I needed to walk off that martini. After we picked up our order from Angel's we headed for the land of the rich and prosperous, also known as Madison Square. We passed the Green-Meldrim House, now part of the Episcopal church and a far better use of the place than the commandeered residence where Sherman set up shop.

Boone's house dated back to the 1880s and had a raised entrance to keep the place clean from back-in-the-day dirt streets. It was Federal-style beige and Savannah lovely with original black shutters and side verandas made for sitting a spell and chatting on a hot summer night. Not that I could see Boone doing much of either on any night.

I took the stairs to the covered porch with lush green ferns and overflowing urns of red geraniums and white petunias. Either Boone had one heck of a green thumb or his gardener knew his stuff. My bet was on the gardener. It wasn't the best of manners to come calling at night unannounced but manners weren't Boone's strong suit. Besides, I had food, some of Savannah's most tasty, and that overrode manners any day of the week.

I whammed the pineapple doorknocker a few times, waited, then gave it another try. "What?" Boone said, yanking open the front door. His eyes were red and bloodshot, chin lined with thick don't-mess-with-me stubble. His feet were bare and he had on jeans and a gray T-shirt that was old and frayed.

"You need to shop."

"Thank you, Christian Dior. Go bother someone else." Boone gave BW a pat, started to close the door till I held up a brown bag, *Angel's* scripted on the side. "I bring tidings of great joy."

Boone parked his hand on his lean hip, the tiniest of smiles at the corners of his mouth. "Angel's. I get it." He grabbed the bag and came out onto the porch. He sat down on the top step, ripped the foil from the sandwich, and took a bite as if he hadn't eaten all day. "Thanks," he mumbled.

"You never thank me for anything."

"That's because until now there was no reason." He took another bite. "We need beer." He handed me the sandwich.

"I'll get it," I offered, handing the sandwich back. "Tell me where."

"And it gives you a chance to check out my house," he said, taking another bite.

"There is that." I dropped Old Yeller on the step, then opened the front door to the entrance hall, living room to the right. In the corner stood one lonely Louis-the-something secretary, a beat-up leather couch facing the fireplace—women had shoes and purses, men had leather couches—a huge desk with the light on, papers scattered over the surface and spilling onto the floor. An ugly table, chairs, and buffet occupied the dining room and more than likely they came with the house, costing more to move them than they were worth. The kitchen had old appliances and a faux wood laminate dinette set the former owners had probably left as well. At this rate I imagined Boone's bedroom possessed an army cot and crates; not exactly in sync with his playboy reputation. I grabbed two Moon Rivers from the fridge and a bag of little carrots. The compatibility of beer and carrots was questionable, but I figured Boone's eyes needed all the help they could get.

"And I thought I lived Spartan," I said to Boone when I got back outside and took the step below him.

"Did you bring a fork for the mac and cheese?"

I dug around in the Angel's bag and pulled out a spork. Personally I hated those things, which looked like they couldn't make up their mind about which utensil to be, but I didn't think Boone would care in his present state of feeding frenzy.

"The carrots belong to my cleaning lady." Guess that was as good an excuse as any to skip veggies, so we twisted off the beer caps at the same time and both took a swig.

Nothing better on a hot summer night in Savannah than cold beer.

"Why are you here?" he asked, looking better than he had a few minutes ago.

"To bring you food."

"Meaning you want information and this is a bribe." Boone leaned against one of the wrought-iron posts, me against the other, BW parked between us. "Where's Hunky?"

"He and Uncle Putter drove to Atlanta for some kind of conference."

"He's not your type."

"He has a job, opens my doors, and picks up the check. That makes him any woman's type. Did Simon sign a pre-nup with Waynetta?"

Boone fed BW mac and cheese right off the spork, then finished the rest himself. "Don't know anything about a prenup," Boone mumbled around a mouthful. "Thought that was your specialty."

"You're mixed up with Reese Waverly some way and my guess is it involves Simon. I'm going to tell you what I think is going on and you can tell me how close I am to being right."

"How's that shop of yours doing these days?" Boone said, scraping out the bottom of the carton for the last bit.

"I'm not great at a lot of things, but I seem to be an ace at stirring up trouble and right now Reese Waverly has my full attention. Everyone thinks Simon intended to marry Waynetta for her money but my guess is Simon signed a prenup with Waynetta. That made Reese trust him, and then to show his gratitude Simon scammed Reese on a nonexistent golf course proposition. Reese realized what was going on and that Simon was also screwing around on his darling offspring so he had Sugar-Ray kill him at the wedding."

"Why kill him? Why wouldn't Reese just turn Simon over to the police?"

"Pride. He'd look like a gullible fool and people would laugh. Not an acceptable scenario for Reese Waverly the almighty."

Boone looked at me for a long moment. He yawned and leaned back, his lawyer face firmly in place. "Someone needs to warn your doctor friend what a pain in the butt you are."

A yawn, the lawyer face, and sarcasm all at the same time! Not fair! Something I said was right on, something close to being right and some part way off base. The question was what part belonged to what?

IT WAS NEAR MIDNIGHT WHEN BRUCE WILLIS AND I finally got home, East Gaston quiet and sleepy as if resting up for the next day. I learned nothing from Boone except he was working on some big case that was none of my business. I, on the other hand, adhered to the kudzu vine philosophy of since I lived in this city anything and everything that happened here was definitely my business.

Tomorrow I'd look up Sugar-Ray and we'd have a chat. He was a little scarier than I remembered, make that a lot scarier, and I wouldn't expect him to throw his hands in the air yelling *I killed Simon*. After the graveyard episode I figured he fit into this murder somehow. Maybe he'd let something slip if I happened to let it slip that I saw him out at Bonaventure swilling white rum and packing a Smith & Wesson.

I pulled my house keys out of Old Yeller and the porch floorboards creaked behind me. It might be a raccoon or opossum but this was a heavy kind of creak making every hair on my body stand straight up and my lungs quit working. Besides, if a night creature did invade the porch, BW would have given chase by now. Instead he flopped down in rub-my-tummy pose, his tail on super-speed. I gripped my keys between my fingers like I'd seen in those self-defense shows and slowly turned around to face Icy Graham, eyes angry, jaw set, body hard and threatening. I needed something more than a house key.

"Hi," I said all smiles. How could someone hurt little Miss Cheerful? "Can I help you with something?"

"You're a pain in the ass."

"Second time tonight I heard that."

"You should pay attention." Icy grabbed my hand and threw my keys to the floor. "I know it was you and your friend talking to my daughter the other day." His voice was low, menacing, fitting the name Icy. He shoved me against the front of the house, rattling the bay window and knocking the breath out of me. His hand closed around my throat, tightening, eyes blazing. "I saw you at the cemetery. Laura Lynn said a lady with a BMW and a woman that needed hair coloring talked to her about Simon. That be you. Stay away from my daughter. You got family. How would you like it if I was out to get them? Stay away from what's mine or you'll be sorry, sorrier than you can imagine."

Icy let me go and ran down the steps to a truck parked across the street. He got in and took off. Jelly-legged I slid to the porch floor, gasping for air. BW came over and licked my face, then sat down beside me as I stroked his back for what seemed like forever, the rhythmic gesture soothing, my life settling back to normal.

Who was I kidding? There was no normal. I was hunting a killer and from what I just saw and felt, Icy Graham would have no qualms killing Simon. He'd have no qualms killing me. Of course the same was true of rifle-toting Reese Waverly. These men were light-years apart in a lot of respects but when it came to protecting their kids they were front and center. As much as I didn't like either one I respected them for that.

I could call the police about Icy but it was my word against his and then he'd be doubly ticked off. I failed miserably at dealing with a singly ticked-off Icy Graham. Best to let this incident go, but I wanted a look at his truck. After our little encounter, I imagined he was the one who knocked me into the swamp and was a prime candidate for I-killed-Simon. Then again Reese had trucks out at the farm and knew I was snooping around and Pillsbury could *borrow* a truck anytime the spirit moved him and didn't think much of Simon either. Even GracieAnn had access to the Cakery Bakery truck. I was running in circles.

I finally felt strong enough to stand. I held on to the

porch railing to steady myself as Chantilly drove up in her Jeep. She kept the car running and hurried up the walk.

"You're still awake, I don't even have to get you out of bed."

"If this is a one A.M. social call because you're having an attack of insomnia, you need to know I'm a quart low on sympathy. Come back tomorrow. I'll be better tomorrow, I promise."

"Look." She held up her iPhone and read, "*Meet me @ Simon's ASAP. Info 2 prove u innocent.*" She grabbed my hand. "Come on, let's go. This is great. We're finally onto something. Someone's helping us."

"And you came here to get me because . . ."

"Because there's a killer on the loose and the condo belongs to someone already dead and buried. It's kind of creepy especially at night and this isn't the kind of thing I want to face alone. But it's still great. We got a lead."

I didn't agree with the great part but the lead reference had merit, and two minutes later I'd locked BW safely inside and was sitting beside Chantilly. She found a parking space courtesy of some late-night barfly finally heading home.

"I've already been though Simon's place," I said as we hoofed it the rest of way to the condo. "I found a book hidden in an ice cream carton in the freezer."

Chantilly stopped dead right there on the sidewalk. "Get out of town! Why didn't you tell me before? What was in the book? More people Simon swindled? What did it say? Now we have other suspects. This is a really good night. About time things turned around."

"Someone knocked me down in the condo and stole the book before I had chance to look at it."

Chantilly smacked her hand to her forehead and closed her eyes. "How could you let this happen? Who do you think took it?"

"Do you know anything about Simon and a golf course?"

"As far as I know he didn't play, but maybe Reese was getting him into the game. Rich man's sport and all that."

We crossed the street and I pointed up to Simon's condo on the second floor. "The lights are off. They're connected to a timer; they should be on."

"Unless whoever's in there is trying to keep a low profile. They didn't want to meet in a public place so that must be it, don't you think?"

"Maybe."

"Maybe's good." Chantilly took a deep breath through clenched teeth and punched the code to get us inside the building. When we reached Simon's door Chantilly knocked softly. She knocked again.

"This doesn't feel right," I said, little pinpricks of unease running up my spine. It was a night full of things not being right.

Chantilly plucked a key from her purse. "Let's hope Simon was a lazy slug and didn't change the locks on me. Last time I was here the key worked."

"Last time? How long ago was last time?"

"About a week. Had a Simon meltdown followed by a doughnut binge. These things happen." Chantilly took hold of the doorknob to insert the key but it opened on its own.

"Hello," Chantilly called out.

"Wait," I said holding tight on to her arm. "Open door means someone's inside. I learned that the hard way."

I took Chantilly's hand and together we stepped inside. "Anybody here?" Chantilly singsonged. "It's me, Chantilly, dying to hear more about the information that's going to prove me innocent."

"Dying? Really?" I whispered, getting a *shush* in reply. I flicked the light switch by the door. No lights. The faint glow from the street sliced in through the blinds casting stripes of bright and black onto the wood floor. I pawed around in the bottom of Old Yeller past two lipsticks, a brush, a second container of hairspray I forgot I had, a pack of gum, nail file, scissors, and *ta-da*, the flashlight. I twisted it on, the beam picking out the humongous TV, debris left over from the fallen bookcase episode, the vanilla candle, and Suellen from the Pirate House lying faceup, eyes wide open, ponytail askew, not moving a bit, and dead as Robert E. Lee, right there on Simon's fine leather sofa.

Chapter Thirteen

"Holy mother in heaven!" Chantilly took a step back and smashed right into me; we both made the sign of the cross. "You were right about someone being in here."

"Not exactly what I had in mind." I used two hands to hold the light steady.

"Who is it?"

"Waitress at the Pirate House. She was at the wedding and found Simon dead right before I did. She was all upset."

"Yeah, well, dead bodies have that effect. Think she sent me the text?"

"I think someone who wanted us to find her sent the text and now I hear sirens. We've got to get out of here right now."

Chantilly pointed at the body, a defiant look in her eyes. "But we're innocent. We didn't do this."

"You used that same line four days ago and yet here we are again. Not a good place to be." I doused the flashlight and using my shirttail swiped off the doorknob inside, grabbed Chantilly's arm and pulled her out into the hall, closed the door, and wiped the outside knob. The sirens stopped; car doors slamming out front. "We're trapped!"

"Back entrance." I followed Chantilly down a hallway leading away from the street, our footsteps muffled by the carpet. Chantilly shoved on a door taking us to a fenced-in area, an ancient fluorescent light suspended overhead from a phone pole. Sirens approached down the alley, our only way out. I nodded at the Dumpster.

"It's August!" Chantilly hissed, eyes huge.

Translation: Bugs, vermin, smells from the depths of hell.

"Jail." I hissed.

Translation: Cavity search, group showers, Brunhilde as a roomie.

We scrambled over the edge, landing on filled garbage bags as a cruiser pulled to a screeching stop outside the Dumpster, sirens echoing off the rusting metal. I could feel Chantilly shaking next to me. Least I told myself it was Chantilly. Something crawled up my leg and I put my hand over my mouth to smother a scream.

"Why did I let you talk me into this?" Chantilly whimpered.

I glanced at her and the biggest roach I'd ever seen— and I'd seen my share—had perched itself on her head.

Another climbed up one of her curls. Something furry sat on a garbage bag behind her. My hand landed in something gooey and I jumped, knocking into another bag that broke open spilling garbage over both of us. Chantilly peered at me, eyes horrified.

"I won't tell what's crawling on you if you don't tell me." I whispered.

I peeled lettuce from my nose and peeked over the edge to the empty cruiser, lights still strobing, no one around. Taking hold of Old Yeller, I hoisted one leg over the edge, then slid down the side of the Dumpster, Chantilly landing beside me. Breathing hard, we flattened ourselves against the building and I glanced down the alley to make sure no cops were coming late to the party. Sidestepping our way around the edge of the building, I peeked to the front now congested with cruisers and sleepy people wandering out onto the sidewalk.

We ducked behind a line of azaleas, all foliage and no flowers this time of year. "We need to look natural," I said knocking a palmetto bug and her family from Chantilly's shoulder as she did some swiping at my hair.

Chantilly swallowed. "Natural? We're covered in garbage and other things I don't want to even think about that are gross and horrible and terrifying and we smell like a sewer."

Actually we smelled way worse than a sewer. I got a stick and flicked a long-haired crawly from Chantilly's shorts. She took the stick from my hand and whacked at my back. "Do you think the cops are looking for us?"

"Maybe." Before she could ask more questions with bad answers I took her hand and ran down another alley of garbage cans, dark windows, and a dog. Not a sweet minisomething who escaped from his loving owner and wanted to go home, but a street dog, saliva drooling from his mouth and pissed that we were on his turf.

"This is what happens when you run from the cops," Chantilly sniffed, tears in her eyes. "The gods line up against you and you get eaten alive by something with big teeth." Step by step we backed up, dog following with his head down, eyes focused, licking his chops.

"Last time this happened I had a package of shrimp and fed an alligator."

"Alligator?"

"It's been a rough week." I scooped the remains of a mangled taco off my shorts. "Here doggie, doggie, doggie. Here it is, the great surprise."

Crouched and ready for attack, doggie came closer, our gazes met, his on fire for me and not in a lovey-dovey way. I tossed down the taco and the dog lunged for it as Chantilly and I ran past him to the Jeep across the street. Chantilly beeped the car open and we scrambled inside, collapsing in the seats, gasping for air. I stomped on a roachy thing that fell off one of us.

"My car will never be the same."

"Just hang one of those little air freshener things from your mirror and you'll be fine."

"This is a nightmare." Chantilly whammed a bug with her fists, the impact popping the glove compartment open.

"I'll never be fine again." She charged up the Jeep as a tear slid down her face cutting across a smear of gravy, or another brown sticky substance I didn't have the courage to name.

"Hey, we're going to find this killer. We have more to go on now. My guess is that Suellen saw who murdered Simon and was trying to blackmail him or her. They wouldn't pay up and killed her instead."

"She should have just gone to the police."

"That's withholding evidence and blackmail, both big no-no's in the world of Detective Ross and others with shiny badges. The killer followed Suellen to Simon's and killed her. Then the killer used Suellen's phone to text you. You're on the ropes for Simon's murder. You're an easy target to take the rap for the second. My guess is that your phone number is in the missing notebook that the killer has. Setting you up to take the fall for killing Suellen was a piece of cake."

Chantilly pulled up in front of my house. "Where do we go from here? Any great ideas?"

"I'll talk to Sugar-Ray tomorrow. He could have easily dressed in the bridesmaid dress and killed Simon. If Suellen was trying to blackmail him, he didn't have the money to pay her off. He's a good place to start."

"Last time we saw Sugar-Ray he was packing heat. I'll pick you up at nine. He can't shoot both of us at once."

I watched the Jeep drive away and kicked off my flip-flops. They were shot. Everything I had on was bug-ridden. I unlocked the front door and started to step inside, then stopped. With the way my luck was running, a pregnant creepy would fall off, hide in the floorboards, and give birth to a bazillion other creepies. It was either risk total embarrassment now and strip on the spot or infest Cherry House forever. I backed into the shadows, ran my hands through my hair to knock lose anything that had taken up housekeeping, ripped off every piece of clothing on my body then grabbed Old Yeller and darted inside. BW gave me one good sniff, barked, and ran for the kitchen. This was the same dog that just a few hours earlier flopped over on his back for the Savannah Strangler. Not a good omen.

I grabbed the baseball bat I kept beside the front door and the three of us—me, Old Yeller, and the bat—headed upstairs. Turning the shower on full hot, I grabbed the bat in one hand, then dumped my purse upside down into the tub.

Two roaches wandered out. My screams temporarily immobilized them till I pulverized the little dears. I swished their remains down the drain, giving them a burial at sea. I joined my purse in the shower—bet you can't do that with one of those fancy Coach bags—lathered and shampooed every inch of me and Old Yeller thrice. I wrapped in a towel, called BW in to have another whiff. After two more barking sessions and retreats to the kitchen, I finally declared myself Dumpster free, set my alarm for 8:45, and collapsed into bed just as the sun peeked over the cherry tree in the front yard.

THE NEXT MORNING MY HAIR LOOKED LIKE IT GOT caught in the blender, if I had one. After five shampoos, all the conditioners in the world couldn't save me from the wild woman of Borneo look. Using my chicken-turning tongs I pinched my clothes off the porch. Holding them at arm's length to keep Dumpster inhabitants as far away as possible, I tossed them into the garbage can, then dropped in the tongs for good measure. I couldn't fry chicken for diddly anyway.

At nine sharp the red Jeep motored up to the curb and I opened the door to a rush of lavender and vanilla. A sleepy-looking Chantilly handed me take-out coffee.

"I scrubbed and Febreezed for an hour last night," she said. "Left the car open to air it out and stomped two more leftover cockroaches on the way here. I think we're good to go."

I took the passenger side. That Chantilly didn't comment on the status of my hair made me rethink what it looked like the rest of the time. I pried off my coffee lid. Bug free. In spite of my hair and questionable infestation of the Jeep, today was already better than yesterday.

Chantilly put the car in gear. "Google says Sugar-Ray's got his marriage counseling office over there on MLK. We need a nonthreatening approach to get him talking."

"Since I'm divorced and Simon is pushing up daisies, coming in for marital advice isn't going to work for either of us. I'll think of something."

But when we walked into the office building and followed the directory to Sugar-Ray's office on the second floor my brain cells still weren't functioning, and I no idea how to get Sugar-Ray to spill his guts. The office was small but smartly furnished with a contemporary flair of cream and celery green, Ikea with taste and pizzazz. There was no one in the reception area so I knocked on the desk. "Hello?"

Sugar-Ray stepped out from a connecting door. I got a better look of him now than at the cemetery. Wavy hair, gym build, beige suit, and yellow silk Versace tie I recognized from a Nordstrom catalog KiKi brought over to keep me abreast of fashions for the Fox.

"Do you have an appointment?"

"Hi." I gave him a little friendly hand wave. "I know it's been a while but if we could just talk to you for a few minutes, Chantilly and I would really appreciate it."

I got the blank stare. "My receptionist doesn't come in till noon."

"Reagan Summerside? High school? The prom?" Worse night of my life and that included the one in the Dumpster.

"Reagan!" Sugar-Ray forced a smile. Guess the prom didn't hold fond memories for him either. We followed Sugar-Ray back to his office, the décor a continuation of the reception area. I took one green club chair, Chantilly sat in the other, and Sugar-Ray parked behind his glass desk, a spray of cream and green orchids on the end pulling the color scheme together.

"You know," he said, looking at Chantilly, then me. "I never expected to see you here."

"Yeah, neither of us have great track records in the marital department."

"Sometimes there's a reason things don't work out and we have to keep that in mind."

I nodded trying to build a rapport. "Hollis, my ex, was cheating on me and Chantilly got dumped and the guy's now dead, just one of those things."

"And then you found each other?"

"Reagan's been a great friend," Chantilly said and gave me a sincere smile.

"Sometimes there are explanations, very personal private explanations why one relationship works and one doesn't." Sugar-Ray came around his desk and put his hand on my shoulder and Chantilly's. He gazed down at me, his smile sweet. "Failure in one relationship doesn't mean all your relationships are doomed to end badly. You need to keep that in mind."

Chantilly scoffed, "I'm just swearing off men."

I added, "The last one I dated kissed like a lizard."

"That's because you were with men who didn't have your best interest at heart. You belong together, it's the way things are meant to be, and don't let anyone tell you differently. I know it's hard, but you came to the right place to talk things over. I understand, I truly do."

My eyes fused with Chantilly's. Oh holy mother! "No," I said, jumping to my feet, Chantilly shaking her head, her mouth opening and closing like a landed fish but no words coming out. "We"—I pointed to Chantilly, then myself—"are not together like *that*. It would be fine if we were, of course." I added, rambling on, "Chantilly is kind of cute and all and I wouldn't mind having access to her wardrobe, but no."

"You're not a couple? As in together?" Sugar-Ray glanced back and forth. "Then why are you here before office hours? I assumed this liaison was something you wanted to keep quiet."

"We saw you out at Bonaventure Cemetery at Marguerite Laveau's," I blurted. "Waverly, money, Simon, white rum. What was that all about? And what's with the gun? It's a cemetery, they're already dead."

Chantilly put her hands on her hips and cut her hand thought the air. "That is without a doubt the worse excuse for clever I ever heard."

"The couple thing caught me off guard," I said as Sugar-Ray's eyes morphed from understanding and sympathetic light blue to bone-chilling navy.

"So I was at Bonaventure," Sugar-Ray said in a flat voice. "So what, a lot of people go there to see Marguerite. My business with her certainly doesn't concern the likes of you two."

I was tired of chasing dead ends and getting nowhere. I was tied of getting knocked into swamps and trapped in gross Dumpsters. I was done with pussyfooting around. I had to start getting some concrete answers. I pointed to Chantilly. "This does concern us. She's accused of a murder she didn't commit. Simon cheated on Waynetta Waverly and then scammed her daddy on a golf course deal that doesn't exist. Rumor is you're hurting for money and Reese Waverly wanted Simon dead. Now that's a marriage made in heaven between the two of you, if you ask me."

Sugar-Ray's eyes shot wide open. "You know about the golf course?"

Bingo! We were right on! "Crinolines are easy to come by and then there's the gun issue."

"Wait a minute, first of all, I do not wear crinolines and I can't believe you think I killed Simon."

"He took your place with Waynetta," I said still on a roll. "Reese couldn't get his hands dirty with murder and was out of time to keep Waynetta from marrying Simon because he's crooked as a dog's hind leg. He hired you to get the job done."

This time Sugar-Ray put his hands on his hips. "Let me tell you about Waynetta; she had an August marriage planned and no intention of canceling it. Simon was focused on getting rich and had no intention of canceling that. I had no reason to kill Simon. I was out of the picture before he came into it."

Chantilly said, "You and Reese have something going or you wouldn't be out there at Bonaventure chanting his name and swilling rum. That brings this conversation back where it started, you and Simon."

Sugar-Ray ran his fingers through his perfectly groomed hair. He paced the room then turned back. "Leave Reese Waverly alone, he's been good to me." Sugar-Ray shook his fist. "Butt out of what's none of your concern, Summerside, and take your friend with you. I'm not your murderer. Look somewhere else." He strode to the door and yanked it open. "Now get out and I don't mean just this here office. You mess up my life and I promise I'll return the favor."

I followed Chantilly into the hall, Sugar-Ray slamming

the door behind us. "Well, girl," Chantilly said as we headed for the car. "I say we done poked the bear. There's something going on with Sugar-Ray and Reese Waverly, and Sugar-Ray is scared out of his designer boxers we'll discover what it is."

"And it has something to do with that golf course. Just mentioning it made Sugar-Ray go crazy and get all defensive."

Chantilly powered up the Jeep and hit the AC, another hot-as-Hades day bearing down on our fair city. When we got back to Cherry House, Chantilly pulled to the curb and killed the engine. Pillsbury gave us a *howdy* wave from the top porch step, BW beside him eating some treat. I'd locked the door to the house, of course. That obviously didn't matter diddly to Pillsbury, of course, because BW was outside instead of inside. "Well now, looky who's come calling," I ventured.

"Goodness me," Chantilly said in a deep Savannah drawl. "He is one mighty fine-looking man. Makes a girl forget all about dead bodies, Dumpsters, Sugar-Ray, and getting fired from UPS."

"Does it make you forget about your daddy?"

"Spoilsport." Chantilly hurried up the steps and sat beside Pillsbury. He took her hand and kissed the back. Okay, I had to admit, that was downright romantic. We should all have a boyfriend like Pillsbury, just with a different occupation and address. I gave Pillsbury a nod when I got to the door.

"Hope you don't mind I let your dog out," he said in

that voice that seemed to come all the way from his toes. "He's right fine company. Gave him some healthy treats."

"It's not you hanging around my dog that's got me worried." I cut my eyes to Chantilly, then went inside and flipped the sign in the front bay window.

"Well, look who's out there on your front porch making goo-goo eyes at Chantilly," Auntie KiKi said, coming down the hall after entering through the kitchen. Sometimes I wondered why I bothered to lock the house at all. Everyone knew how to get in. I should pass out keys and charge rent. KiKi fluffed her hair. "He is some kind of stud."

"Thought you were married."

"It's like Cher says, *You don't go looking for men, they just fall in your lap.* This morning I'm appreciating the fall. Who is he?"

"A banker. Hear anything from Putter?" I headed to the kitchen to get the money and set up business for the day.

KiKi called after me, "Putter misses my pot roast and Doc Hunky wants to see more of you. Don't know quite how to take that but it sounds mighty interesting."

"This is not going to be one of those interesting relationships." I pulled out the Rocky Road container. "This is going to be a let's-do-dinner, have-a-nice-chat, and I-get-the-doggie-bag relationship. Period."

"Honey, with that hair you should take what you can get, but right now you got yourself some mighty unusual visitors coming your way."

"Customers already! Do they have expensive pocketbooks? You can always tell a money-spending customer if she's toting an expensive purse."

"Two cops, Detective Ross, and they're toting badges and unfriendly expressions."

My stomach jumped to my throat. I hurried in from the kitchen and KiKi grabbed my shoulders. She looked me dead in the eyes. "Detective Ross is not here to pick out a new wardrobe, is she. What in the world have you gone and done now to have the police here first thing in the morning?"

"There may have been a dead body over at Simon's place last night and Chantilly and I sort of stumbled across it." KiKi and I made the sign of the cross for the dead body.

"And you didn't call the police?"

"They came of their own accord and hanging around a corpse didn't seem like a good idea at the time so we left."

"Who was it?"

"Suellen, that waitress from over at the Pirate House with the side ponytail and blue eye shadow."

"And I'm just now hearing of it?" KiKi slapped her palm to her forehead. "This is what I get for forgetting to turn my phone back on and checking my tweets. Your mamma's running for office, remember? Family drama does not get people elected, it gets them on *The Daily Show* with snide comments and unflattering pictures. If she finds out about this, she'll have a canary."

"Can we send her on a cruise?"

Detective Ross and the policemen strode onto the porch and Auntie KiKi followed me out to meet them. Ross nodded to Pillsbury, then her gaze landed on me, her expression way less friendly. Not a good sign when the police greet you with less congeniality than the local gang member. "How do you keep winding up in the middle of things?" Ross grumbled.

"There's a full moon."

She walked over to Chantilly. "You're under arrest for the murder of Suellen Hamilton."

"No!" Chantilly said, holding up her hands defensively and taking a few steps in retreat. "This is not fair. I didn't do it, I swear. I hid in a Dumpster for crying out loud. No way could you have seen me. I suffered through bugs and slop and creepy things I'll be dreaming about for months, and my car has roaches in it and—"

Pillsbury clamped his sizable hand over Chantilly's mouth. "Babe," he said in the deep calming voice of someone who knew the police drill. "You need to chill. Don't say another word now, you hear."

I ran our escape route in my brain. Chantilly was right, there was no way the cops saw us. They would have given chase and nailed us in that alley if they had. "What makes you think Chantilly killed Suellen, because she didn't. Why would she? She didn't even know the girl."

"How can you be sure about that?"

Because she told me when she saw the body was on the edge of my tongue till I caught a warning glance from Pillsbury. "Just a guess."

"Guess again," Ross said. "Chantilly's fingerprints were on the murder weapon."

"I was giving myself a mani-pedi." Chantilly pointed to her peep-toe sandals and held out her fingers, all twenty nails broken and chipped from the Dumpster dive.

Ross looked at me. "Unless you have one heck of a good alibi between ten and midnight I got a feeling you're mixed up in this someway."

"There was this guy trying to strangle me."

THE INTERROGATION ROOM WAS PUTRID GREEN, the table gross and sticky. The worst part was that this was no surprise because I'd been here before. On second thought that wasn't the worst part of this whole affair at all, not even close, because Mamma came through the door in her perfect navy suit, cream blouse, and coiffured hair with natural silver streaks.

"Reagan, what's going on?"

I should have stayed in the Dumpster. "How did you know I was here?" Mamma took the seat across from me.

"Honey, what did you do to wind up in this place?"

Those were the exact same words she used in Principal Stiller's office when I got caught skinny-dipping in the high school pool. That the rest of the soccer team managed to get away scot-free should have been a warning that a life of crime or almost crime was not for me. I never was good at warnings. "Well, there was this dead body."

Mamma looked pained. In my thirty-two years of life there'd been quite a few *oh honeys* and pained looks.

"Detective Ross doesn't have anything on me. She's trying to pin the murder on a good friend of mine because her fingerprints just happen to be on the murder weapon. There are other suspects; I just have to make Detective Ross aware of them."

Mamma nodded. "My guess this murder is connected to the one out at the plantation?"

I took Mamma's hand. "I'll try to keep things on the down low and not sabotage your chances for alderman and I'll keep Auntie KiKi safe though I don't think I've got a prayer of carrying off that last part."

Mamma grinned. "Do the best you can on that score." She checked her watch. "I have to get to court. Don't fret over the alderman election, you just do what you have to. If you need anything, anything at all, call me and don't let my sister talk you into a bunch of trouble." Mamma kissed me on the cheek. "That's what she used to do to me all the time and you be sure and tell her I said so."

Mamma opened the door then looked back, her expression serious. "I'm not going to try and talk you out of helping a friend because that's who you are. But you need to be right careful, Reagan; one hand for your friend, and one for yourself." She gave me a little wink then left. I let out a pent-up lungful of air, and relaxed. Not that I was afraid Mamma would yell and throw a hissy, that was not her way. Even though she was a judge and a lot of times my judgment sucked, we saw eye to eye on most things, my marrying Hollis being one of the great exceptions. My biggest concern at the moment was that I'd disappoint her. Least that *was* my biggest concern till Walker Boone came through the door, hands in pockets, holier-than-thou smirk firmly in place, and the last person on earth I wanted to see.

"What mess have you gotten yourself into this time, Blondie?"

Chapter Fourteen

"WHAT are you doing here?" I asked Boone when he sat down across from me. "Just happen to be in the neighborhood and thought you'd catch up with the local felons and the soon to be incarcerated?"

"Pillsbury called. Said Chantilly was booked on her second murder in less than a week and you were keeping her company. Couldn't turn that one down, now could I?"

"Someone's out to frame Chantilly and right now it's not all that hard to do. She's innocent this time just like before, though I doubt you or anyone else around here believe me."

"I believe you're loyal to a fault and would jump under a bus before you threw a friend there."

"Chantilly didn't even know Suellen; why would she kill her?" I pushed back my chair and paced, sitting still driving me nuts. "Chantilly got a text to come to Simon's condo for information that would prove she didn't kill the man. We went in and found the body."

"We?"

"There's a murderer running around and it's a little scary going to meet someone you don't know at midnight. Chantilly came to get me. We went to Simon's and there was Suellen. I wonder who called the cops?"

"Ross said that someone in the building heard a scuffle and yelling."

"See, there you go. There was no scuffle or yelling. The door was open so we went in. The body was on the couch and . . . Wait a minute," I said, my brain starting to function. "My guess it that whoever killed Suellen was watching the condo. When Chantilly and I got there they called the police." I spun around and faced Boone. "Chantilly still has that text message that said to come to the condo on her phone. That proves someone set her up, got her there to pin the murder on her."

"Not quite." Boone sat back in his chair, looking as if he were at Tubby's having lunch. "The cops think Suellen saw Chantilly kill Simon. Suellen tried to blackmail Chantilly and Chantilly panicked and whacked Suellen over the head with Simon's Employee of the Year trophy."

"The trophy? You have got to be kidding."

"Like I could make that one up. The cops traced the text on Chantilly's phone. It came from Suellen's phone, and no one can find it. The cops think that after the murder Chantilly texted her own phone from Suellen's, then ditched it.

That would make it look as if Chantilly got set up. She got you involved to add substance to her story."

I leaned across the table. "You really think UPS Chantilly could come up with that big, detailed, well-thought-out plan after killing Suellen and being scared half to death? This is way beyond riding a horse naked, this is the work of someone who took time and planned the whole thing beginning to end to frame Chantilly. She's at the top of the list for Simon's murder. It's easy to stretch that into two murders. Doesn't that smack of a little too convenient?"

"Chantilly has motive, method, and the opportunity for killing Suellen. She knew the code for Simon's building and probably still had the key. And there're fingerprints."

"Chantilly was in that condo a week ago having a last-minute coronary over Simon marrying Waynetta."

"That adds to her motive for killing Simon in the first place. It all goes to motive."

"Are they going to arrest me, too?"

"The only thing you're guilty of is stupidity. A strangler? That's the best you could come up with for an alibi?"

I shrugged.

Boone's brows arched and he sat straight in his chair. "It's true?"

"For heaven's sake, Boone, it's all true. Every single word I've told you, and I have no idea how to prove it or find the real killer. Any suggestions?"

"None you want to hear. You were run off the road, attacked, and now set up for murder. I think it's time you butt out and let the cops do their work."

"Would you butt out?"

"I'm me and you're you and I'm not going to be the one to put your neck in a noose. Stay out of trouble for a change. Go home, sell some clothes."

Go home? Sell clothes! I braced my arms on the table and met Boone eyeball to eyeball. "I'm going to find this killer and I don't need your help to do it."

I grabbed up Old Yeller, slammed the door behind me, paid homage to the nearest vending machine, and walked out of the station. This time the police would hold Chantilly without bail, I was sure of it. I was exhausted from no sleep and a sucky night of hide-and-seek in the Dumpster. With the police station on Bull Street and Cherry House a good forty-five-minute hike away, I ate my Kit Kat and headed for the bus stop as a gray SUV pulled up beside me, the window powering down.

Pillsbury stuck his head out the window. "Coffee?"

"Throw in a burger and you got yourself a deal."

"See Chantilly?" Pillsbury asked as I got in.

"No. I hate this." I broke my Kit Kat in half and shared, Pillsbury popping the offering in his mouth.

"I'll drop by, see how she's doing," he said around a mouthful of candy. "Give her survival tips. I got cop friends who owe me."

"You got them a good price on a hot car?"

"Good advice on a hot stock."

"Maybe you should stay away from Chantilly."

I got a hard look in return that made me reconsider whom I was talking to. "You and her dad duking it out during visiting hours isn't going to help her case, you know. Why were you at Simon's wedding?"

Pillsbury's jaw clenched. "Chantilly caused a commotion once naked and chances good she'd repeat the performance one way or another. She was hung up on that Simon dude. You don't like me much, do you?"

"I know you like Chantilly and would do anything to have her for yourself."

"Like off Simon?" Pillsbury laughed deep in his throat, a sinister grin curling his lips. "That part no sweat, but I don't let my woman go down for my deeds. You best be thinking who you give orders to, white woman."

He pulled up for a traffic light and I hopped out of the SUV, the friendly portion of our conversation having come and gone. I swallowed, trying not to look petrified. "I'm doing what I think is best for Chantilly."

Pillsbury jabbed his finger in my direction. "Don't much care for what you saying, you got that."

"Just stay away from her for now." The light changed and Pillsbury drove off. Well gee, here it was a little after twelve and so far I'd gotten threats from Sugar-Ray, told Boone to take a flying leap, and royally ticked off the hood. It was shaping up to be quite a day. Being that I was a quart low on caffeine and trans fats and a block away from Cakery Bakery, I decided on a detour. Maybe Percy had some information other than that GracieAnn was the love of his life.

Savannah in the summer is living under one giant canopy of oaks and awnings. Walking from one to the other was the only way to survive. I started to open the door to the bakery and caught sight of Tipper Longford sitting alone at one of the outside tables off to the side, his gray

Confederate hat kittywhumpus on his head, his face buried in his hands. Not that Tipper and I were BFFs but something was wrong. Besides, how could I turn my back on a soldier so ready to defend this fine city?

"Are you okay?" I asked Tipper, taking the seat across from him.

He looked up, eyes bloodshot and sad. "She's gone."

"Delta?"

"Lordy, no. That woman's still alive and kicking. It's the good who die young. My Suellen is gone. Delta will live forever. How could such a thing happen?"

In the mad dash to find Chantilly innocent I completely forgot about Tipper and Suellen. Last time I saw them together at the Pirate House they were all smiles and snapping pictures. Tipper sniffed. "The only consolation is that the police found the person who killed her. They say it was the same girl who killed Simon." He gazed at the bakery. "I was happy here once, but that was a long time ago when Delta and I were first married. We sort of just drifted apart. Now I have no one."

"Did Suellen ever mention Simon?"

A tear slid down Tipper's cheek, which he quickly wiped away. "The police think Suellen must have seen Simon's killer at the wedding then got herself killed so she wouldn't tell who it was."

Meaning your little girlfriend was into blackmail and extortion. Not that Tipper needed to hear that right now. "Want me to bring you out some water or sweet tea?"

"Don't tell Delta I'm here; she wouldn't like it. We'd

just fight and I'm not up for it right now. I didn't know where else to go and I've always loved the bakery. The person who runs it, not so much."

I went inside and eyed the one and only sprinkle doughnut, just waiting for me in the display case. For sure it was the best thing to happen to me all morning. GracieAnn cut off my mouthwatering view with, "Well now, looks like your friend, Chantilly, got herself into even more trouble. Imagine that."

"What?"

GracieAnn grinned, a sinister glint in her eyes. "I hear she got arrested for killing off that waitress at the Pirate House and she's sitting in the slammer this very minute just where she belongs." GracieAnn tipped her chin and folded her arms. "Guess there'll be none of her getting out this time."

"Except she's innocent," I said, peeking around GracieAnn to Delta slipping *my* sprinkle doughnut into a white pastry bag and handing it off to another customer. You weren't supposed to cry over spilled milk and I figured that applied to lost doughnuts as well, but I was sorely tempted.

"What goes around comes around," GracieAnn droned on. "I do believe justice is served right well now and you'll have to accept that."

Sounded like Walker Boone, part two. I wasn't in the mood for him or GracieAnn. "Did you ever get over to Boone's office to talk about the case? He's been wondering where you are. You should catch up with him at his house. He spends a lot of time there." I grabbed the pink order pad and cupcake pencil from her apron and jotted down the address. "Big white house with geraniums and petunias. Just keep going back till you connect with him. He'd consider it a personal favor."

GracieAnn's eyes narrowed. "I don't have anything good to say about Chantilly. Why are you sending me to Boone? I'll just prove her guiltier, and I thought he was out to prove her innocent." A sassy grin pulled at her thin lips. "But I wouldn't mind spending a little time with that man all the same. He sure is fine."

I held up my hands all little Miss Righteous. "Boone just wants to get at the truth. It's the way he is. Like you said, what goes around comes around. You should know he talks about you. I told him you were coming to call and he said, '*Me?*'" I didn't see any reason to add the *why* in front of the *me*.

"Is that right." GracieAnn smoothed back her hair that didn't need smoothing since it was trapped under a net. She strutted off humming what sounded remarkably like "Happy Days Are Here Again." Either she was a closet Democrat or tickled pink about seeing Boone. For sure I was tickled pink about her seeing Boone but it made me wonder about her loyalty to Percy.

The undercover repairman was nowhere in sight. I'd have to catch up with him later. I bought two glazed doughnuts always in abundant supply at any bakery and added a supposedly low-fat brownie for Auntie KiKi. I never really trusted the no-fat part. My food philosophy was if it tasted good, it landed on your hips no matter what the sign said. I left the bakery and gave Tipper one of the doughnuts. He took a few bites and gave me a little smile. He looked a little better, a bit more relaxed. I headed down Broughton and pulled out the other doughnut just as Percy yanked me into a side gravel alley between the bakery and the art supply store.

"How's Chantilly doing?" he asked.

"I think I just chipped a tooth. Chantilly's getting strip-searched and fitted for a new wardrobe of bright orange. I'd say her day's pretty crappy."

Percy wrung his hands together, worry creasing his forehead. "I'm not having much luck getting information on the real killer. Mostly this place is just a bakery with lots of butter and sugar. I've put on five pounds." Percy pinched his middle to show his flab.

"Delta seems pleased that Tipper's girlfriend got knocked off," he went on. "GracieAnn thinks those two were fooling around when Delta and Tipper were still married, though best I can tell it wasn't a great marriage anyway for a lot of years. Maybe I should give it up here and work Chantilly's case with you; the girl's in a world of hurt. I could be asking questions like I was before instead of just fixing stuff that's not really broken."

Oh, Lordy. I'd stirred up enough problems on my own without bringing Percy onboard. "See if you can find out if there was any connection between Simon and Suellen. There was some reason she was at his condo. How are things with you and GracieAnn?"

Percy rubbed his chin. "Well, she's a little possessive. Yesterday she saw me chatting with Pastor Liz. GracieAnn followed me home and parked outside my apartment in the bakery truck for two hours just staring at my window."

"You sure it was GracieAnn?"

"Cakes and pies painted on the sides, but I was too afraid to go check it out for sure. GracieAnn and Delta are the only ones who drive that truck. It's a little scary, don't you think?"

"I think it's stalking." Or GracieAnn's a sociopath, but I didn't want Percy to fret even more. "Stay in public places, lock your doors. Be careful. Don't get in that truck."

"That bad?"

"She bakes dead-people cookies. Keep nine-one-one on speed dial."

By the time I got back to the Fox, Auntie KiKi was running around the shop like a headless chicken trying to check out customers and take in consigned clothes. The brownie perked up her spirits, the sight of customers perked up mine, but neither of us had time to put two thoughts together till five when the last customer left. I flipped the sign in the bay window as Reese Waverly stormed in the front door before KiKi could lock it.

Not many men in Savannah shopped the Prissy Fox unless their wives gave explicit instruction like, *Honey could you please pick up that there pink sweater hanging in the front window for me* or maybe if they were a performer at Club One and in need of a new sparkly dress and accessories for their act. Reese's wife died ten years ago and last I heard the man hadn't taken up life as a crossdresser, though that sure would be some sight and draw one heck of a crowd.

"I think you know why I'm here," Reese said, his eyes cold and calculating.

"You wanted to buy a little something to support the cannon for down on River Street?" I ventured, trying to defuse the moment.

Reese ignored me and kept his eyes focused on Auntie KiKi. He braced his hands against the checkout counter. "You took something that belongs to me and I want it back."

Auntie KiKi mixed and mingled with the best families in Savannah and took no prisoners when someone got on her turf, messed with her kin, or especially if they got in her face while doing it. She braced her hands on the counter and leaned right into Reese. "The last time I was visiting your home was to offer my sincere condolences for your most tragic loss, Reese Waverly, and that I took something from you is outrageous. What in the world could you have that I could possibly want?"

"You swiped a flash drive that has information on it. I what that drive back."

KiKi's eyes narrowed. "You can't come around here accusing me of being a common thief. I believe you need to get yourself out of here."

"Or what?" he sneered.

"Or I'll tell your mamma how you came barging right in here all full of unwarranted accusations and embarrassing me to no end. She can still take a piece out of your hide like all good mammas can. You best mind your manners, Reese Waverly."

Fear flickered in Reese's eyes. Good Southern mammas had that kind of effect. "I suggest you and your interfering niece here keep what's on that drive to yourself if you know what's good for you," Reese went on. "This here is business, my business, that no one needs to know about. Stay out of it."

"I don't take orders from the like of you, *Mr.* Waverly," Auntie KiKi declared. "I'll do what I want, when I want, and how it suits me." KiKi pointed a stiff finger at the door. "Go intimidate your employees. They have to put up with your undignified behavior, but I sure enough do not."

"You two are always sticking your noses in where they don't belong and this time you're playing with fire. Be careful or you'll get burned." Reese turned on his Italian-loafered heel, then slammed the door behind him, rattling the glass in the bay window.

"Sweet Lord!" I said, watching Reese drive off in his black something-expensive car. "Maybe we should just give him back the flash drive."

"He's fishing, honey. There were tons of people in his house that day and he has no idea that I'm the guilty party."

"I think he's considering our reputation."

"There is that, but I won't be intimidated by that upstart. His mamma and daddy owned a bait store over there in Whitemarsh. Not that there's one single thing wrong with a bait store, mind you, and his mamma and daddy are the salt of the earth kind of people, but now he acts so high and mighty like he's better than anyone else. Putter comes running every time that rich hypochondriac calls. He's always thinking he's having a heart attack and dying. If he wasn't dabbling around in shady tomfoolery, he wouldn't have heart problems in the first place, now would he?"

"But why is he so upset over a fake golf course that doesn't even exist?"

"I think our embarrassment theory hits the nail right square on the head. He got duped and Waynetta nearly married the scallywag who did it to boot. That makes Reese Waverly a laughingstock in anyone's book. He surely can't let that happen, no sirree." KiKi let out a deep breath. "Well, that's enough excitement for today, and I have yet to hear about your sojourn to the police department this morning. Did you drop Chantilly off at her apartment before you came here?"

"Detective Ross saw fit to give Chantilly a change of address. I just hope it's not permanent."

"Jail! Mercy, how could this be happening? I feel terrible for that girl." KiKi sat down on the stool.

"I'll get you some water."

"Oh, honey, water's for medicinal purposes only. I'm thinking Jen's and Friends and a double martini. Walk BW, get that pocketbook of yours, and be ready in ten minutes. We are in serious need of libation to try and figure out how to make things right around here."

Chapter Fifteen

JEN'S and Friends was packed, but on a hot summer night in Savannah at the corner of Bull and Congress that was pretty much the norm. Waiters were up to their eyeballs in customers so KiKi and I elbowed our way though the crowd to the bar to take care of our own alcoholic needs. She got a strawberry shortcake martini and I opted for the Snickers martini, the rim of the glass coated in chocolate, caramel, and nuts. A martini and a candy bar all at once, what could beat that? Probably a healthy diet. Instead I added a Snickers candy bar on the side in case I didn't get my fill in the martini. Since business at the Fox was on a roll I could even afford it.

"So how is Detective Ross these days?" KiKi asked after we hunted down an outside umbrella-topped wrought-iron table. "You two exchanging Christmas cards this year?"

"Ross is skinny and cranky. When she walks down the hall people dive for cover including me. To add to the perfection of the day, Walker Boone was at the station. He wants me to butt out of Chantilly's case. Why does he care what I do? What's wrong with that man?"

KiKi stirred the martini with her skewered strawberry, a little smirk on her lips. "I'd say the man doesn't know himself what's bothering him, but right now we have to focus on the fact that Chantilly's innocent and we can't let her stay in jail forever because it's the easy thing to do."

"Amen." I clinked my glass to KiKi's in agreement, then told her about Chantilly's text message, finding the body, hiding in the Dumpster, and how Chantilly's prints got on the trophy. "So now we have two murders to consider."

KiKi munched the strawberry. "One murder you look for motive, two murders you look for a connection, that's what Rick Castle says."

"New dance student?"

"Yummy guy on TV. But who would want Simon and Suellen both dead? I'm not even sure they knew each other?"

I licked the chocolate concoction from the edge of my glass and thought I saw Jesus. "Tipper was outside the Cakery Bakery today. He's a lost soul with Suellen gone. He thinks the reason she was killed is that she saw who killed Simon at the wedding. He or she then killed Suellen to keep her quiet. That's what the police are going with too and Chantilly fits the bill."

"But Chantilly wasn't the only one out to get Simon. What about Icy Graham, Pillsbury, Sugar-Ray, or Waynetta?

There's even GracieAnn; she was baking celebratory cookies for crying out loud. They all had motives to off Simon and they were all at the wedding except Sugar-Ray and with the grounds wide open and wearing costumes like we were, he could have sneaked in easily enough."

"Except there's the little matter of Chantilly's fingerprints on the murder weapon. The question is did the others have alibis for last night? There's only one way to find out. Ask!"

Auntie KiKi put down her glass and hunkered over the table toward me. "We have ourselves two murders now and if you go snooping around, we could have another." She made a finger gun and pulled the trigger. "Maybe there's a way to back into this. You know, ask around and find the connection between Suellen and Simon first. Tick off as few people as possible or at least the ones least dangerous."

The bells bonged out seven and KiKi gulped down the last of her drink, then licked her lips savoring the taste. "I need to get on home, Putter's calling at seven thirty sharp." She leaned closer again, this time devilment in her eyes. "Gonna try that phone sex stuff going on these days. Heard about it on *Oprah*. Now that she has her own channel she can talk about anything she has a mind to. Gets me all twitterpated just thinking about it."

I slapped my hands over my ears. "TMI . . . too much information. Do I have to hear this?" I dropped the Snickers in KiKi's new purse. "For stamina."

KiKi left in a state of giggles and I tried to forget the last minute of conversation with my dear auntie. I decided to walk home and maybe stop by Pinkie Master's. With a little luck Pinkie's was Bridesmaid's new haunt and she was there again. Bridesmaid knew Simon and she was the only person I hadn't managed to tick off in the last twenty-four hours who might know something about Simon and Suellen and if they had a connection.

I headed down Drayton, the sun finally dropping behind the trees, Pinkie's outside tables jammed. I ducked inside to loud music and an elbow-to-elbow crowd munching Tabasco-flavored popcorn and downing forties. Bridesmaid sat on a stool at the end. She spotted me, smiled, and gave a little finger wave.

"I want to thank you for putting me in a cab the other night and being nice," she said over the din.

"Looks like you've recovered."

"Some things are meant to be. I never really did fit into the highfalutin social scene with the Waverlys. Mamma wanted me to better myself with being a debutante but truth be told it wasn't better at all." Bridesmaid nodded to a guy by the jukebox with the body of a lifeguard and the looks of George Clooney, the younger years. "I met TJ." She laughed. "He's a janitor. Actually he owns the company but he's a hardworking guy."

"Brown Eyed Girl" filled the bar and Bridesmaid beamed. "He's playing that for me. He says I'm his brown-eyed girl. Isn't that the sweetest thing ever? Did you come here to try and meet somebody, too?"

"Did Simon know a waitress over at the Pirate House? Young, blonde, wears her ponytail to the side, lots of blue eye shadow."

"Blue eye shadow and ponytail." Bridesmaid nodded. "Simon was with her at the restaurant one time. It was a year or so ago before Waynetta came into the picture. I was meeting Simon at the Pirate House for a drink. The place was crowded and I parked in the back lot. Those two were there by his car all cozy like. I remember because I was fuming mad thinking Simon was two-timing me. If I'd had an ounce of sense, I'd have realized Simon was probably three- and four-timing me but that's another story. Anyway, he said he owned her money and it was all just business and nothing more. Monkey business if you ask me."

I congratulated Bridesmaid on her delish guy, slipped the waiter a few bucks for some take-out popcorn for KiKi, who would no doubt be famished after her phone rendezvous, and turned for home. The one thing I knew for sure now was that Simon and Suellen did indeed know each other and something had been going on between them. Simon got GracieAnn to send him clients from Wet Willies so it made sense that maybe Suellen did the same at the Pirate House. They'd overhear someone talking about their financial situation and tell them about Simon. No better advertisement than word of mouth.

GracieAnn was involved because she was hard up for guys and had a crush on Simon. Suellen was good-looking and a sexpot and in it for the money. Simon and Suellen were partners and that explained how she got into Simon's condo last night with the security code. The idea that Suellen met with the killer at Simon's to get paid off was more valid than ever. She probably set the location and she had to trust this person to meet with him or her alone.

That ruled out Pillsbury for sure. Nobody would meet one-on-one with a known member of the Seventeenth

Street gang if he were indeed the killer. I figured the same was true for Icy Graham except he had a daughter. Maybe the daughter killed Simon or helped her dad? Lord knows she had motive and she would also fit nicely in a peach dress with crinolines. Maybe Waynetta? Suellen wouldn't feel threatened by her and as for wanting money from GracieAnn that seemed unlikely.

It was after nine when I got back to Cherry House. A humid breeze carried in from the ocean and clouds paraded across the quarter moon. I retrieved BW for a potty break and we started for Rose Gate to deliver the popcorn, the only lights the ones on timers. KiKi should be watching Fox News by now, but the bedroom was dark. Good grief, how long did phone sex last? Personally I had no idea, but two hours of long-distance hanky-panky seemed a little extreme.

A phone rang inside and kept on ringing, Auntie KiKi not picking up. Oh, Lordy, maybe KiKi fell? Maybe she was in the shower? Maybe all that phone sex brought on a heart attack? I found the spare key under the third rock in the garden and let myself in, the kitchen dark and quiet except for the ringing phone in the hallway. The answering machine clicked in with Uncle Putter saying the Vander-pools weren't available and if this was a medical emergency to call his answering service or 911. The caller didn't leave a message.

"KiKi?" I yelled, my voice echoing in the house I'd known all my life. This wasn't just my auntie's house, you see, this was the house I'd grown up in. With mamma being a working single parent and KiKi and Putter having no children I was pretty much joint property. I knew which steps creaked, which windows stuck, and which toilet handle needed a good shake to flush. I flipped on the kitchen lights. "KiKi!"

My heart hammered in my chest. The phone rang again and again. No other sounds. Something was wrong, really wrong. I could feel it in my gut like when I was speeding and knew there was a cop around the next corner and there he was, big as you please, and sure enough I had myself a ticket. 'Course that was back in the day when I had a car. "KiKi!"

I flipped on the living room lights and snagged the phone on the hall table. "Hello?" I said, taking the cordless phone with me as I searched.

It was Uncle Putter. He'd been trying to reach KiKi for two hours now. He sounded fine, his soothing cardiologist voice steady and even, dealing with whatever comes, making light of his wife forgetting a phone call. But he wasn't fine. He knew his wife and I knew every nuance of Uncle Putter's voice probably better than I knew my own. He may not be my father but for sure he was my dad.

KiKi wasn't in the parlor, dining room, bedrooms, library, bathrooms. I was scared and shaking and no way could I convey this to Uncle Putter four hours away in Atlanta and who could only worry from afar. I lied my little heart out that Auntie KiKi got asked at the last minute to sub at the canasta club and had to do Mildred Kincaid a favor and was out for the night and wouldn't you know it here was her cell phone on the table and gee, she must have forgotten Uncle Putter was going to call. When I hung up I realized Uncle Putter didn't even ask why I was in his house alone at night, meaning he knew my voice too and would be on the next flight to Savannah.

This was my fault. Icy Graham, Reese Waverly, and Sugar-Ray were seriously worked up over me digging around in their lives and they'd all threatened to do something about it. There was no better way to get my attention than through Auntie KiKi, everyone knew that. Boone made it clear at the police station he wouldn't help me and I couldn't call the cops. What would I tell them, my auntie didn't show up for phone sex?

I needed help. I needed someone who knew the city and had eyes in every nook and cranny. What was that old saying about not burning bridges in case you had to walk back over them? Rain fell as I kissed BW on the nose, then closed the door behind me. No cabs would go where I was headed. I held Old Yeller tight to my side and took off in a dead run.

SEVENTEENTH STREET WAS DISMAL IN BROAD daylight with full sun and blue skies. At midnight in the rain the place was downright miserable. That I was soaked to the skin and had four guys in do-rags following did not help my opinion. I didn't belong here. I knew that and so did my escorts. I imagined the only reason I got this far without being run off or robbed was sheer curiosity of what the likes of me was doing here in the first place and what would a woman with a plastic purse have worth robbing.

In the dark all the houses looked alike and my brain was too scrambled to think of the exact address where I'd made the UPS delivery. A light spicy scent breezed by me and I remembered the red crape myrtle bushes next to Pillsbury's house. I took the worn steps of the gray bungalow with faded green shutters, the boys waiting on the sidewalk to see what happened next. Yeah, I wondered that myself.

An AC unit sticking out the front window purred at full tilt, an old wicker rocker with threadbare cushions sat by the door. I took a deep breath to keep my teeth from chattering and knocked on the weathered screen door making it rattle in the frame. The door opened to someone I didn't know dressed in jeans, a faded red beater shirt, some very impressive muscles, and a *17* tattoo on his shoulder. Word was that the Seventeenth Street boys all had *17* tats. Word also had it that Walker Boone sported that very same tat and Dr. Gilbert's nurse nearly peed her pants giving him a flu shot last year. "I'm looking for Pillsbury."

"Who you?"

"Reagan Summerside. I have a problem. I need to talk to Pillsbury."

A deep laugh sounded from inside. "Git lost."

I knew this would happen. You didn't tell a guy to not visit his girlfriend then hit him up for a favor. I knew it was a long shot but Pillsbury was my only shot at finding KiKi. Now what? There wasn't any plan B; this was the only plan I had and it sucked. "I can't get lost," I sniveled, my insides going to jelly. "My auntie KiKi's missing." Hearing the words come out of my mouth made KiKi's disappearance all the more real and I started to cry. "I know someone's got her and it's all because of me and I have to find her before Uncle Putter comes back from Atlanta and I know he's worried something terrible and—"

The door slammed shut in my face, leaving me with mad boys of the hood inside and menacing boys of the hood outside. My crying turned to flat-out fear. Slowly I turned around to cold stares. The door behind me opened again. This was one of those rock and hard-place situations. Who would have me for dinner first?

"Dr. Putter?" muscled guy in the doorway asked. "The guy who carries that golf club around with him everywhere?"

"The heart guy?" one of the boys on sidewalk cut in, his eyes warming.

I nodded like a bobblehead doll and swiped my runny nose with the back of my hand. "Auntie KiKi was supposed to be home and she's not and Uncle Putter called so they could have phone sex and I brought popcorn from Pinkie's, that Tabasco kind she likes, and now someone has Auntie KiKi and it's all because I ticked off the wrong people."

"You? Tick off the wrong people? Imagine that," Pillsbury said, his big hand taking my arm and leading me inside to a nice leather chair and Pottery Barn interior that did not match the exterior at all. A new meaning to keeping a low profile. Big Joey handed me a glass.

I met up with Big Joey a few months ago when trying to save Cherry House and he helped me break into Boone's office for less-than-legal purposes. "Drink this fast."

Brown liquid in a crystal glass, the hood's version of a red apple offered by a sinister queen? I had infuriated Pillsbury after all. "Poison? You're going to kill me?"

"That give the street a bad name." Big Joey grinned,

the light catching his gold tooth. "This be single-malt scotch. Drink."

Like I had a choice. I gulped it down and saw stars, choked, and instantly felt warm all over and revived. "You know my uncle Putter?"

"A truly righteous individual," Pillsbury said in his James Earl Jones voice. "He took care of Mamma when she had a heart attack some years back. Did it all for free, didn't charge a dime 'cause she had no insurance. Did the same for Tiny's grandmamma back in '08." Pillsbury nodded at one of the boys who was anything but tiny and who'd been on the sidewalk and now stood inside. "'Course that's changed now," Pillsbury added. "We have a group plan with low deductibles and minimum co-pays."

"You have medical insurance?" What did I expect form someone who had the cloud. "I don't have medical insurance."

"Need to get you on the plan, babe."

Another Rambo-built guy hunkered down in front of me, iPhone in hand. "I put out the word on your auntie," he said.

"KiKi is fiftyish with curly auburn hair and about five-four and probably could stand to lose a few pounds but don't tell her I said that and—"

"This her?" Rambo held up the iPhone screen, a picture of KiKi staring back at me. He touched the screen again and the Beemer came into view complete with *Foxtrot* license plate. "Google knows all. Got a tweet that *Foxtrot* head south on Bull two hours ago."

I gave another bobblehead nod. "Thank you, kindly. I'll start looking for her," I said, getting to my feet.

"We find her. You'll get in the way. Make the brothers nervous." Pillsbury put his heavy hand on my shoulder. "Sit tight."

"I suck at sitting tight."

"Try real hard."

And I did, I swear. The thing was I got Auntie KiKi into this so how could I sit around sipping scotch and wait for someone to clean up my mess? Besides, I knew KiKi and how she thought and now I had the Bull Street information to go on.

Wherever KiKi was she wouldn't be sitting around either. It was in the Summerside genes to do something even if it got us into more of a mess while doing it. Even Mamma had her moments. We couldn't help ourselves, like scratching an itch. I waited till the Rambos went on the porch to plan strategy, then I snuck out the back door.

Chapter Sixteen

B ULL Street ran north and south, bisecting the city into east and west and was broken up by the squares, Johnson, Wright, Chippewa, Madison, and Montgomery, in that order. It took an eternity to traverse around the squares, all of them one-way. That was fine when out for a casual evening or admiring the loveliness of the city, but KiKi was on a mission to get where she wanted to go. She'd never take Bull Street. Instead she'd take Congress to Price.

I figured there were only three things that would keep Auntie KiKi from her phone call tonight—me, Mamma, and Uncle Putter. Uncle Putter was on the other end of that call and Mamma was at a debate for city council over at the Marriott. That left me hunting a murderer and if I threw Bull Street into the mix that led back to Simon's condo that faced Wright Square. I couldn't imagine why KiKi would go there and no one had seen *Foxtrot* parked nearby, but it was the best lead I had and I needed to start somewhere.

The rain let up, leaving the city neon-shiny with lights reflecting off puddles, wet streets, and sidewalks. After my trek all the way to Seventeenth Street and adventures in the hood, I looked like something the cat dragged in so I couldn't use the hot-slut routine with Beau to gain access to the condo building. I went with drunk and toasted. I waited till a weaving young male occupant meandered his way up to the front door with a to-go cup in hand, accessed the code, then I quietly slipped in behind him.

I got to Simon's condo and stopped at the yellow crime-scene tape across the door. Last time in here I found a dead body, the time before it was assault with a near-deadly bookcase. Bad juju. I opened the door. Surely the police locked up? More bad juju? Stepping between the crisscross of plastic tape, I went inside and flipped the lights. I ignored the little yellow numbered tents marking where the body and trophy had been. Suellen dead once was enough. I rounded the leather couch, a Snickers wrapper on the floor. *Sweet mother in heaven!* I gave KiKi that Snickers. "KiKi!" I yelled.

I ran in the dining room, then the kitchen, flipping on lights as I went, my heart tight in my chest, my legs like rubber. Why didn't she answer? I stopped dead in Simon's bedroom, KiKi's blue straw bag hanging on the far closet doorknob, a chair jammed under to keep it closed. I kicked the chair out of the way and flung the door open to a stack of boxes. Period. No auntie. Putting my hand to my head I leaned against the jamb to catch my breath. Bull Street,

Snickers, closed closet, blue purse meaning KiKi should be here. A breeze ruffled through my hair and I looked up to an opening in the ceiling.

See, this is what I meant about not sitting still. Could my dear wonderful auntie just wait here till I came to get her? Heck no! She had to go all Indiana Jones on me and escape or at least try to. "KiKi? Where the heck are you!"

I parked Old Yeller on the floor and kicked off my flip-flops. I gazed up at the black opening in the ceiling. I sucked at sitting still. I sucked more at getting into small spaces with little light. I think it came from reading scary stories under the covers by flashlight for all those years.

The opening looked so tiny. Very dark and tiny. I started to sweat. Breathing was hard. Losing KiKi would be worse, much worse. I gulped in a few deep breaths, to clear my head, and climbed the boxes. I reached into the dark abyss. If something bit me, I'd die of heart failure or maybe rabies. Balancing on the top box I stuck my head through to see KiKi's shoes at the side and a window at the far end lit from the alley below. I was hot on KiKi's trail and figured I was about a minute's shimmy away from the window, the only place KiKi could be. Okay, I could do this.

Belly-scooting across the floor, I counted seconds, telling myself I was getting closer, forcing myself to think of something other than being in a small, dark, smelly space. All of these buildings were well over a hundred and fifty years old and had been used during *the* war as hospitals, barracks, brothels. At the very least, this floor was covered in bat poop; at worse I'd come across a dead Union soldier. Savannah folk didn't take kindly to having Yankees in their midst. Not a pleasant thought but sure got my mind off small, dark, and smelly.

I yanked open the window at the end and siphoned in a lungful of fresh air. Peering over the side, I caught sight of an old rusted fire escape that snaked up a bricked-in side of the building that had once sported windows and now sported KiKi. "Lordy, woman, what in the world are you doing out there!"

"Why there you are, honey." KiKi grinned up at me, dirty faced. She stood on one rung and held on to another, then waved.

"Both hands, KiKi! For the love of God, both hands!"

"Been a while since I did something like this. Cher would be mighty proud. Good thing it's nighttime. Some scalawag could be looking right up my dress given a chance."

"I think I've been insulted," came a voice from below and unfortunately I knew that particular voice.

"Boone?"

He stepped into the light. "Half the city's out looking for you two. Pillsbury's having an aneurism that you went missing on his watch; Big Joey had to give him mouth-to-mouth. Wish I'd been around to see that one."

Ignoring my sage advice of *hold on*, KiKi waved at Boone. "Can you take my picture with your phone, honey? This will look great on my Facebook page. I hate that timeline thing, don't you?"

Boone raked his fingers though his hair, looking exhausted. "Miss KiKi, why are you out here . . ." His eyes widened, his voice trailing off, then I heard it too, the grunt of old steel under duress.

"KiKi!" Boone and I yelled together. "Get down," Boone added. "Put a move on."

"Oh, Lordy, this here contraption's moving right under me." KiKi gripped the rungs, the fire escape lurching.

"It's not going to hold. Jump for it!" Boone yelled. "You're about twelve feet up. I'll catch you."

"Do it," I said, the top brackets by me tearing free.

"Well, I do declare." KiKi kicked one leg over the edge just like those Rockettes at Radio City Music Hall then kicked the other. "Geronimo!"

She jumped, Boone breaking her fall just as the fire escape tore completely loose. Boone rolled out of the way taking KiKi with him, the tangle of metal crashing down beside him. My gaze connected with Boone's though the darkness, a string of Seventeenth Street expletives filling the air ending with, "Holy crap!"

Boone sat up and helped KiKi off the ground. "The cops will be here any minute," he called up to me. "You're interfering in a crime scene. Get out of there."

That meant another trip back though the dark hole of Calcutta. The alternative was a trip back to the smelly room of the police station. I closed the window, scooted back though the poop, snagged KiKi's shoes, then dropped down into the closet. I slipped on my shoes, grabbed Old Yeller, ran for the front door, then doubled back and snagged KiKi's blue straw purse. Sirens pulled to a stop at the front of the building just like last time, and I turned for the back entrance, a police officer coming right toward me. Was this better or worse than the Dumpster?

Think, Reagan, think! "Why, mercy me," I said, scrambling for an explanation as to why I was here in the hall, purse in hand and filthy. Make that two purses in hand and an extra pair of shoes. I slid KiKi's things behind my back and said, "I just heard the most awful noise outside."

"You live here?"

"Third floor."

The officer tipped his hat to the back of his head, his look critical. "There're only two floors in this building."

"Why see there, I'm flustered by all this commotion and can't even remember where I live." I pointed to the door. "You best hurry, something terrible's going on out there, I just know it. Sure was a big crash. Bet it's that C-4 stuff that blows things up on TV all the time. What's this city coming to?"

The officer did an eye roll then headed for the back entrance. I followed him out the door, looking all interested till Boone yanked me behind the stand of azaleas, KiKi beside him. She slid on her shoes and without saying a word we crept toward the alley, KiKi limping and Boone helping her along. He flashed a smile at the local attack dog and I swear the dog smiled right back at him, not so much as a hint of a growl anywhere. We stepped onto the sidewalk and I felt ten years older than I had that morning.

KiKi kissed Boone on the cheek. "My hero."

I was sure Boone wanted nothing more than to shake me till my teeth rattled but instead he said to KiKi, "Happy to be of service, ma'am."

"Where's the Beemer?" I asked, the three of us piling into Boone's convertible without one word about getting white upholstery dirty. If it had been just me in the car, I'd be relegated to the trunk.

"My guess is your car's in your garage," Boone offered as one who knew about such things. "Whoever got you in that condo didn't want the cops involved. If you go to the police telling what happened, you're in trouble for crossing the yellow crime tape."

"How did you wind up at Simon's condo in the first place?" I asked KiKi, Boone pulling away from the curb into light traffic. "You were supposed to be going home for a phone call, remember?"

KiKi dug around in her purse. "There was this note on my car. Wouldn't you know it the thing's not here now. It was a yellow sheet off one of those legal pads and said something like *Have proof Chantilly's innocent. Meet you at Simon's.* There were some numbers to get inside the front door. I figured it was on the up-and-up. Why else involve me?"

I could hear Boone's teeth grinding all the way in the backseat.

"But when I got there," KiKi went on, "someone shoved me into that there closet and grabbed my purse. It was so dark I couldn't make out who it was and then they locked the door on me. I waited for a bit, knowing someone would come looking, but I had to use the girl's room something fierce after that strawberry martini. I found the opening in the ceiling."

KiKi tsked. "Putter's going to be mighty upset I missed

his call. Like Cher says, *Husbands are like fires, they go out when left unattended.* My plan was to get the information from Simon's place, then be on my way back to the house in time for Putter's call."

"About that," I said. "I told Uncle Putter you did an emergency fill-in for the canasta club."

"I can work with that. Say I twisted my foot on Sally Newton's stairs. Those things have been in need of fixing for years and she's just too cheap to part with the money to have it done. I sure don't want Putter to know about tonight or he'll put one of those ankle monitors on me and I'll never get beyond the mailbox."

The three of us trooped into KiKi's house, and BW did the happy doggie dance around Boone. "Putter's always wanted to go to Pebble Beach, that fancy golf course out in California. I'll tell him I've made plans, that'll take his mind off the phone call." KiKi cast a look at Boone. "Think that will work?"

Boone sat KiKi in a chair and elevated her leg. "Men are easy. All you have to do is show up wearing a smile. If you bring along a bucket of chicken and a six-pack, so much the better."

I put ice in a baggie for a makeshift cold pack, then wrapped it in a towel. I put it on KiKi's swollen ankle and nearly threw up. I could have lost her.

"You okay, honey," KiKi patted my hand. "You're looking kind of peaked all of a sudden."

"Tea," I said because I had to say something. "We need tea."

Truth be told, I could do with another hit of Pillsbury's

scotch. I went on autopilot and filled the blue kettle. Boone located cups and saucers and set them out along with the sugar bowl and spooner that held KiKi's sterling spoons collected over the years.

"What was all this foolishness tonight about anyway?" KiKi asked. "Whoever locked me in that closet had to realize you would find me sooner or later."

"It was a warning," Boone offered, rhythmically dunking his tea bag. "Someone's not happy with Sherlock and her dancing sidekick prowling around in their affairs. They wanted to tell you to buzz off."

"And that's exactly what's going to happen," I said as evenly as I could without bursting into tears. KiKi's cup clinked to the saucer, and I knew I was in for an argument. "Look," I said, beating her to the punch. "I'm getting nowhere with all these questions and causing a lot of problems for everyone. It's over. The police can handle this. I'm making things worse for everyone."

KiKi put her hands flat on the table and scowled. "That there's crazy talk. We can't stop now when it's just getting interesting." She stifled a yawn. "But I'm plum tuckered out right now. I'm calling it a day, children." She took a sip of tea, then grabbed her ice pack. "I need to phone Putter and save him a plane flight home. You two lock up when you leave. Try not to behave yourselves."

I watched KiKi shuffle off toward the steps and felt a tear slide down my cheek.

"I know you," Boone said, standing beside me. "You're not giving this up. Someone messes with your family and you're not going to just forget it happened."

I picked up the cups and took them to the sink. "Thank you for saving KiKi like you did. That was really sweet. Tell Pillsbury I'm sorry I worried him tonight but if one of his own was in trouble he'd do the same thing I did, except he'd probably do it a lot better."

Boone put his hands on my shoulders, looked me in the eyes. "Reagan, you need to talk to Ross, tell her what you think. See if she'll look into it."

"According to Detective Ross, she has the killer and there's nothing more to look at, end of story. But now *I* have something else to go on. Whoever got KiKi into Simon's apartment knew the access code and had a connection to him."

Boone collected the saucers. "Or has my tax gal. Your little speech about the case being over was for KiKi's sake, wasn't it? You should be the one wearing the ankle monitor."

I stacked the dishwasher, then leaned against the counter trying to put pieces together. Boone turned a kitchen chair around and sat backward like guys do. "So now what?" he asked.

"The idea that Suellen saw the killer and wanted money to keep quiet makes sense."

"But?"

"How do you know there's a but?"

"You're flipping your hair."

I folded my arms so I wouldn't do any more flipping. If Boone hadn't saved KiKi, I wouldn't tell him squat. He'd find holes in my theory and try to talk me out of doing anything other than selling clothes and visiting Chantilly every other Thursday. But Boone did save KiKi. Why did it always wind up this way, me owing him and not the other way around? "Why do you care about any of this?" I asked him.

"Your stirring up trouble has collateral damage. I want to know what's coming my way."

"Before GracieAnn worked at the Cakery Bakery, she was a barmaid down at Wet Willies and fed Simon clients for his loan-sharking venture. I think Suellen did the same thing from the Pirate House. The three of them were in the business together, that's their connection, though I think GracieAnn had a crush on Simon. When he dumped her for Chantilly and then for Waynetta, GracieAnn was irate and bitter and depressed and Delta took her in at the bakery. It didn't matter to Suellen that Simon went for Waynetta. All Suellen was interested in was the money."

"And when Simon died, why let a very lucrative business she'd helped establish go down the tubes." Boone gave me a long look across the short distance between us. "That night at Simon's place, when you got the bookcase pushed over on you, you weren't admiring Simon's big plasma TV."

"There was a notebook, Simon's records as best I can figure. Someone knocked over the bookcase and took the notebook. Suellen maybe or GracieAnn."

Boone shook his head. "Suellen's the one in the morgue. That points to GracieAnn knocking her off."

"Unless there's something else in those records worth killing for. Like maybe information about a golf course?"

Boone went perfectly still, his expression lawyer-blank. "How do you know about the golf course?"

Well, dang. Pay dirt! "A little birdie told me?"

"Forget this. Forget the golf course. Forget it exists."

"Because it doesn't." I took in Boone's forever five o'clock shadow, short black hair, eyes darker than midnight, and could easily imagine the build under his navy polo. Boone's face was unreadable but there was always that barely contained hum of danger just under the surface. You can take the boy out of the hood but the hood's always a few short blocks away. "Why did you leave Seventeenth Street? Lose your bad-boy streak?"

A menacing spark lit his eyes, that half smile back on his lips. The bad boy was alive and well, he just stayed out of sight, usually. "Watch your step, Reagan."

"You never give me a straight answer."

"I just did." Boone made a two-finger salute, kissed BW on the snout, and left.

I dropped one of those green soap cubes in the dishwasher, wiped off the table, then stood at the bottom of the steps and listened to make sure KiKi was okay. A soft voice and giggles drifted down from her bedroom. I guess it was never too late for phone sex. BW and I headed across the side yard serenaded by late summer crickets and other things that sounded a lot nicer than they looked. I unlocked the kitchen door and went in, the peace of home-sweet-home wrapping around me like a warm, welcoming blanket after a hard day at the salt mine.

"Yo, white woman. 'Bout time you show up."

Chapter Seventeen

PILLSBURY stepped out of the shadows and gave BW a good rubdown. "What on earth are you doing here?" I ran my hand over my face to keep from fainting dead away and gulped in deep breaths. "Not that you're unwelcome, but you scared the liver right out of me!"

"Living a little lean here, babe. Your fridge is bare. Hot dogs? Nitrates? That stuff will kill you."

"They're for BW. He's addicted."

"Doggie abuse. An ice cream container? Ever hear of a bank?"

"You came here to criticize my culinary and monetary skills?"

"Among other things." He took my hand and dropped a black phone in it. "Stay connected."

"Says who?"

"Can't have you running around without hookup. Your auntie went missing and you want to find who do the deed, I get that. If you're in need of assistance." He plopped a set of keys on top of the phone. "Wheels."

I handed back the phone and the car keys. "I thank you kindly, but you've done enough. I'm okay here." I pictured my pants on fire after that big, fat lie.

Pillsbury shoved a note at me. "On your door. *Next time it's for keeps.* Don't think this be in reference to a marriage proposal."

Two death threats in less than a week; just call me little Miss Popular. I took back the phone and tried to keep my hands from shaking.

"You scared?"

I nodded.

"Good. Keep you from being stupid. My digits' on speed dial."

"What do you know about Simon being involved in loan-sharking?"

Pillsbury did the raised-eyebrow thing, then stuffed his hands along with the car keys in his jean pockets and rocked back on his heels. "Nickel-dime stuff at first. Lately he built up a clientele, mostly hard-ups who didn't know what they getting into. Hired Tiny to do repo."

"So how did he build up the clientele? I mean if he was lending out larger amounts lately, he had to be getting the cash from somewhere and that takes a while, not just all of a sudden. Any ideas where Simon got a sudden influx of capital?"

"Inheritance, take on an interested partner for a cut of the action, twenty-to-one on a fast filly at Belmont Park."

"What about a golf course." I had no idea how this played into anything but it sure got a rise out Boone and Sugar-Ray when I mentioned it.

Pillsbury's eyes turned to thin slits and he shook his head. "Not good if that got out. Make a lot of folks mighty unhappy."

"My lips are sealed and thanks for the info."

"Later, babe." Pillsbury left out the front door, the house now eerily quiet. I was absolutely sure no one else was lurking about in my partially restored humble abode or Pillsbury would have squashed them flat. On the way to bed I stopped and sat on the stairs with BW beside me. Together we gazed over our little shop, BW thinking about hot dogs in the fridge, me thinking about martinis to mayhem all in one night. I'd pushed somebody's buttons and they were pushing back hard by messing with KiKi. I knew stuff that the killer or killers were not happy about and they were warning me to stay away. But I couldn't and now I'd always be looking over my shoulder, wondering who was after me.

There was no turning back till this was over and I got the killer. Problem was I didn't have much to go forward on either. I didn't know who killed Simon. I didn't know if that same person knocked off Suellen or if the two nasty-grams warning me to back off were from the same person. I didn't even have the blasted notebook to give me a lead, and how did a fictitious golf course play into all this?

Did Simon swindle Reese and the boys of the hood to

invest in this golf course? There was some reason they got all jittery when I mentioned those two little words. Was the golf course scam how Simon got his seed money for loan-sharking? I could see Simon hustling Reese, but getting the hood involved smacked of blatant stupidity. Right now all I had was a whole lot of nothing for a whole lot of trouble.

THE NEXT MORNING THE SULTRY BEAT FROM *The Devil and the Dancer* filled KiKi's parlor along with the Silver Spoon Girls and lots of their friends. Finger cymbals clinked, hips twitched, setting off the tinkle of little bells on filmy skirts, and we all shook our booties for an hour, pretending we were somewhere exotic and maybe losing a few pounds along the way. As I gyrated and twirled around I considered what to do next about who killed whom over what.

The first thing was to find Simon's killer; everything else hinged on it. That brought me back to the usual suspects of Reese Waverly, Sugar-Ray, Icy, and GracieAnn, though I had no idea how GracieAnn figured in with the golf course. I needed to talk to them. The problem was to get them to talk back. I'd use the direct approach, say if they answered my questions I'd quit bothering them. Of course if my poor lifeless body got dumped in Gray's Creek, I wouldn't be bothering them any longer either.

"That's all for today, ladies," I said at the end of the hour.

"But where's Walker Boone?" Lilly Crawford asked, looking around, the other girls nodding.

"At his office?" Or waking up in some cutie pie's bed, which was always a distinct possibility.

Marjorie Lambert added, "So he doesn't always come to watch you dance?"

"Me?"

"The way he looks at you one would think there's something going on."

Like an attack of gas last time he was here, but I didn't think the girls were looking for that answer.

"We just want to look back," Marjorie added. "Having that man around is a fine way to start the day. He's kind of a bonus for coming and exercising, if you know what I mean. We're all married but some eye candy first thing in the morning gets our juices flowing."

I wanted to tell them to try Starbucks but I didn't think that's what they had in mind either.

"Think you can persuade him to be here next time?" Lilly asked, a glint in her green eyes. "We'd all be mighty appreciative."

I considered the overflow class and how much I made in one hour. "You bet."

KiKi hobbled in using one of Uncle Putter's golf clubs as a cane as the girls left. "That was some big group; you're really good at belly dancing. I had no idea you'd attract such a crowd. We should have done this years ago."

"They came to see Boone. They thought he'd be here again and wanted to start their day off with their juices flowing. I told them he'd show up next time. The class should be packed, I'll make a killing."

"Honey, you can't make money off that sweet man. He just saved my life."

"That sweet man made *my* life living hell and he made money off my divorce without batting an eye. I figure it's my turn."

"What are you going to tell him?"

"Don't shave and wear something tight. Can I borrow the Beemer tonight?"

"I knew it." KiKi thumped the golf club against the floor. "That little speech you gave last night was a bunch of hooey. You're going to find Simon's killer and I'm coming right along with you."

I shook my head and crossed my fingers behind my back to offset a whopper of a lie. "I'm going to Beaufort to pick up some clothes from a new consigner over there."

KiKi gave me long, steady look and tapped her foot. "First you're pimping out my hero and now you're lying to your dear auntie who spent hours and hours drumming the multiplication tables into your head."

What I was trying to do was pay my electric bill and keep my dear auntie out of harm's way. I crossed my fingers a little tighter. "I'll be back by ten."

I headed across the yard to the Fox. BW was taking his morning snooze on the front porch, customers already shopping inside. Elsie Abbott straightened racks of clothes while AnnieFritz manned the checkout counter. Brownies and chocolate cookies sat at the end in a pink basket with matching napkins. Social media had its place, to be sure, but tried and true social graces counted for so much more, especially when you could eat them!

"There you are, sugar," AnnieFritz beamed. "I knew you had to be around here somewhere. Elsie and I were coming in from a funeral Mass over at St. John Cathedral this morning. Last week we showed up at St. John's Episcopal by mistake and set about crying something fierce at little Lucy Ryder's baptism instead of Roland Sim's funeral. You'd think with all the saints in heaven like there are, this here city didn't have to settle on two St. John churches. Anyway, Burl Ramsey's heart finally gave out on him and had one of those oversized coffins to contain his hugeness; the big chunk of gray metal could pass for a battleship. Doc Griffin tried to convince Burl that biscuits and sausage gravy every morning was not a particularly good idea but there was simply no convincing the man."

"I guess you remembered where the spare key is hidden?"

"Honey, everyone knows where that key's hidden. I must say your outfit's mighty fetching, like you're going into telling fortunes. All you need is one of those fancy crystal balls and a tent."

If it paid the water bill sitting on the kitchen counter, I'd give it serious consideration. I promised to be back in ten minutes, then snagged a brownie and hurried upstairs to change. When I came back down, Icy Graham's daughter stood at the counter, state-of-the-art stroller by her side, pile of toddler clothes in front of her. I couldn't remember what Icy said her name was when he came to visit the other night. I was too busy trying to breathe.

"Aren't these the cutest little boy clothes ever?" Annie-Fritz gushed, holding up a pair of blue Nike gym shoes.

"I didn't know they made these things this small. Looks like a Christmas tree ornament." She gave me wink. "Doesn't it make you want a bunch of little darlings of your own?"

That's what happens when Auntie KiKi and the Abbott sisters gossip and I'm not around to supervise.

"Hi," Icy's daughter said. "I'm Laura Lynn. We met the other day at my daddy's seafood shop down by the docks. I didn't know you owned this place. A friend said you might consign children's clothes, and I have some nice ones. Daddy bought so many things for little TJ when he was born that he never got a chance to wear them before he was too big."

"Your daddy said to bring the clothes here?" I pictured a sawed-off shotgun hidden in the pile.

Laura Lynn laughed. It was one of the infectious laughs that make you happy, too. Laura Lynn was a darling girl and if Icy didn't kill Simon for threatening to take her baby away, he should have.

"Lordy, no," Laura Lynn said. "Daddy doesn't have time to think about such things. Shrimping is mighty hard work. Except for yesterday, when he took TJ and me out to Tybee for the day, he's been out on his boat every night. He gets bigger catches when it's not so hot. Yesterday was TJ's first birthday and we didn't get home till late." She glanced down at the toddler in the stroller. "You were one tuckered-out little boy."

"Children's clothes are a fine idea." I grabbed the pile and put them behind the counter and handed Laura Lynn a paper to fill out to open an account. I never really thought about opening up a children's section at the Prissy Fox, but considering the customer and her daddy and the possibility of another late-night visit from Daddy, a children's section seemed like a fine idea indeed.

By noon things calmed down at the Fox and AnnieFritz and Elsie headed home to get ready for the Delroy Farber viewing. Delroy had been a used car salesman over in Garden City. When you turned sixteen and had saved some cash from babysitting or packing groceries at the Piggly Wiggly, you paid Delroy a visit and he fixed you up with a decent car and decent payments. God bless Delroy. The place would be packed.

At one o'clock, KiKi meandered through the door minus Putter's golf club/cane but she still held on to the ice bag. "You're doing better?"

KiKi parked on the stool behind the counter and elevated her leg onto a pile of clothes not suited for the Fox and headed for the local thrift store. "Gave me an excuse to cancel Bernard's lesson." She angled the ice on her ankle so it wouldn't slide off. "I saw Icy Graham's cute little daughter and her baby come in here earlier and it got me thinking."

"No babies. I barely remember to feed BW. I have some old romance novels upstairs you can read to take your mind off things so you don't have to think so much."

KiKi made a sour face and brushed her hand though the air as if chasing black flies. "Why would I want to read when I have our current situation staring me in the face."

For once I was glad there was a murder around if it kept Kiki's mind off babies and the state of my love life. I wrote up a sale for a denim skirt I wished I could afford, then KiKi added in a low voice, "I don't believe the shrimp guy's our you-know-what. He wouldn't risk going to jail and leaving his daughter and grandson to fend on their own. This is a man who goes to sea every day. He's not some hothead who acts on impulse. He understands consequences or he wouldn't still be alive. Doing you-know-what to you-know-who had some big consequences no matter how much the you-know-who jackass deserved it."

I stood with my back to the customers and dropped my voice. No need to share everything with the gossips and that pretty much included the whole town. "The daughter said they were all out at Tybee yesterday. The night our waitress got whacked our shrimp guy was out on his boat. I can't see him sending his daughter and grandbaby here to lie for him. That also gives him a good alibi for when you were lured into the closet."

"He still could have done in the jackass; our shrimp guy was right there at the wedding."

"Let's go with the idea that the same person did both. Too much of a coincidence for it not to be."

"Well, there you go, shrimp guy drops to the bottom of our suspect list and pushes that infuriating skunk of a human being who accused me of out-and-out blatant thievery to the top along with his grave-visiting henchman."

"What about GA and her dead-people cookies? She sure has motive."

"I can't see her knocking off you-know-who. The infuriating skunk on the other hand didn't like the loan-shark jackass for multiple reasons, and he and his henchman are all in a sweat over that there golf course. There's no connection between the golf course and GA. We'll run out to

Whitemarsh after you close up and ask the infuriating skunk point blank what's going on. Don't dawdle."

"We? I'm going to Beaufort tonight remember? Clothes? New consigner?"

"Doc Hunky wants to take *you* dancing. A little birdie told him that you had some mighty fine moves and are even teaching classes to perfect them. That birdie said you are one sexy dish and have the skirt to prove it and can even be persuaded on occasion to wear it. All he has to do is call you over and over and over again till you say yes."

"You didn't."

"Not yet but if you keep up this nonsense about Beaufort and a new customer, I have Doc Hunky's number committed to memory."

Chapter Eighteen

"WELL, come on," KiKi said to me at six o'clock as I closed up the Fox. "You're late. We got to get moving if we're going all the way out to Whitemarsh."

"I had customers, paying customers. I just couldn't tell them to go away, now could I?"

"There're more important things than money."

"Spoken by someone who has more than enough." I scooped up Old Yeller, clipped BW to his leash, then locked the front door behind me.

"Honey," KiKi said, looking at Bruce Willis. "I like this here dog and take my grand-auntie status right serious but I don't think he should be coming with us out to Waverly Farms. We'll be unwelcome enough as it is and I do believe that's putting it mildly."

"We're not going to Waverly Farms and it has nothing to do with me heading over to Beaufort without you so don't be having a hissy right here on my front porch and dialing up Doc Hunky. The thing is, we can't just walk up to Reese and say, hey, Reese, old boy, why did you go and have Sugar-Ray kill Simon?"

"Well, he accused me of walking into his house and stealing his flash drive easy enough."

"He knew there was a good chance he was right and I'm not so sure he had Sugar-Ray do in Simon. Besides, there's a big difference between being accused of flash drive–napping and murder." I held up the ice cream social card I got in the mail. "We're going here instead. One of the gals from the Daughters of the Confederacy shopped at the Fox today and said she was in a state of total astonishment and needing something perky. Seems Waynetta Waverly had just volunteered to help out at the ice cream social to raise money for the cannon. Everyone's scrambling to look their best or Waynetta will gossip about them behind their backs. Waynetta never volunteers for anything."

"Why now, I wonder. I surely can't see her having one of those life-changing revelations of doing good for all mankind and saving the world because Simon up and died on her."

"It's more like saving Waynetta. When we were out at Waverly Farms dropping off the deviled eggs and you were busy fainting on the stairway, I was spending time with our local princess, remember? She had a meltdown about needing to be in mourning for some months over Simon's untimely kicking the bucket. The reason she's volunteering tonight is to get out of the house and this is a respectable way of doing it."

"Well, if that don't beat all. It's worth a trip to the park just to see Waynetta doing something helpful for a change." KiKi patted BW and we started down Gwinnett.

"The plan is for us to be friendly and sympathetic and pump her for information," I said. "She could very well know something that she doesn't realize is important. You have to admit that us meeting up with her is a lot safer than a face-to-face with Reese and his gun collection."

"I suppose I could do with a scoop or two of Old Black Magic. Lord knows I'll have to get my fill now before Putter comes back in town. I think the man's getting right serious about me losing weight. This is what happens from marrying a heart surgeon."

Hot and humid made for perfect ice cream weather. "Georgia on My Mind" drifted out of the park, people mixing and mingling. Two kids stopped to pet BW, their faces painted to look like Mickey Mouse and Elmo. We walked past the fountain, the mere sound of splashing water dropping the temperature a good ten degrees. Under the expanse of oaks, crowds gathered behind long tables lined with gallons of ice cream packed in iced tubs. The daughters scooped cones and cups and passed around chocolate sauce and sprinkles.

KiKi nodded at the end of the line to Waynetta dressed in a simple white dress, hair pulled back in a clip, Daddy Waverly no doubt nixing the usual tiara. "Look who's in charge of handing out spoons? I imagine an ice cream scoop is pretty much a foreign instrument."

"Hi," I said to Waynetta as we came her way. Wonderful night for—"

"Jeez Louise, that is your dog?" Waynetta asked taking a step back and pointing to BW, her lip doing the Waynetta curl. "Why?"

If I stabbed that *witch* with a *b* right here on the spot with one of her own spoons, I'd never get the answers I needed for Chantilly. I'd have to just suck up the insults for now but one of these days . . . "This is Bruce Willis."

"Crying shame to disgrace a fine actor in such a way, if you ask me."

BW flopped down and rolled over on his back, tail wagging and waiting for Waynetta to scratch his tummy. Like that was going to happen. I gritted my teeth and said, "KiKi and I were wondering how you were doing."

"I'm doing fair, thank you kindly for asking, that's mighty neighborly of you."

KiKi smiled but it wasn't the natural kind that comes with being happy and wanting to spend time with a friend. It was more of a sneer-smile. Auntie KiKi was never good at sucking it up; she was an ace at subtle warfare Southern style.

"Why, honey," she cooed. "With that vicious old rumor making the rounds about how you did in Simon at your very own wedding, Reagan and I thought you might be a bit upset this evening and we were deeply concerned for your welfare."

Waynetta blinked a few times, not quite believing what she'd just heard. Heck, I blinked a few times myself not quite believing it. Waynetta dropped the basket of spoons, white plastic littering the ground. "Wherever did you hear such an outrageous lie?" she whispered in a tight panicked voice, cutting her eyes side to side to see if anyone overheard. "Mercy me, how do these things get started?"

"So it's not true?" KiKi asked, brows arched innocently in surprise. "Not that I ever considered it was, of course. Why, sugar, you're looking a little under the weather. How can I be of assistance?" Without waiting for a reply, KiKi kicked the dirty spoons under the table and handed off the basket to an unsuspecting Mayor Gillespie as he walked by. Being this was an election year the mayor took on the job all smiles and KiKi led Waynetta to one of the tables out of the flow of traffic.

"Here," I said, handing Waynetta a bottle of water I bought from a vender. We all sat down, BW on the alert for a dropped cone and me on the alert in case the cone was chocolate. "This will make you feel better."

"Why would someone think I killed Simon of all things?" Waynetta gasped between gulps from the bottle.

I patted her hand. "I'm sure some folks figure that Simon doing the afternoon delight with your bridesmaid must have given you cause for concern and made you act in haste. If you gave Simon what he so richly deserved, everyone would understand completely." *They might put you in jail for the rest of your natural life, but they would understand.*

Waynetta stared wide-eyed. "That is truly what everyone thinks?"

KiKi and I gave a solemn and sincere nod and hoped to not get struck dead by a righteous lightning bolt out of the blue.

"Oh, dear." Waynetta guzzled more water. "Daddy tried and tried to warn me about Simon, but I wouldn't listen. When I heard that no-good varmint grunting and groaning in that closet I decided to cancel the wedding on the spot. I went back to my room and was in the process of taking off my dress to end it all when one of the staff came to fetch me saying I needed to come right quick to the dining room, that something fearful had happened to Simon. I was terrible afraid Daddy had enough of Simon's shenanigans and went and put a bullet between his beady little ratty eyes. My only regret was that I didn't do in Simon myself, though it would have taken some doing to snatch that peach dress, get out of my wedding dress, meet up with Simon, then get back to my room and redress and all the while not be seen. Being that I was a simply stunning bride, surely someone would notice me out and about like that."

The stunning part was up for grabs but getting noticed was dead-on. "Of course," I said in agreement to keep Waynetta talking. The one thing for sure about Waynetta was if you kept the topic centered on her, she'd keep on chatting away. "Did your daddy know what was going on with Simon and his escapades in the closet?"

"I suspect he knew Simon was fooling around all along and deep down I knew it, too. I just didn't want to admit it, and daddy didn't want to tell me and get me all upset. I'd planned the wedding of my dreams after all. Least I was smart in one way and got that dirtbag to sign a prenuptial agreement. If we'd married and it didn't work out, he wouldn't walk off with all my money, just a hundred thousand or so."

Just and *hundred thousand* didn't fit in the same sentence as far as I was concerned. "Your daddy was involved in building a new golf course?"

Waynetta gave a little pout. "Don't know why it couldn't be a shopping mall. I despise those little carts people ride around in. They're not even air-conditioned, for Pete's sake. Simon and Daddy knew all about the new golf course. Fact is, they had words and Daddy told Simon to keep his mouth shut if he knew what was good for him. I do believe the whole affair is rather hush-hush."

Waynetta took another gulp of water. "I need to get back and hand out more spoons. The Daughters are going to be upset with me if I shirk my responsibilities and right now a little volunteer work is all Daddy's allowing me do. He said I needed to be respectful of Simon's memory if I'm ever to marry into a nice Savannah family."

"Did you ever think about not marrying?" I blurted, thinking maybe Waynetta would get the hint that she had really bad husband karma.

Waynetta threw back her head and laughed. "You say the funniest things, Reagan Summerside. Whatever would I do without a fine man on my arm? What would any girl do?" She gave me a *Waynetta the superior* look. "You know right well how it feels to be all alone. It's just plain terrible, don't you agree? 'Course some things can't be helped now can they? I'll have Daddy make a donation to the children's hospital in my name with some kind of ribbon-cutting ceremony involved. Everyone will forget Simon even existed and simply focus on that till this here ugly gossip goes away."

Waynetta wandered back to her station at the ice cream table and reclaimed her basket from the mayor. Only someone running for office can make handing out a spoon look like an accomplishment. KiKi rested her chin in her palm. "Money may not buy happiness, but for Waynetta it sure covers up a lot of messes."

"Well, she was right about one thing, she couldn't have knocked off Simon. Getting in and out of the dresses was impossible considering the time line and for sure she would have been noticed. But did you catch the part about dear old daddy wanting to put a bullet between Simon's eyes?"

"Add to that, Reese found out the golf course was a hustle and Simon was taking him for a bundle, he had to be fed up with his future son-in-law." KiKi sat back in her chair. "But this is all guesswork on our part. We need proof, something in writing. A check from Reese to Simon for the golf course would be nice."

"What we need is Simon's notebook. I bet the information in there might be enough for Detective Ross to at least consider that someone else, like Reese Waverly, had a motive to kill Simon. My guess is Suellen took it from me to carry on with Simon's sharking business or to hide the fact that she and Simon were partners in something totally illegal, or Sugar-Ray took it because it implicates Reese."

"Why didn't Simon just put the thing in a safety-deposit box to begin with?"

"Too much trouble to record information if he did that.

I'm sure he had the information on a computer somewhere but that's probably in the nearest landfill by now. Since Suellen's place is unoccupied we can start looking there for the notebook. The waitress at the Pirate House said Suellen had one of the new town houses on East Taylor."

"That's two short little old blocks from here." KiKi wiggled her foot. "I can make it that far but how will we know which house is Suellen's and how are we going to get inside the place?"

There was no *we* to this little dilemma. When it came to verbally duking it out with the local snobs, no one put them in their place faster and with more finesse than Auntie KiKi, but this was different. This was breaking the law and Mamma asked me to keep KiKi out of trouble. That she'd already fallen off a fire escape and gotten caught pilfering a flash drive meant *mission not accomplished*. Maybe I'd luck out this time, though truth be told, keeping Auntie KiKi out of trouble was like herding cats.

"You know," I said, studying KiKi's ankle. "It seems a little swollen. You need to rest tonight; we can hit Suellen's place some another time."

I got the beady-eyed glare as an answer; so much for lucking out.

"You're not fooling me," KiKi huffed. "You don't want me around in case something goes wrong, and my guess is your mamma put you up to this, telling you to watch out for me or some such nonsense. I'm no coward. I watch *Law and Order*. I can take the heat."

"Of course you're not a coward. You escaped from a

closet and crawled though bat poop. That's brave in anyone's book."

"And I can get along on this here ankle just fine, thank you very much. But . . ."

Oh, thank the Lord in heaven, there's a but*!*

"Putter's due home this evening and I want to be there. After the phone-call situation I need to show him I care. Besides, I missed the dear man something fierce."

It took as long to walk back to East Gwinnett as it did to polish off double scoops of Old Black Magic. I promised KiKi we'd visit Suellen's house tomorrow but she and I both knew that was a lie. It was night, we needed answers, and Suellen's place was empty. Easy-peasy.

As if reading my mind, KiKi took both my hands in hers. "Maybe you should get Walker Boone to go with you."

"Maybe I should get a root canal."

"You have that new phone. If there's a problem, I'll be there right quick with one of Putter's golf clubs." She grinned. "And a .38 or two for backup."

Chapter Nineteen

B W and I agreed on a lot of things, like that hot dogs rocked, mean people should rot in hell, and the best thing about the heat of summer was that it made you really, really appreciate the cool of autumn. Together we swam our way though the humidity to East Taylor, my capris and tank top stuck to me like a second skin by the time we drew up in front of the town houses. For the most part all the houses looked alike, distinguished by an occasional wreath on the door, doormat in front, and assortment of flowerpots overflowing with multihued impatiens.

I assumed Suellen's house was third from the end, with drooping flowers from lack of watering, letters and the like sticking out from the stuffed wrought-iron mailbox, magazine on top. I had to be certain this was Suellen's address and not someone too lazy to pick up their mail. Breaking into an occupied house meant another visit from Detective Ross and winding up as Chantilly's roomie in jail. Casually, BW and I wandered down the sidewalk, girl walking her dog, all's well with the world. I sat on Suellen's steps and pretended to mess with BW's collar slowly inching my way toward the mailbox.

Bingo! *Glamour* magazine addressed to Suellen. I hid a spare key outside, KiKi hid a key, and so did Suellen under the second pink-and-white flowered pot. I read somewhere occurrences of breaking and entering in Savannah were way down. Heck, there was no need to break in anywhere with keys hidden in every nook and cranny.

With my recent bad luck of unlocked doors, the good news was that Suellen's door was indeed locked. BW and I went inside; light slipped though the trees, casting the living room in weird dark shadows. BW stayed close as I hunted for my flashlight, twisted it on, and realized the place was trashed. Drawers dumped, books scattered, and papers littered on the floor.

"And you thought I was a bad housekeeper," I said to BW to lighten the creepy mood of a ransacked room and dead occupant. "My guess is Reese beat us here, or more to the point his gofer Sugar-Ray did. Either way I bet the notebook's long gone and it must have some juicy information to warrant all this."

BW yawned and sniffed out a cushion flung behind the couch. He circled it in true doggie fashion then curled up for a nap in the AC not caring diddly that a killer might be lurking about. Doggie bliss.

I picked my way over upturned chairs and a broken

lamp and made my to a small painted-white desk. The notebook might be gone but maybe I'd find out something that would lead me to Reese. Right now I'd settle for a golf tee. I found nothing but a few stamps honoring Elvis, a reminder postcard that Suellen's Civic was overdue for maintenance, and a Snickers that needed eating.

The kitchen was a wreck, boxes of cereal, pancake mix, protein bars, and such strewn across the counter, Pirate House glasses on the floor beside a pencil with a cupcake eraser and two cork coasters from Pinkie Master's. Suellen had sticky fingers syndrome. If she liked it, touched it, it was hers! I checked the freezer. Rocky Road ice cream, the universal hiding place? I tore it open to . . . ice cream? The girl had no imagination.

The bedroom reflected the rest of the house. Costume jewelry spewed across the dresser, clothes on the floor, tumbled bed. I felt under the dresser and nightstand. Sometimes important stuff was taped there; I saw it in a movie once. The town house was standard décor, nothing unusual except for the front door opening.

"Sweet mother, now what?" I flipped off the flashlight, then picked my way around stuff and crouched low in the doorway, peering into the living room. The outside light silhouetted a guy, a big guy. Why did people always have to show up when I was around? Why couldn't they just wait their turn? Big Guy took a few steps and BW wandered over, licked his hand, and flopped on his back for a tummy rub.

"Blondie."

"Boone?" I flipped on my flashlight and picked out his

face in the darkness, Boone putting up his hand up to block the glare.

"Do you mind?"

"Why are you here?"

"Why are *you* here?"

"Looking for evidence to put Reese Waverly in jail and get Chantilly out. Your turn."

Boone made his way to me, took the flashlight, and doused it. "The thing's like a beacon from outside. Look," Boone said, sounding exasperated. "Reese had nothing to do with Simon's murder, or Suellen's. Simon dead isn't exactly a hardship to Reese but he isn't responsible, and why would he kill off Suellen? He didn't even know her. You're barking up the wrong tree."

"More like the wrong branch. I get that Reese wouldn't pull the trigger or in this case wield the cake knife and the trophy, but Sugar-Ray would for enough money. He's a man with expensive taste. He wears Versace, for Pete's sake, and his office belongs in some artsy-fartsy magazine. Sugar-Ray has to support his addiction and it's not by his faltering marriage counseling practice, we both know that."

"What's Reese's motive in all this?"

"Get rid of bad rubbish. If Simon married Waynetta, he got a hundred thou just for putting a ring on her finger, and then there's the golf course scam. Who knows how much Simon swindled out of Reese on that little deal."

Boone sat on the end of the couch and exhaled a long deep breath meaning he was going to tell me something he didn't want to tell me. Sweet! Finally Boone was going to cough up some information.

"Reese Waverly wouldn't kill over a hundred thousand dollars. It's not exactly pocket change but not a reason to risk going to jail."

"What about the golf course? That's a big motive and probably big money. Reese went ballistic when he thought KiKi took a flash drive with the information."

"She *did* take the flash drive."

"That's not the point. Simon persuaded Reese to invest in the golf course because it was the hottest thing since Vegas and Reese took the bait hook, line, and sinker."

"No bait, no sinker, the golf course is for real. Reese is getting influential backers to support it. If word gets out, property prices in that area will skyrocket and tank the whole project before it gets off the ground. The golf course will bring in jobs, conventions, and tournaments."

"Make Reese a lot of money."

"For sure, and somehow Simon found out about it and wanted in on the action, not the other way around."

I took a few beats for this to settle in. "If that's true, then Reese had Simon knocked off to keep him quiet."

"Pillsbury and his crew are silent partners in the deal. Simon knew better than to cross them. No one has any idea how Simon found out about all this in the first place."

Beware the girl who wears the tiara. If Waynetta heard her daddy talking about the golf course, it's not much of a stretch to think she'd mention it to Simon. That's how he found out about it . . . maybe. "I think you're lying. I think you're making this up to keep me from suspecting Reese. *SA* was written on the flash drive, that's Simon Ambrose, and how does Sugar-Ray fit into a golf course? And he sure does somehow."

"*SA* is Savannah Arbors, the name of the course and Sugar-Ray has a special friend in Atlanta who runs a five-star restaurant there. Sugar-Ray convinced him that Savannah is a great place to live and work. Reese brought Sugar-Ray on to show his appreciation for getting the chef here. It'll establish Sugar-Ray as a designer. You should see what he did with Reese's office. I'm going to get him to do my house."

"Ditch the leather couch."

"I love that couch."

"Blast it, Boone! Would it have killed you to tell me about the golf course from the get-go?"

"Yeah, right, you and Auntie Twitter." A slow grin spread across Boone's face, his body relaxing. The Sphinx goes happy.

"I'm glad *you're* enjoying this." I punched his arm. "This leaves *me* with no good suspects for who killed Simon and Suellen and I've been running around in circles over the blasted golf course and all for nothing."

"Kept you out of trouble for a little while." He put up his hands to block another punch. "Can you sit on this golf course information for another week? We should have this sewn up by then."

"We?"

Boone shrugged. "I did some of the legal work."

"Invested some money?"

"Way out of my league. Pillsbury would take it as a personal favor if you kept this to yourself."

"What about you?" I had no idea why I threw in that last part. Fatigue no doubt or just something to say in the dark of night. Something flickered way back in Boone's eyes. Slowly he took my hand and pulled me a step closer.

"For some reason everything between us is personal, Blondie." Then his eyes suddenly focused, the smile gone. "Cop cars."

"I don't hear anything." Boone and his days-in-the-hood spidey senses were on full alert. He picked up BW's leash.

"Neighbors probably saw you come in."

"Hey, you're not invisible. They could have seen you."

"Yeah, right. We have to get out of here." We ran to the kitchen, BW in tow. Okay, now I could hear the sirens. This was a way of life for me lately that I could darn well do without. Boone opened the back door to a driveway that led around to the front, the rest of the yard enclosed with a privacy fence. I hate fences. "Now what?"

"Over."

"BW? No man left behind?"

"We'll get him a good lawyer." Boone made a cup with his hands. "I'll boost you. Get a move on!"

I kissed BW on the head, hitched Old Yeller onto my shoulder, kicked off a flip-flop, then stepped into Boone's hands and hoisted myself up. Struggling, I grabbed the top.

"Don't you ever work out?"

I felt something on my butt. Boone's hand! "What are you doing!" I stage whispered.

"Saving your ass!"

There was no safe reply to that one. I gave one final tug and catapulted myself to the other side, falling in a heap of shrubs and grass, Boone landing on top of me, his breath in my ear coming in quick pants. Been a while since I was in this sort of position. Never in a million did I think it would be with Walker Boone. "You're squashing me."

"You smell like Snickers." The back door opened and we froze where we were. A man's voice said, "Nothing out here but a dog with a shoe in his mouth. Whoever broke into this place is long gone. Probably knew the girl was dead and took advantage of the situation, heisting her stuff."

We could hear movement on the other side, then the door closed and all was quiet except for BW making pitiful whiny doggie sounds on the other side and breaking my heart. Boone flopped over on his back and I glared at him. "We are bad, bad doggie parents. How are we going to get BW?"

"He has his leash on. You say he got away from you. Unless it's Detective Ross in that house the other cops will buy it. You look innocent; if they only knew. I'll get the car and pick you up out front."

"I have one shoe? What will people think if I'm walking around with one shoe on?"

Boone kissed me on the forehead, laughter in his eyes.

"They'll be too busy looking at your hair to think about your feet." And then he was gone.

Chapter Twenty

"WELL, I'll be," Auntie KiKi said as she drew up next to me on the sidewalk, the red Chevy turning the corner into the night. "You did call Boone after all." KiKi had on a blue robe, matching slippers, mussed hair, and a sleepy satisfied look in her eyes. Some marriages really did last forever. She gave me a sly smile. "I know why I look a mite disheveled, honey; what's your excuse?"

"I fell in the bushes and Boone fell on top of me."

"Is that what you kids are calling it these days," KiKi said with a laugh, following me to the front porch, the two of us taking up our perch on the top step. BW sniffed and pawed around at things we couldn't see and seemed okay after his temporary abandonment. I on the other hand had guilt issues over leaving him. Heck, I had guilt over anything, the residual effect of being a judge's daughter, no doubt.

"I met up with Boone at Suellen's and then the cops came. We had to make a mad dash for it."

KiKi leaned back against the railing. "You two need to do something about this while you're still young."

"What does that mean?"

"Nothing if I have to explain it. So was Boone there to save Reese Waverly's miserable hide and find the notebook that more than likely had his name all over it? Did he mention how much Reese lost on the golf deal? Bet it was a pretty penny from all the commotion it's caused."

I didn't want to lie to KiKi, but I couldn't level with her about the golf course being real. Pillsbury helped me find KiKi when she went missing so I owed him. As for Boone I didn't owe him a blasted thing. So my hair was a little messed up; it was his fault. "Simon didn't swindle Reese, I had that all wrong."

"So you did find the notebook?"

"There was some other information at Suellen's." Namely Walker Boone. "Reese is off the hook for both murders. He and Sugar-Ray were involved in some other business dealings, nothing that Simon set up. That's why Sugar-Ray was protective about Reese; he's helping him out. My guess is he did Reese's office that you liked so much. All this brings us back to square one. We know Waynetta couldn't have killed Simon, Icy was at sea, Pillsbury would never do anything to get Chantilly in trouble, and he certainly wouldn't let her take the rap for something he did." BW wandered back and put his big head in my lap.

"That leaves us with GracieAnn," KiKi said not sounding all that convinced. "GracieAnn and two murders? Hard to imagine."

I petted BW. I had no idea how anyone figured out anything without a pet in the lap. "Well, Percy did say GracieAnn was a little schizoid. Seems she's all sweet and lovey-dovey when she has him to herself. Then he had a casual conversation with Pastor Liz and GracieAnn went nutty and staked out his apartment in the bakery truck. Maybe she did in Simon because he dropped her or because Simon took on Suellen. Jealousy is a big motivator. Maybe Simon was paying GracieAnn to refer clients, and if he cut her out when he took on Suellen, that's a good reason to be mad at them both. That's jealousy *and* greed for motive."

KiKi gazed up at the stars and yawned. "GracieAnn can't be making as much at the bakery as she was at Wet Willies. She has to be tight on money. Delta has some part-time employees and took GracieAnn in because she felt sorry for her. They'd both been involved in bad relationships and bonded."

"Can you really see GracieAnn Harlow as loan-sharks-r-us?"

"Two weeks ago I never thought the girl would be making dead-man cookies and biting off the heads. Have you seen Percy lately? Maybe he has some other information for us. If GracieAnn is acting off-the-wall, she won't suddenly jump back to normal." KiKi stood and stretched. "Tomorrow we'll go to the bakery, check on Percy, and pay GracieAnn a visit."

"If GracieAnn's serving up another batch of weird cookies, I say we're onto something."

AT SIX A.M. BW AND I SAT ON THE FRONT PORCH, me in old shorts and a T-shirt I'd worn to paint the upstairs hall, BW in the fur coat he'd been born with. I tied on a pair of running shoes I'd bought during a health-kick craze some five years ago. The good news was I kept the shoes. The bad news was the health kick lasted for about twenty minutes till I realized how much work it was to actually run. I wouldn't be contemplating this suicide-mission now if Boone hadn't made that crack about not working out and actually put his hand on my behind to get my out-of-shape self over the fence. That took embarrassment to a whole new level.

I slid my phone in my back pocket in case I had a heart attack along the way and had to ring up Uncle Putter. I did a few run-in-place jogs to get my blood flowing. Except my blood didn't flow at six A.M. but stagnated in my veins waiting for coffee and a jolt of caffeine. I took off anyway. Halfway down the block I glanced back at BW on the porch snoozing. Smart dog. I decided the best way to handle this morning burst of insanity was the bat-poop approach of thinking about something else till this horribleness was over.

Running down East Gwinnett was a crappy way to start the day, but I was sure Chantilly's start of the day was a million times worse. I needed to visit her but just couldn't do it without good news and right now I had nothing but rotten news. Panting and sweating like a roasting pig and wondering if embarrassment was all that bad after all I turned up Abercorn. Gulping air, I contemplated my heart actually exploding out of my chest till I heard footsteps behind me closing in fast. A fellow jogger? A mugger? Yeah, like I had so much to mug. Little prickles of alarm skated up my spine anyway.

"Hey, lady. What you doing?"

I stopped and turned around to . . . "Pillsbury?"

Pillsbury drew up beside me dressed in expensive work-out shorts, T-shirt, and some fancy shoes that probably ran all by themselves. He jogged in place, looking like a TV commercial or a model for *Muscle and Fitness* magazine, not that I subscribed but alphabetically it was next to *People* in the grocery store and there were always dynamite guys on the cover. "I needed some exercise," I said.

"Same here." He studied my color-splashed outfit.

"New look."

"Sweet. Let's roll."

"I'll be holding you back."

"That's cool. I already did a few miles." From his build I'd say he did about ten miles a day and never broke a sweat. Pillsbury and I together was something like a golf cart keeping pace with a Corvette, but the man wasn't moving without me. I started off, Pillsbury beside me taking baby steps. "Find who snuffed Simon?"

"My suspects alibied out." Running was tough. Running and not looking like a wimp and talking at the same time could be downright fatal.

"Who's on radar?"

"What are you going to do to them?"

A big smile split Pillsbury's face. "Not my turf. You're the Sherlock. I just want my babe out of the slammer."

I took that to mean he hadn't visited Chantilly and I knew it was tough. Pillsbury cared for her; anyone could see that. "Maybe the killer's someone Simon lent money to and they couldn't pay him back. Or there's GracieAnn Harlow over at Cakery Bakery. Simon treated her bad. She's a little hard to figure, but I can't see her as a cold-blooded murderer just because Simon messed her over." I sucked in a lungful of air and managed, "Seems a bit extreme."

"How'd you feel when your man ditched you?"

"You know about that?" I asked as we took a right onto East Huntington and I prayed not to drop dead.

Another smile split Pillsbury's face.

"Right." The hood knew everything. Twitter for badasses. "Truth is, I wanted to put a bullet between Hollis Beaumont the Third's eyes or more righteously between his legs considering what he had going on while still married to me."

Pillsbury laughed deep in his chest as we jogged in place to let a car pass. I promised the Lord I'd light two candles in thanksgiving for the car allowing me to catch my breath.

"Maybe GracieAnn feel the same with Simon. Bet he kept more than one squirrel around."

"Squirrel?"

"Hot lady. Jealousy cuts deep. You need the dope, that be evidence."

I nodded in agreement about the evidence as we turned onto East Gwinnett. I nearly wept with joy when I spied my house. "Got any ideas," I asked as we pulled up to my front porch, not a dry spot on my body, hair plastered to my scalp. "Have you heard anything on the street?"

"Nada. Not our game. This be a personal hit. Someone felt the man needed killing. Bush league."

"Meaning not professional. GracieAnn fits that bill. I just need the dope."

Pillsbury nodded with a smile. "Keep it one hundred, babe. Later." Pillsbury jogged off still without an ounce of sweat on him anywhere.

I wasn't sure what keeping it one hundred was but it felt like a compliment. I grabbed a shower and slipped into navy capris fresh out of the dryer and smelling like Spring Mist. I added a white T-shirt. I'd flip on a cute scarf when I came back from the bakery and be ready for a day at the Fox. Scarves and earrings dressed up anything. 'Course dying my hair might help, too.

"How can you look alert at eight A.M.? Only time I'm up at this hour is when strung out on caffeine," KiKi said to me while we walked toward the bakery. "I think you need to open the Fox at noon, then we don't have to do stuff at this ungodly hour and I can get my beauty rest."

"I went out jogging and met up with Pillsbury. The man is built like an armored truck. He must have run all the way over here from Seventeenth Street and didn't even look winded."

KiKi's eyes rounded and she sucked in a deep breath. "Why on earth would you jog of all things? Have you done lost your senses? It'll make your boobs sag and your baby-maker fall out, every woman knows that."

Least the ones who needed an excuse not to jog. I stepped up the pace. If I didn't, all the sprinkle doughnuts would be gone . . . again. "I have no boobs to sag and as far as I can tell my baby-maker's still where it belongs. Besides, I need to get shaped up. Yesterday when Boone and I played escape artist there was a big fence. Boone had to boost me up."

"So?"

"He had his hand on my butt and shoved me over. Talk about awkward."

"I could call it something else but you wouldn't believe me. Did Pillsbury have any ideas on who's our killer? He hears stuff out there on the streets."

"His take is that it's someone with a personal score to settle and thinks GracieAnn is a good candidate. See if anything sticks out as being a little off with GracieAnn this morning. Something unusual."

Cakery Bakery was in full swing, the little white tables out front under the trees filled with customers sipping sweet tea and coffee and eating pastries. Inside the lines were long, Delta loading fresh baguettes into a tall basket, GracieAnn scribbling orders and filling cups of coffee. Three sprinkle doughnuts sat in regal splendor under a glass dome at the end of the counter.

"Well, would you look at that," KiKi said nodding at the display case. "Snickers bar cookies. Never knew such things existed." KiKi craned her neck to get a closer look. "They even have peanuts and caramel drizzled on top. Snickers cookies and Snickers martinis, this is one mighty fine city."

BW eyed the doughnuts, now two under the dome, little drops of doggie drool pooling at the corners of his mouth. When we got to the front of the line GracieAnn sneered at the BW. "He shouldn't be in here. Board of Health would have a fit."

"We'll say he's a little person in a fun coat. Where's that repairman that's always hanging around? I haven't seen him lately."

"What's it to you?"

"My AC is down. I need a repair guy."

"Well, I don't know where he is, the no-good rat. I think he's two-timing me. Why do men do that? Think they're so important they can treat women the way they do." GracieAnn snapped the cupcake right off the top of her pencil. "I baked toolbox cookies today, chocolate, they're cooling in the back. I wonder what he'd think about that. So what's your order?" she asked, broken end of the pencil poised over the pink order pad. "Make it quick."

Toolbox cookies! KiKi and I exchanged wide-eyed *holy mother-of-pearl* looks.

"Order or move on," GracieAnn hissed.

"Two sprinkle doughnuts and coffee for me," I said in a rush and KiKi chimed in with, "Plain doughnut. Part of my diet, but I'll get a half-dozen of your Snickers cookies for Putter. The man's skinny as a lamppost and the cookies do look amazing."

GracieAnn's face morphed into a sincere grin. Miss Jilted to Miss Sweet-as-sugar in two seconds. "You mean it?"

"Oh my goodness, yes." KiKi nodded for emphasis.

GracieAnn held up one of the Snickers cookies. "I've been eating the candy bars for the past week trying to get the recipe right. I put on five pounds along the way but that's the price of success. Delta and I need to make sixty dozen tonight. The Daughters of the Confederacy wanted something unusual and scrumptious they could use as a fund-raiser."

GracieAnn flipped cookies into a white pastry bag, then headed for the glass dome. "One sprinkle left," she called out to me. "I'll substitute a plain." She added coffees at lightning speed. I hitched Old Yeller onto my shoulder, then picked up the order. KiKi snagged us an outside table.

"Did you see that?" KiKi said as we plopped down, her voice a strained excited whisper in deference to big ears and loose tongues lurking nearby.

I looked at BW, all smiles, his tail wagging in anticipation, big puppy-dog eyes staring up at me.

KiKi leaned across the table. "Toolbox cookies, Percy's gone MIA, and then there's GracieAnn's rendition of *Sybil Does Savannah* when I told her the cookies looked good! The girl's nutty as a fruitcake, I tell you. Lord have mercy, what's going on around here?"

"Forget fruitcake. I hate fruitcake. They don't make

enough sprinkle doughnuts is what's going on!" Feeling guilty for leaving BW at the fence, I fed *him* the doughnut and swore to get him on a healthier diet starting tomorrow when my abandonment remorse subsided. I hunched across the table. "GracieAnn's always a little loopy. I think it's the men in her life. I can relate. It doesn't mean she's a killer."

KiKi gave me the thin-lip expression and beady-eyed stare. "What do you want, a Broadway show of *How I Killed Simon and Suellen and Got Away With It*. I just hope she hasn't added Percy to the list. I know what's going on with you, it's that jogging. Your baby-maker and boobs are okay, but your brain's all jiggled up inside and your energy's spent doing something stupid like running around for no good reason. You should be all excited we're onto GracieAnn."

"I'm all out of excitement. In case you haven't noticed I've been wrong a lot in narrowing down the suspects. Every time I thought I knew who the killer was, it wasn't."

KiKi sat back and studied my plain doughnut and glanced down at hers, both blah pastries untouched. "It's the sugar thing all over again," KiKi said. "There's no jolt to get our brain cells functioning." She pulled out two cookies from the little white bag and handed me one. "These will have to do, but it's a rotten shame I had to throw away the Snickers you gave me from Jen's and Friends the other night. We sure could use it now. That would be one big old sugar rush."

"You didn't eat that candy bar when you were at Simons place?"

KiKi broke off a piece of Snickers cookie. "Started to melt before I even got to the car. I had to get rid of it right quick. Breaks the heart." She nibbled the edge dieter's style to make the deliciousness last. "If I got chocolate on the leather upholstery, Putter would have a canary and buy two more golf clubs to settle himself down. Pretty soon we'll have to put on an addition to house all of them." KiKi took another nibble.

"But there was a Snickers wrapper on the floor at Simon's place when I came to find you. I thought it was the one I gave you and you'd dropped it. It's one of the reasons I knew you were at Simon's and kept looking around."

KiKi stopped the next bite halfway to her mouth. She held up the chunk of cookie, both of us studying it like an insect stuck on the end of a pin. "I saw that wrapper at Simon's place, too. I didn't think anything of it till now. I mean everyone likes candy bars including a certain someone who's been eating them for a solid week."

"There was a Snickers on Suellen's desk at her town house and I found one of GracieAnn's cupcake pencils on the floor. I thought Suellen stole the pencil because she liked it and because she had other pilfered items lying around, but what if she didn't steal the pencil? What if GracieAnn left behind the candy while she looked for the notebook and accidentally dropped the pencil? She'd be in a hurry and nervous in case someone saw her go inside and called the cops."

"You think GracieAnn would bring along her own candy? And how would she get in the town house in the first place?"

"I'd say GracieAnn's a stress eater. She said she'd been eating nonstop. And there's a key under the flowerpot. That's how I got in."

KiKi gave me a big, toothy grin. "Well, there you go, we're right back to GracieAnn. Suellen took the notebook from you at Simon's. GracieAnn wanted it. When GracieAnn couldn't find the notebook at Simon's she figured Suellen had it. Suellen wasn't in the mood to share and GracieAnn whacked Suellen over the head with the award trophy. GracieAnn then went to Suellen's to find the notebook. It all adds up nice and neat."

KiKi popped the rest of the cookie in her mouth and said around a mouthful of crumbs, "We did it. We have motive and opportunity and a candy bar and cupcake pencil as evidence."

"Pitifully weak circumstantial evidence. Ross would laugh what's left of her behind right off if that's what I brought to prove Chantilly innocent. Chantilly's still the front-runner with her fingerprints on the murder weapon. It's going to take something sincere and monumental to trump that. Something big."

"The truck, that's big. What if GracieAnn's the one who knocked you and Big Brown into alligator alley? That could link her to the murder."

"Or it could have been Reese or Icy warning me to quit poking around in their lives."

"The killer had the most motive for trying to scare you off and we know Reese and Icy are innocent. If the Cakery Bakery truck has brown paint on it, that's another nail in

GracieAnn's coffin, right?" KiKi scooped the plain, untouched doughnuts into the bag. "We're here now. I say we go around back and take a look-see at that the bakery truck. I just bet it has that UPS brown paint scraped all over the front bumper."

Chapter Twenty-one

"THE truck's not here," KiKi said to BW and me, the three of us standing in the empty gravel alley behind the bakery. "Do you think someone's out making a delivery? Maybe we can wait a few minutes till the truck comes back."

"Percy said Delta and GracieAnn are the only ones who drive the truck and they're both inside. Maybe the truck's having repairs done, like for a dent in the front." I called myself every name for stupid. "I should have checked this out sooner. If GracieAnn did run me off the road in the bakery truck, all the evidence will be gone under a new coat of paint. See, I get distracted and don't follow through and this is what happens."

"Because we had other suspects who looked guiltier. But this isn't all bad, honey. In fact it's good news. If the truck *is* getting fixed that means there's a reason. Something happened. Maybe we could make a few calls to body shops, see if the Cakery Bakery truck is there and what the problem happens to be."

"Why would the body shop tell us anything?"

"Because Ace Auto Insurance Company needs to know about the truck for the claim adjustment."

"Who in the world is Ace Auto Insurance Company?"

KiKi raised her hand, a devilish glint in her eyes. "You're looking at her sweet little old self right here."

BY NOON I'D OPENED UP THREE NEW CONSIGNMENT accounts at the Fox and accepted a date with Doc Hunky when he stopped by to bring me yellow roses. If he ever got on that bachelor show, the women would be lined up across America to marry the guy. Business was brisk, my social life out of the toilet for the moment, BW dug a new hole in KiKi's flower garden that I was sure to catch heck for, and I hadn't heard anything from dear auntie on Ace Auto Insurance.

I found a nice navy skirt and peach sweater to add to the display in the bay window that needed sprucing when *pssst* sounded from the hallway leading to the kitchen. I looked over to see Percy hiding around the corner hooking his finger at me in come-here fashion.

"What's going on?" I asked when I met up with him in the hallway.

"GracieAnn," Percy whispered, little beads of sweat across is brow. "She thinks I'm cheating on her and she's baking toolbox cookies. I can't decide if that's a good thing or not so good and sort of hanging low till I figure it out."

I took Percy's hand. "Honey, when Simon bit the big one GracieAnn baked dead-man cookies."

Percy faded to paste white. "You think she killed Simon?"

"It's a possibility. Did you ever hear Delta say anything to GracieAnn about putting a dent in the delivery truck?"

"Not while I was around, but they work together a lot when I'm not there."

"I feel terrible that I put you in this predicament. Maybe you should go on vacation. Get out of town for a while till I can find out what's going on with GracieAnn. I'll keep in touch. I have a phone now."

"I can help Uncle Chicken. He's swamped with AC repair jobs." Percy gave me a quick kiss on the cheek, then looked around at the shop. "You better be careful yourself. If GracieAnn can bake toolbox cookies, she can bake dress, skirt, and shoe cookies. She's a little left of center if you get my drift."

After Percy hustled out the back door I considered his warning. A little left of center? Make that out in left field. GracieAnn had stabbed and knocked two people to death; murder by clothes hanger wasn't that far of a stretch. I wrote up two more sales and stuffed the money in the Godiva candy box. I started in on another display in the dining room when KiKi rumba'd her way through the front door, waving a piece of paper in the air and swishing her skirt side to side. "Am I a genius or what?"

"You found the truck?"

Before she could fill in the details, two more customers wandered in. I welcomed them to the Prissy Fox, explained about the store, trying not to rush, but I really wanted to hear KiKi's news.

"I located our pigeon," KiKi gushed, the customers heading off to shop. "Roy's Body Shop over on Montgomery."

"The front bumper has brown paint and there's a dent in the hood?"

"Well, sort of. There *was* brown paint and the dent. The bumper was sold off for scrap this morning and the brown paint is under a fresh coat of white paint. Delta needed the truck for a delivery so they worked on it all day yesterday. But it *was* all there like we suspected. It's just not something we can show to Detective Ross." KiKi put her hand on my shoulder. "I'm sorry about that, honey."

"So we can't use the truck as concrete evidence," I said, trying to figure out a way to turn this information into something significant. "The guys at the body shop could say there was indeed brown paint on the bumper and truck but there's no way of knowing it was from the UPS truck or not. The thing is, we know and that's what counts."

"That's what I think, too," KiKi said, all smiles. "And we also have the cupcake pencil and Snickers wrappers plus motive and opportunity." KiKi glanced at the two customers shopping. She came a little closer and dropped her voice. "GracieAnn was at the wedding and knew how to get into Simon's place. They were in business together and now we have the truck. I think with all the information we have, our favorite detective would listen to what we have to say. At least she'd talk to GracieAnn, don't you think? Ross is one scary gal. If she gets GracieAnn alone in one of those interrogation rooms like you see on TV, the girl will crack like a rotten pecan."

KiKi gave me a sassy wink. "Roses? Tell me you're not just using the guy for the free food."

"He's interesting and a fine doctor," I said, giving myself a Doc Hunky pep talk. "He saves people and is a true humanitarian."

"That's what I want to hear. Putter and I are going out for dinner. I've got our vacation to that Pebble Beach golf course place all set up. He's been working so hard. You have fun tonight and tomorrow we'll go together and pay Ross a visit. She has to see that all this GracieAnn stuff is more than coincidence. We'll bring her carrot sticks."

When the last two customers left I closed up shop, put away clothes, tidied up, and tried to convince myself to feel good about the evidence against GracieAnn. It didn't work. Maybe because I'd been wrong on every single suspect so far it was hard to believe I was right this time.

A tapping on the front window drew my attention to Tipper Longford standing on the porch. "I need to chat with you for a minute," he said, his muffled voice drifting in. "It'll just be a minute."

I couldn't think of a single thing I had in the Fox that would appeal to Tipper, not one Confederate soldier jacket or saber in the whole place.

"I know you're closed and I actually waited till you were," Tipper said when I let him inside. He took off his hat and ran his fingers through his thinning hair. "This is sort of awkward for me. I'm not the kind of person who goes around accusing people of things unless I'm sure." He took a deep breath. "Everyone knows you're a friend of Chantilly's and trying to prove her innocent of killing Simon and my Suellen, and I would have bet my last dollar Chantilly was guilty as all get out but now . . . Well, maybe not."

A forlorn expression pinched Tipper's face. "I miss my Suellen something terrible. The funeral's tomorrow. I still can't believe she's gone, and who could have done such a terrible thing to my sweet, sweet girl? She was the light of my life, the song of my soul, the reason I got up in the morning, and—"

"Mr. Longford?" I interrupted, suspecting if I didn't there'd be a half-hour eulogy for Suellen right here in the Prissy Fox.

"The reason I came here is that GracieAnn Harlow, the young girl who works for Delta over at the bakery, had on Suellen's pearl bracelet the other day. I stopped in at Pinkie Master's for a beer with some of the other soldiers and GracieAnn was there with one of the part-time help at the bakery and I noticed the bracelet. I nearly spilled my drink all over myself."

I patted Tipper's shoulder. "You're grieving. For a while everything is going to remind you of Suellen. When Granddaddy Summerside passed away, every time I ate mashed potatoes I thought of him. The man loved his potatoes." With lots of butter and gravy and half the reason he was at the big mashed potato gathering in the sky.

"That's right sweet of you but I know it was Suellen's

bracelet because I gave it to her, you see. GracieAnn saw me looking at the bracelet and took it right off and dropped it in that big purse she hauls around with her. I know it was Suellen's bracelet because I had a special charm put on for her, a magnolia blossom. She was right partial to magnolias, springtime being her favorite time of year and all."

Tipper sniffed and blinked back tears. "Suellen told me that Simon treated GracieAnn bad. Suellen said he even tried to come on to her a few times. I'm thinking GracieAnn got jealous and killed Simon, then Suellen, too. How else would she get Suellen's bracelet?"

"Why don't you take this to the police?"

Tipper shrugged. "One little piece of jewelry is hardly enough evidence for the police to act on but people say you've been nosying around. If I think GracieAnn had a hand in these murders, maybe you do too, is all I'm saying. You've been nice to me and if I can help you get your friend out of jail, I'd be pleased as punch. Do you have anything that points the finger at GracieAnn?"

"I was going to talk to the police tomorrow. I can tell them about the bracelet."

"Maybe they can get one of those search warrants? Nothing will bring back my Suellen, but knowing her killer is going to pay is some consolation. If the police need to talk to me, they can after the funeral of course." He took my hand. "I knew I could count on you to do the right thing."

Tipper let himself out and BW came around the counter for a post-nap stretch and scratch behind the ears. "What do think?" I asked BW. I swore he said, *You better get yourself gussied up so you don't look like something the cat dragged off the river.* BW had quite a way with words.

"NOT EXACTLY THE PINK HOUSE," I SAID TO DOC Hunky over a din of voices as we polished off a pizza at Vinnie Van Go-Go's, the zip line carrying orders to the kitchen whirling over our heads.

"Salami, spinach, artichoke, and sun-dried tomato are my favorite toppings. And the atmosphere is great. But that might have something to do with the company." Hunky clinked his beer to mine.

KiKi's crack about dating for free food wore heavy on my Catholic education conscience, and whereas pizza and beer were not exactly quid-pro-quo for pan-seared scallops and French wine, City Market was fun, with vendors, people mingling, and all the outdoor eateries. Plus I could afford to pick up the tab.

"Well now, what's this," Hollis-the-horrible said, swaggering up to our table as if he owned the place. He glanced from me to Doc Hunky. "Trying to sell Cherry House to the first person who comes along?"

"And you are?" Hunky leaned back in his chair giving Hollis a cold *she's mine* stare. Not that I was all that sure since no one had ever stared on my behalf before.

"I'm her ex. Bet she's told you all about me."

"Didn't have to. I know you're a jackass since you let her get away." Hunky tossed double what our dinner cost on the table and held out his hand to me. "I think we're done here, Reagan."

I took Hunky's hand, him leading the way, me in a fog. "You okay?" he asked when we got outside.

"My plan was to pay your way tonight and you go all Prince Charming on me, and I think I'm babbling."

Hunky laughed and actually blushed. Couldn't remember the last time I saw a guy do that. "Don't know about the prince part," he said. "But the expression on that jerk's face was payment plenty."

He put his arm around me as we made our way toward the jazz group setting up. We paused under the trees, dim light slipping though the branches swaying gently in the breeze. He looked into my eyes and I looked into his and waited for my heart to skip a beat.

And it actually did because someone over at City Market yelled, "Help! We're in need of a doctor over here! Hurry."

"Do you think your ex put them up to this?" Hunky smiled nonchalantly as if someone had called for a taxi. He took my hand and we ran back toward the square. A woman had collapsed and instantly Doc Hunky morphed into Doc Superman; actually he did that when he squashed Hollis. Fifteen minutes later Hunky accompanied the paramedics to the hospital amid a round of applause from the crowd of onlookers and my assurance that I could indeed get home safe and sound.

"You have yourself a fine man there, honey," a woman said as the ambulance drove off.

"You need to hang on to that one," offered another. And they were right as rain of course. The Doc Hunky/Superman types didn't come along every day of the week and it wasn't just because he lived in Charleston and only got to

Savannah once in a while. The man was truly fine. Any woman would be lucky to have him in her life. Right?

I headed for home, passing a Gloria Summerside poster adorned with a handlebar mustache and devil horns. Guillotine Gloria was not loved by one and all. Storefronts sat lonely and dark, businesses closed for the night. One pink neon cupcake sign lit the front part of Cakery Bakery, but around back the kitchen blazed bright and lively, the heavenly aroma of Snickers cookies drifting out to the sidewalk. Delta and GracieAnn were hard at work for their catering gig the next morning.

I wandered down the alley and there parked in the gravel, pretty as you please, was the white Cakery Bakery delivery truck with cakes and pies and cookies painted on the sides. It had a spanking-new bumper in front and no dents anywhere to implicate wrongdoing.

Could I really convince Ross that GracieAnn was the killer and Chantilly innocent if all I had was a bunch of theories and hearsay? Tipper was distraught, the bracelet sighting not something Ross would put much stock in. Heck, I didn't put much stock in it. Maybe the bakery truck didn't knock me into the swamp after all. The truck could have crunched into anything brown and I was so busy trying to stay on the road I didn't pay attention and seeing directly behind was nearly impossible anyway. Truth be told, I couldn't swear beyond all doubt that this bakery truck was the one that hit me. Little twinges of doubt skirted across my shoulders. I needed something concrete to take to Ross. I needed something of GracieAnn's that said *guilty*!

The back door to the bakery stood wide open, only the screen door in place, letting the oven heat escape into the night air. If Tipper did see GracieAnn drop the bracelet in her purse, there was a chance it was still there. I looked at Old Yeller hanging off my shoulder. Big purses were like that, a bottomless pit of catchall for weeks at a time and longer. It was worth a shot. I crept up the wooden steps and peered into a storage room piled with boxes, sacks, drums, extra chairs, and tables. Delta and GracieAnn's voices drifted out from the kitchen area but most words were lost in the racket of baking and exhaust fans.

The corner of GracieAnn's purse protruded from under her blue sweater hanging on one of the pegs by the hall. All I needed was a little peek inside to confirm what Tipper had said. Then I'd know I was on the right track and feel more confident when I met up with Ross tomorrow. Maybe I really could persuade her to get a search warrant. Ross may not take to heart my evidence of candy wrappers and the like but she couldn't discount evidence from Tipper *and* me.

Slowly I slipped inside, easing the screen door closed so it wouldn't bang. Tippy-toeing, I made my way across the room toward GracieAnn's purse till I heard footsteps crunching on the gravel outside. I ducked behind a clothes hamper of dirty aprons and towels as the screen door opened, steps creeping my way. I held my breath, didn't move a muscle. The footsteps stopped by the hallway. I peeked one eye around the hamper and saw . . . Tipper Longford? What in the world was Tipper doing here? Stealing an apron from Delta? Sabotaging her business? Borrowing a cup of sugar?

He pushed aside GracieAnn's sweater. He methodically pulled on a pair of gloves then opened GracieAnn's big purse and removed her wallet, brush, a blue scarf, a canister of hairspray, some other stuff, and her cell phone. He dropped a pearl bracelet in the purse along with the brown notebook I'd taken from Simon's and a pink-jeweled iPhone I recognized as Suellen's. He put the other things back on top then rearranged the sweater over the purse like it was before.

He smiled as he took off the gloves and stuffed them in his pocket. It wasn't the smile of good-old-boy Tipper Longford, reenactment soldier and sorrowful lover, but a sinister smile of satisfaction mixed with a huge dose of pure evil.

Chapter Twenty-two

T IPPER retraced his steps back to the door then let himself out into the night. I sat on the floor and collapsed against the sack of dirty laundry, my brain on overload. If I hadn't seen Tipper Longford plant that evidence with my own two eyes, I never in a million years would have believed the man was capable of framing GracieAnn. Worse still, Tipper Longford was capable of two murders! Sweet Jesus! How did that happen? Why?

I retrieved GracieAnn's purse off the peg and walked into the kitchen, stacks of cookies cooling on racks, mixes whirling around and around. GracieAnn's apron was smudged with caramel and chocolate and she looked tired clear though. "What are you doing here," she bellowed across the kitchen when she saw me. "And what are you doing with my purse?"

I turned off the mixers. "We need to talk. You're not going to believe this."

"What I believe is that we have baking to do." GracieAnn elbowed me aside, flipped the mixers on, then grabbed her purse right out of my hand. "Get out of here before I call the police on you for stealing." She turned to Delta. "Call nine-one-one right now. She was probably going to sell my purse in that shop of hers."

"If I was stealing your purse, why would I bring it to you?" I grabbed the purse back and dumped it upside down on the stainless counter, the comb, wallet, hairspray, scarf, lipstick, and cell phone skittering across the counter followed by the pink iPhone, notebook, and Suellen's bracelet.

GracieAnn stared, blinked, then stared more. "How did all this stuff get in there? That's not my fancy phone or bracelet and what's with the notebook?"

"Tipper put them in you purse," I said. "I just saw him do it in the back room. All this stuff belongs to Suellen. He's trying to frame you for her murder, GracieAnn, and Simon's, too."

GracieAnn gave me a mean, hateful look. "Well now, that's crazy talk. How do I know you didn't put those things in the purse to make me look guilty? Everyone knows for a fact you'd do anything to get Chantilly out of jail and now you're setting me up for murder."

Delta shook her head, looking sad. "Oh my goodness. You saw Tipper do this? That's just plain terrible."

GracieAnn rubbed her hands on her face, turning her cheeks white with flour. "Tipper couldn't do this. He loved

Suellen to pieces, everyone knows that. Why would he kill her? You're making this up."

"Tipper was jealous, that's the best explanation I've got. Suellen was involved with Simon. Tipper knew it and killed them both. Blaming it on Chantilly was easy with all her motives for wanting Simon dead but I was determined to get Chantilly off so Tipper tossed me another bone, namely you." I nodded at GracieAnn. "After one bad relationship with Delta and the divorce, the thought of two women betraying him sent the man over the edge."

Delta picked up the iPhone. "What I want to know is what you're doing here in my kitchen late at night in the first place. Maybe you got these things from Chantilly and planted them in GracieAnn's purse and made up the part about Tipper."

"The killer had that iPhone," I said. "It's how he lured Chantilly to Simon's condo with Suellen's dead body, making Chantilly look guilty. Tipper just told me today that GracieAnn had Suellen's bracelet. He wanted me to take that to the police along with the other information he'd planted. He left a Snickers wrapper at Simon's place to point the finger at GracieAnn being there and again at Suellen's along with one of her cupcake pencils."

GracieAnn sank to the floor, her legs sprawled out like a dropped ragdoll. "I don't even know where Suellen lives," she wailed. "I've never even been to Simon's in my whole life. How could this happen to me? I'm innocent. I haven't done anything wrong."

I said to GracieAnn, "I figured you were the one who locked my auntie KiKi in a closet to get me to back off the case, but all the while it was Tipper. What I don't get is how he used the bakery truck to knock me into the swamp and Delta not wonder how the truck got all banged up?"

"Because Delta did know," Tipper said from behind me, my heart dropping to my toes. I turned to face him, gun in his hand, every hair on my body standing straight up in flat-out terror.

"*I* drove the truck," he said, that evil look still in his eyes. "Chantilly came in here for a doughnut and said you had her truck out at Waverly Farms making deliveries for her. I wanted to scare you away from poking around but in the end it turned into another way to implicate our little GracieAnn here."

I looked from Delta to Tipper and GracieAnn on the floor. GracieAnn started to cry. All things considered that wasn't a half-bad idea. "You and Delta? Together?" she whined. "You hate each other. You're divorced. All you do is argue and make a scene."

Tipper kissed Delta on the cheek. "That's what we wanted everyone to believe, especially you, especially Simon and Suellen. Delta here just sent me a text from Suellen's phone, that's how I knew there was a problem and came right back. For the final installment to our plan GracieAnn will realize you're onto her as the murderer and she'll kill you. You'll be her third victim. GracieAnn knows where we keep the gun at the bakery. Delta will be distraught over the situation, tie GracieAnn up with an apron, then call the police. All the evidence for the other two murders is right there in GracieAnn's purse so when the police come that's what they'll find, plus you dead of course."

Delta took off her apron and handed it to Tipper. Gra-cieAnn sobbed louder. Feeling weak, I stumbled back, my hand knocking over a sack of flour and two boxes of Snickers cookies. "What is all this about? Why would the two of you want Simon and Suellen dead?"

Delta let out a deep sigh. "It was me being stupid."

"We were both stupid," Tipper cut in, hugging Delta close to his side. "Simon was young and handsome and made a play for Delta here. Suellen did the same with me over at the Pirate House when the boys and I would come in for a beer or two. Simon convinced Delta to sign over the bakery to keep it out of the divorce settlement and said he'd give it back. They were to be married after all. He'd proposed and she'd accepted all on the QT of course so I wouldn't know she was trying to walk away with the bakery when she divorced me."

"He swindled me." Delta said, a tear trailing down her face. "He sweet-talked me and nobody did sweet talk bet-ter than Simon Ambrose, the lying bastard, I can tell you that much. Tipper and I weren't getting along and Simon and Suellen played right into that."

"They were in it together, Suellen making a play for me so I'd be all starry-eyed and get a quickie divorce from Delta no matter what and Simon making a play for Delta to keep the bakery. Those two played us against each other," Tipper said. "Simon wouldn't give back the bakery, his plan was to make Delta buy it back. Delta came to me and we suspected what was going on. Then we saw Simon and Suellen meet up behind the Pirate House. Delta and I pooled our money. Took all our savings to get back our own business and we swore to get even. Killing Simon was easy and we knew if I kept Suellen hanging on that sooner or later we'd get the chance to kill her, too. They both deserved it."

"You could have gone to the police."

"What they did was legal and we'd just look like two old foolish people who got swindled. Plus if we didn't buy the bakery, we'd never get it back."

"And you paying Simon is how he got the seed money for his loan-shark operation," I said, pieces falling into place. "You realized Simon had other enemies and killing him at his own wedding made for a lot of suspects all of them right there. The bridesmaid dress on the floor made for a nice cover."

"How do women stand those crinolines things? They itch something terrible." Tipper made a sour face and scratched his legs.

"But that meant they'd be looking for a woman and not a man or a man with a woman's help and you fit neither scenario," I added, seeing this all from a new angle. "You got Suellen to Simon's place and killed her, then texted Chantilly from Suellen's phone to have her standing over the body when Ross showed up, except we got out the back. Delta stole the notebook from me because it had the information on paying Simon for the Cakery Bakery. That would make her a prime suspect."

"In the beginning all the evidence was stacked against Chantilly nice and neat, even down to me stashing the dress in the UPS van," Tipper said, he and Delta hauling the sobbing GracieAnn off the floor. "But you just had to keep on digging around. Good thing we had GracieAnn here at the wedding so everything we did could also fit with her. We manufactured a few other details, threw in the bracelet, and got you to go to the cops for us."

"You used me, and I fell for it."

"We learned from Simon and Suellen how it's done. If you hadn't come snooping around tonight, Chantilly would have wound up free as a bird. That'll still happen, but now you'll wind up dead."

"I don't want to die," GracieAnn blubbered.

"You're not going to die," I said, stalling for time, trying to figure out what to do. GracieAnn was a loose cannon. I needed a fuse. "You'll go to prison for a while, Percy will lose your appeal, and then you'll die. It'll just take a while."

GracieAnn's face got all red and blotchy, her eyes little slits. "First Simon treats me bad! Then Percy! Now you!" She glared at Tipper. "Men! I hate you all!" She kicked Tipper in the shins.

"Ouch!" he yelped, grabbing his leg. I snagged the sack of flour, closed my eyes, and flung it at Tipper and Delta, great white clouds billowing everywhere. "I can't see!" Tipper scratched at his face and I tackled him to the floor. If the gun went off, I'd die quick. If I had a sprinkle dough-nut in my hand instead of Tipper's soldier hat, I'd die happy. Instead Boone grabbed the gun out of Tipper's hand, then flipped him over on his stomach like an egg in the skillet.

"Let me go!"

"Apron?" Boone grunted, pointing to the floor, holding on to a struggling Tipper.

"What are you doing here?" I asked.

"Apron?"

"Where'd you come from?"

"Blondie, the apron if you please. The guy's little but he's scrappy."

I handed over the apron. "Suddenly you show up out of nowhere?"

Boone hogtied Tipper, then dusted the flour from his hands. He gave me one of those half smiles. "I'm a sucker for Snickers cookies, smelled them all the way out on the sidewalk as I was passing by. What can I say, I'm a fan."

Sirens sounded a few blocks away. Boone stood and flicked off more flour. "I think they're playing our song."

"Sweet Jesus in heaven! Delta!" I said, scrambling to my feet. "We need to get her."

Boone snagged a towel and walked over to the oven as if he owned the place. "Not to worry. GracieAnn tore out after her like greased lightning. I think the girl's downright pissed. I feel right bad for Delta."

He slid out a tray of cookies and set it on the counter. He plucked two, juggled them in the air to cool, then tossed one to me. "So did you and Hunky enjoy the pizza?"

Cruisers screeched to a stop in front of the bakery, Detective Ross dressed in workout clothes and three uniforms hustled in the back door. Ross surveyed the room blanketed in white and Tipper on the floor. She looked from me to Boone, then back to me and snarled, "I was in the middle of my elliptical routine."

"Tipper and Delta killed Simon Ambrose at the wedding," I said. "Then they killed Suellen because she and Simon swindled them out of the bakery. They tried to pin the murders on Chantilly and when that didn't work they planted evidence in GracieAnn's purse to make it look like she was the killer." I pointed to GracieAnn's purse on the counter. "Then they wanted to kill me."

"I know the feeling." Ross looked at Boone. "And how do you figure into all this?"

"Me? I just stopped in for cookies."

"You couldn't wait for us to go together to see Ross, could you," Auntie KiKi grumbled the next morning as I sat at her kitchen table drinking coffee, telling all. I knew KiKi would have my head on a platter if she got the news of Tipper/Delta and the great bakery caper via Twitter. As it was, she just pitched a fit.

"If I'd waited and not gone in the bakery last night, I wouldn't have caught Tipper in the act of planting the evidence in GracieAnn's purse. It was meant to be."

"Phooey!" KiKi folded her arms and tapped her foot.

"Chantilly's out of jail."

"You could have been killed, you know."

I considered countering with her near-death balancing act on the fire escape, but when KiKi was on a tirade it was best not to egg her on. "I could be killed crossing the street," I soothed. "Besides, Boone was there."

KiKi stopped her foot tapping. "Now how did he wind up at the bakery on a nearly deserted street at midnight?" KiKi snatched the coffee cup out of my hand. "Never mind. It's nearly nine. The Silver Spoon Girls will be here any minute now. They're all geared up for another belly-dancing class this morning and looking forward to seeing Walker Boone. Any idea how you're going to get him there?"

"Knock him over the head and strap him to the hood of the Batmobile is the best I came up with, but it never happened."

"The girls will not be amused."

And they weren't. But it did get me to thinking about what KiKi said as I cranked up the volume on *Gypsy Fire* and started the belly-dancing warm-up routine. What *was* Boone doing on Broughton at midnight? City Market and River Street and Bay Street were all about nightlife but that end of Broughton was small shops and daytime eateries.

And why did he suddenly show up at Suellen's when I was there looking around? Then there was Pillsbury suddenly behind me without an ounce of perspiration and wanting to jog with me? Why was he over here in the middle of the Victorian district when he lived on the west side? And what about that crack of Doc Hunky and enjoying the pizza!

I told the girls to keep dancing for a minute and ran into the kitchen. I picked up Old Yeller and handed it to KiKi. "Take this for a drive over to Forsyth Park."

"Why on earth would I take a purse for a drive?"

"You'll see and when you do tell him he better get his fanny back here right now and not make me come after him." KiKi gave me a quick once-over. "Fanny, huh. This should be interesting." She grabbed the purse and hoofed it out the door.

Belly dancing is always passionate but when I tossed in ticked off, mad as a hornet, riled up, and genuinely ready to strangle someone with my bare hands, passionate took on a life all its own.

"There he is," one of the Silver Spoon gals sang out as the last song wound to an end. She nodded to the back of the room, all eyes following. The women filed past Boone with sultry *hellos* and *how are you doing this fine morning* and *it's mighty nice to see you again.*

When the last of the class paraded out the door Boone ambled over to me, Old Yeller balanced on the tip of his fingers. "You rang?"

"Blast you, Walker Boone!" I grabbed Old Yeller and dumped the contents on the floor, empty wallet, brush, flashlight, flip-flops, phone, dog collar, dog treats, dog doo-doo bags, gum, water bottle, all piled in a big heap. "Okay, where is it?"

Boone folded his arms and stared, humor brightening his usually dark eyes. I punched his arm. "You held my purse when we were at Simon's and I was under the bookcase."

"I rescued you from under the bookcase."

"I could have crawled out. Did you put it in then?"

"Put what in?"

I rummaged through the pile and picked up the phone. "Pillsbury and you together! That's how he knew where I was jogging. You bugged me."

"You always bug me. Seemed fair."

I faced him nose to chin . . . unshaved chin at that. "You had Pillsbury give me the phone so you would know where I was all the time and if I was someplace questionable, one of you would show up. Right?"

"Why would we do that?"

"Because you think I can't take care of myself, and I can, usually. Sometimes I just need a little assistance."

"Sometimes?"

"I'm going to get you for this."

The superior smirk was firmly in place. "This should be interesting."

"See all those lovely women who just paraded out of here gaping at you like a piece of raw meat. You just invited them for dinner. I'm sending a text message from the phone you so graciously gave me with time, date, and directions. Twenty women will be camped on your porch Saturday night at seven."

The smirk slipped a notch. "You wouldn't."

"Wanna bet?"

Boone grabbed for the phone and I dropped it down my blouse.

WELL-CRAFTED MYSTERIES
FROM BERKLEY PRIME CRIME

- **Earlene Fowler** Don't miss these Agatha Award–winning quilting mysteries featuring Benni Harper.

- **Monica Ferris** These *USA Today* bestselling Needlecraft Mysteries include free knitting patterns.

- **Laura Childs** Her Scrapbooking Mysteries offer tips to satisfy the most die-hard crafters.

- **Maggie Sefton** These popular Knitting Mysteries come with knitting patterns and recipes.

- **Lucy Lawrence** These brilliant Decoupage Mysteries involve cutouts, glue, and varnish.

- **Elizabeth Lynn Casey** The Southern Sewing Circle Mysteries are filled with friends, southern charm—and murder.

Enjoy rich historical mysteries...

Ariana Franklin
Mistress of the Art of Death Mysteries

Victoria Thompson
Gaslight Mysteries

Margaret Frazer
Dame Frevisse Medieval Mysteries
Joliffe the Player Mysteries

Kate Kingsbury
Manor House Mysteries
Pennyfoot Hotel Mysteries
Holiday Pennyfoot Hotel Mysteries

Robin Paige
Victorian Mysteries
Edwardian Mysteries

Bruce Alexander
Sir John Fielding Mysteries

Maureen Ash
Templar Knight Mysteries

Solving crimes through time.

penguin.com